LASTING IMPRESSIONS

YANIQUE
BELIARD MICHEL

Lasting Impressions

 www.trafford.com

North America & international
toll-free: 1 888 232 4444 (USA & Canada)
fax: 812 355 4082

ACKNOWLEDGEMENTS

IN THE SPRING OF 2005, I learned that a famous writer was offering her advice to potential aspirants at the East Fishkill Library. I rushed on the occasion to present the rough draft of my book, *Lasting Impressions*. During the session, Doreen Rappaport twice asked me to read from my text. She concluded that I needed to develop my synopsis into chapters.

A year later, I presented part of my manuscript for consult at the Wesleyan Writers Conference. Alexander Chee patiently exposed to me the flaws of my book.

I spent the next six months trying to apply Professor Chee's recommendations. Then, I contacted Nancy Butler-Ross of The Book Muse to edit the fruits of my labor. Nancy thoroughly reviewed my work and offered her honest and practical literary judgment.

Along the road, my daughter, Christie Michel, provided me with her enthusiasm, support and guidance. To Doreen, Alexander, Nancy and Christie, I say, "Mille mercis."

College Regina Assumpta, my high school in Cap-Haitian, Haiti, gave me the intellectual knowledge to complete a book such as *Lasting Impressions*. Their teaching, coupled with the dedication of my mother, Marie Therese Dassas, and my grandmother, Camise St. Juste, prepared me to sustain the course and be who I am today. To them I also say, "Mille mercis."

For shelter, support, care, nourishment and advice I present my gratitude to Cindy Michel, Martiza Hyacinthe Blemur, Rachel Jean Marie, Carole Walker, Shona McMilan, Brunel Michel, Marie Moise, Marcelle St. Juste, George Madhuro, Judith TeleMaque, Professor Verdejo Duarte, Ursule Laroche, Paulette Ford, Florence Graft and Jessica Keet.

For my daughters,

Cindy and Christie

INTRODUCTION

"ROMANTIC," ONE WOULD BE tempted to call Cap-Haitian, Haiti's second-largest city. Serene, some folks would argue, describes the location better. Still, some hard-to-please natives would prefer their land to be considered as an original gem. In fact, the island's northern shore stretches into an oyster-shaped promontory with the Caribbean Sea kissing its shell. It's "the cape" which is circled by the ocean on the north and a chain of mountains on the south. Its population is bounded by the geographical seclusion, a thick patois accent, and their complexion.

Contrary to other parts of Haiti, 95% of Cap-Haitian inhabitants have dark brown skin. They are people set in their own ways, a people who pass family traditions from generation to generation. Their coarse, direct manners have won them the title of being rebellious; they claim that they are only courageous.

By 1960 not one household had benefited from the commodity offered by the telephone system. Instead the city prided itself on the old telegraph service and a public telephone office sitting in a battered building at the corner of Rue 16A. The telegraph linked the city to the world, and was charged with carrying international news for the local radio stations. In that respect it was revered. However, the population resented its use on different occasions. For example, a telegraph message was always a precursor of trouble. It conveyed sorrow in the form of announcing a grave accident, a terminal disease, or death of a family member abroad.

In 1960, two theaters brought to the city an era of movement on the screen. They were the only places where such novelty could be watched, since no family owned a television set. However, transistor radios sprouted in most homes. The two radio stations repeated with legendary morbidity the news of the day, which meant those that were not censored by the government, as well as local and international events and music. At night they were closed, but some men in the intimacy of their homes listened to Radio Cuba, a station that provided them with the latest political news about Haiti. In that way the Cap-Haitian population learned information that was not exposed by the regime of Papa Doc Duvalier, the Haitian dictator.

The church services, from Catholic to Baptist to Protestant, exploded with devoted worshipers praying with fervor to lessen the abuse of the despotic regime that had befallen them. Their fear was nourished by a series of events that had flourished recently in the city. Cap-Haitian was a city that felt like a town. Its twenty-thousand inhabitants commented eagerly on the town's activities, and the art of gossiping had reached its perfection among them.

In 1960s Haiti, the army and police were entangled into a single unit. Their khaki uniforms generated a profound respect, blended with a paralyzing fear, from the population. Three years into the Duvalier regime, the northern population of Haiti, ridiculed for being suspicious, grew more cautious. Their attitude was warranted by the resentment they nourished for the oppressive practices of the government. The imposed discipline did not frighten them, but some occurrences that sparked in the city did.

At a soccer match, a fanatic openly manifested his enthusiasm for his preferred team, which had won the game. He was arrested by one of the military officers who supported the opposing team. He was beaten publicly, and to discourage him in case he or any other zealots had not learnt from that experience, he was thrown in jail for four months.

Cap-Haitian had only a few cars, twenty-five at the most. Three of them were taxis, the drivers of which were men from the community. A taxi ride was an occasion to socialize; the many customers sharing the ride were always excited and talkative on their way to the bus station or the airport. On a serene afternoon, Sam, a grandfather and the oldest cab driver in the city, was in a hurry to drop his customers off at the bus station and he passed a Colonel's Jeep. The Colonel sped up, passed Sam, and with a gesture of his arm ordered him to stop. He summoned Sam out of his car and solicited an apology. The old man rejected the solicitation, proposing instead to pay a ticket if he had committed an infraction. The Colonel grasped Sam's collar, almost choking him, knocked his head against the hood of the car, then slapped him. Under the bewildered eyes of the witnesses, he climbed into his Jeep and drove away, leaving Sam bleeding. The victim's lip was cut and his left eyelid was swollen shut. When the humming of the Colonel's vehicle had faded long enough for the bystanders to assume he was gone for good, they rushed to Sam's aid.

Saturday and Sunday afternoons were when most adults spent quality time with their children. It was also the time when they proudly exposed the clothes they had fabricated for their progeny during the week. Some well-to-do families could afford more than clothing; their acquisitions could be a new toy or instrument that surmised the admiration of the population, and a hint of envy. The sidewalk or parks were the designated places for the show-off.

On a Sunday afternoon around 5 p.m., when the sun was gentle and the breeze cool, Mr. and Mrs. Bachat took their four-year-old to the park of Notre Dame. Mr. Bachat had all week long helped his son on his tricycle. Little Joe had made great improvement and with a big smile, he directed his bike. After grasping the park visitors' attention, Little Joe concentrated on learning different maneuvers at a certain speed. The park was big; he could pedal faster than at home. Suddenly, a strident whistling made him stop briskly, almost falling off his seat. His parents' eyes, which had been glued on him, abandoned their observation. Turning their attention in the direction of the sound, their faces changed from relaxed to concerned, as a veil of dark thoughts crossed their minds. The town's military captain was advancing toward them.

Cap-Haitian sported one bank, which was owned by the government. Mr. Bachat was the director of that bank, where he had met the captain in his office, so he stood to humbly present his respect. The captain ignored his gesture with a question that sent a chill of terror down Joe's parents' spines.

"Who gave you permission to use the bike here?" spat the captain.

Mr. Bachat mumbled a shy, "No one," and added a comment that one could interpret as a critique or a protest against the captain's question. "In the past, we did not need a permit to use the park; we just had to make sure that our activities left enough space for our friends."

"Ah, ha!" retorted the captain, "From now on you need a permit. This is the Duvalier regime, and I represent law and order. I'm going to prove it right now." The captain snatched

the tricycle out from under Little Joe, who had been looking at him with dilated pupils, his mouth hanging open.
He handed the frantic child to his mother and left with his
prey.

Little Joe began to scream. Strident, prolonged howls
that invited the curious to share his pain filled the air. His
father took him from his mother and cuddled him, prom-
ising him another bike, one even more beautiful. But his
intervention made the child even more upset. Afraid that
Little Joe's attitude could anger the captain, Mr. Bachat beat
his son until he stopped crying.

It became a habit to discuss every night in the safety of
one's home what the population had termed as the "new
tactic of the military": the improvised schemes as described
above, accepted with reluctance and chagrin by the townsfolk. They would not dare present their recrimination to a
judge. He was nominated by the president and teamed up
with the military.

The victimized population grew weary of the authorities. The rare generous acts of the individual military members—one gave a mother and her epileptic child a ride to the
hospital, another sponsored a football team, and another
bought medicine for a poor patient—could not redress the
military's numerous affronts. The townsfolk planned ways
to eliminate the military's venom. They armed themselves
with a cold passivity, playing dumb as a way of resistance
and an avenue to strive.

It was in that atmosphere that the Arab-Haitians, Cap-
Haitian light-skinned descendants of 18th century Arab
immigrants, felt the most unlucky. They had arrived in Cap-
Haitian with the first wave of Middle Eastern immigrants
from Syria to Haiti during the middle to late 1800s. While
most members of their population resided in the capital

and were regarded as part of the upper class, the ones who had elected to thrive in the countryside towns were seen as ordinary citizens. However, all of them, no matter where they lived, maintained their unique presence separately. Due to their light complexion, they were considered Caucasian by the general population. The natives had always regarded them as uneducated merchants who were all involved in business. In Cap-Haitian, their members, representing less than 1% of the population, could not hide their assets or prosperity, since they owned most downtown businesses.

To survive, they faked approval of the action of the military that they feared, buffering themselves by paying hefty ransoms to government representatives. During those years, children were aware of the military activities. Their parents compared them to werewolves or *loupgarou* that could come at night and take them away forever. So they, too, were raised with a fear of the police.

It was in that town of Cap-Haitian that Fritz Jean Lucas was born and raised. His Arab-Haitian parents had decided to send him to Paris for his university years, so he would be more mature when he was to take over their business. It was also a way to protect their son. On the last weekend of September 1960, Fritz left Cap-Haitian eager to begin his studies in Paris, nourishing the plan to return to his native town four years later to marry his girlfriend, and replace his parents at their store.

————

MONDAY

June 14, 1965

———

FLAP, FLAP, FLAP.

Fritz Jean Lucas awoke suddenly.

Flap, flap. The chaotic, unfamiliar noise persisted.

"What's going on here?" Fritz groaned. He sat up in bed briskly. His heart drummed loud, rapid beats; his respiration whistled short, panting wheezes, joining the outdoor cacophony. He slit his eyelids open and squinted at his surroundings. He followed the morning's orange ray from the window, like a laser blade piercing the darkness, zooming on the wall to end on a deformed mass crouching on the console facing him.

Fritz drew the sheet tighter around himself. He rolled his eyes searching for an opportunistic weapon. His sight met with the massive three-panel oak armoire made by his great-grandfather looming in the right corner. Fritz exhaled, relieved. He eased his grip on the sheet as he recognized his family heirloom. The armoire had been passed down to him, the only male child on his maternal side. His parents were descendants of Syrian immigrants who had adopted Haiti as their country. Fritz was designated to carry the torch, which meant to continue his family's trade business.

On Monday, June 14, 1965, two days after his return to Haiti, he was to fulfill the expectations of the tradition of the Arab-Haitian community, but with a twist. Instead of

15

pursuing the import-export services that his parents were so proud and fond of, he was embarking on a venture to manufacture baseball caps and balls. He had elected to invest in a factory, a whole new field to his parents. To further upset the balance, he decided to place the factory in the airport vicinity of Port-au-Prince, Haiti's capital, and had chosen Kenscoff, located 15 miles from the factory, for his residence. In all, he would settle 90 miles from Cap-Haitian, the town where he was born, and where his mother—in Arab-Haitian tradition—had joined his father.

The noise outside Fritz's window intensified to a loud clatter, then stopped. It was a dead silence cut sharply a few seconds later by a short cascade of raucous *coco ricos*.

"Noisy roosters, go to hell!" Fritz grumbled. He reached for the box of matches he had placed on the nightstand, grabbed one, and snapped it. The sizzling noise, the dancing flame, the odor of sulfur brought life to the bedroom. Fritz slowly identified the target of the laser. The monster was just a pile of photographs of his former girlfriend, Crystal Dijon, a non-Arab-Haitian.

Fritz sighed.

He forgot that he had left them on the console. It was his luck that he had met Crystal's twin brothers at the dance on Saturday night, the night he had returned to Haiti from the U.S. He did not ask about Crystal but as soon as he was at home he had rummaged through his suitcase for those pictures. However, he did not have the courage to look at the proof his mother had victoriously dashed on him four-and-a-half years earlier to confirm her assumption.

She had always claimed that a woman of a different race would not befit her son. She would first pretend that their ignorance of Arab-Haitian customs was reason enough not to include them in the list of potential aspirants. But when she was cornered in familial discussions, she revealed her fear, her prejudice against black women. She assumed they would not be faithful to her fair-skinned son and would make a cuckold of him. The pile of photos had been abandoned, untouched for years. Painfully, Fritz acknowledged that the photographs and their implications were the main reason why he had opted not to join his parents at the familial business in Cap-Haitian. He felt himself reeling back to Saturday and his trip from the airport.

———

Fritz had been sleeping in the airplane from New York, going back to his native country of Haiti, when the pilot's voice thundered a message through the overhead speaker requesting the passengers to stay in their seats, and the crew to get ready for landing. Fritz opened his eyes and was blinded by the brilliant rays of light invading his window. He promptly shut his eyes again, breathed deeply, and smiled as he realized that this was what he had wished for during the past five years: to come back to his native country. The prospect filled him with excitement and he grew restless as a surge of vibrant energy spilled over his entire body.

The airplane brusquely touched the firm ground, pirouetted a few times around the deserted *piste*, steadied itself to switch to a gentle ride, then stopped smoothly in the middle of the track. A wheeled ladder was placed against the exit door and the travelers were invited to leave. Fritz abandoned his seat, grabbed his travel bag from the overhead compartment, and thanked the flight attendants on his way out. The bright Caribbean sun and a wave of hot air welcomed him; his skin blushed under its assault as he descended.

When he reached the pavement he placed his free hand to his brow, squinting as he scanned the airport balcony to locate his family members. He recognized them easily. They formed a flashy trio at the edge of the crowd, their skin glazing fiery red in the baking sun. Fritz saw his mother's dark auburn hair flowing with the breeze, the hat that she should have been wearing to protect herself pinned under one arm. She pointed a commanding finger in his direction, as if the two men at her side could not identify him. Then she waved animatedly toward her son, a warm smile displayed on her face. Fritz waved back.

He joined the line to the customs department, was cleared, pushed his carriage along with his luggage, and hurried to the waiting area. Arianne, his mother, stood at the front of the party, as always, her arms extended wide to receive her son. Fritz let go of his carriage and flew into his mother's embrace. They exchanged a long, tight hug. His father, Curtis, patiently awaited his turn, and then came Uncle Michael's turn. Fritz retrieved his luggage and they left the airport, packed his belongings into his uncle's trunk, and drove away.

Fritz shared the front seat with his uncle while his parents sat in the back. As the car attacked the dense traffic under the expert command of his uncle, Fritz turned to face his parents. His mother had a grin on her face, which to Fritz seemed strangely malicious.

Her eyes beamed with pride and she began, "You look good, son! What a difference the four months since we last visited you made! The young women of the capital are going to have their heads turned by your charm."

Fritz responded, "Thanks for the compliment, Mom. But remember, the last time you saw me was February, in the deep winter. You know that season and I don't mix well. That's part of the reason I came back."

Fritz accepted the unflattering criticism that he had violated the family tradition by rejecting to continue the import-export business his family had maintained for eight generations and were extremely proud of. The Lucas business provided the countryside with all kinds of goods: generators, fabric, buttons, etc. But, even with Fritz's factory construction almost completed, his mother still nourished the secret hope of having him come back to live in Cap-Haitian. She did not want to upset Fritz by openly reproaching him for his business choice. So, she presented her plea with formality to mask her disapproval, and saved her dignity. She said, "My offer still stands, Fito. Come join us at our store in Cap-Haitian!"

"You and Dad are managing it well enough, you don't need me. Didn't you expand it threefold?" Fritz replied.

Arianne answered, "Yes we did, but that's not the point. Don't you get it? With your looks and wealth, the women in Port-au-Prince will prey on you. How will you be able to resist them?" She glanced furtively at her husband, then fixed her son with a stern stare and added confidently, "Fortunately, Curtis and I have already chosen a wife for you. We will be able to follow our Arab-Haitian tradition. She is out of the country right now, but she should be back by the time you settle things in the factory. We will be ready to speak to her parents again."

Fritz cut her off sharply, "Come on, Mom, wait a minute! How many times do I have to tell you that I will only marry the woman I love? As a matter of fact, race has no role in my choice. She could be Arab, or white, or black!"

Curtis, sensing an argument and wanting to avoid it, pitched in, "You know that we are here for you, son. How was your trip? How are you doing? Did you bring my whiskey?"

Fritz exchanged a grateful look with his dad and answered, "I'm fine. I survived the stay at the university. Now I want to visit the factory and find out."

Arianne interrupted him briskly, "Find out what? The factory will make it. Didn't you claim that you signed some baseball cap contract or something, as part of your graduation project?"

Fritz answered, "Yes. I do have the contract, but the factory isn't much of a concern. I want to integrate into Port-au-Prince society, make a life for myself, and find out."

"Are you going to run for mayor?" Arianne asked sarcastically. In a more serious tone she warned her son, "Don't look for any trouble. You're an adult now, and we won't always be here to protect you. Stay with your own people, in the Arab-Haitian community."

"Don't worry, Mom. I will," replied Fritz dismissively. "But I intend to catch up on those years I spent in seclusion. My stay in the U.S. after Paris was not a happy one, as you know."

Arianne continued determinedly, "Well, Fritz, it was your choice. What you need now is a good wife. Your father and I must leave first thing in the morning. We already visited the factory and the construction is almost done. The site being close to the airport is perfect."

"You mean you aren't staying to participate in my first meeting with my firm's engineers?" Fritz asked incredulously.

"Son, don't worry. Your uncle will introduce you. Didn't he direct all the procedures during your absence? Your mother and I plan to come back on Friday for the factory's inauguration!"

Switching gears Fritz commented, "So you won't be at the factory blessing on Thursday? Oh well. I hope that Father Ignacio will make it simple. From what I've learned, uncle, your experience with the firm was positive. The engineers were serious and the work was done as scheduled."

He glanced at his uncle and then turned back to his parents. "Can you believe the piece of gossip he fed me? He told me the firm's architect was a woman, a black Haitian woman. And to quote him, 'She's pretty in her own way, intelligent, and the driving force of the firm.'"

"She's probably a *diaspora*. Can you imagine a female architect working at the same level as men in Haiti? Things sure are changing in this country. It is nice to have a woman working in a field that is considered taboo by us. The general population only accepts women as teachers, nurses, or nuns. Now with the *diaspora*, those Haitian citizens who have been living abroad for so long and have decided to come back to Haiti, we are in touch with the modern world. I guess women will have the right to choose; no more staying home to take care of her children and husband. I wish her the best, even though I presume she must have a tough time dealing with her colleagues. And we Arab-Haitians must follow in their footsteps; we need female architects, physicians, engineers. A female architect is exactly what we need in the Arab-Haitian community," Arianne exclaimed.

The three men in the car burst out laughing at her audacity. She never missed an occasion to promote her partial views as an Arab-Haitian mother and wife.

Michael tapped Fritz on the shoulder, "Wait until you see her. Let me know what you think."

———

The heat of the match teased Fritz's fingertips, bringing him back to his room and the photographs. Fritz cautiously advanced the flame to the wick. The candle caught fire. He shook his hand to put out the match and at the same time nodded his head in disbelief to deny one more time the accusation carried by the photographs. That morning in bed Fritz had re-examined his mother's comment about women and work in Haiti. He agreed that it would be a big change to have female architects in his country. But he concluded that it was a good move, that they would bring their sense of esthetic to soften the angles of the sterile buildings recently arisen in the country.

How would the patronizing males treat them? Fritz wondered. In the Arab–Haitian community, women worked with their husbands in their stores; they did not go outside to mingle with the general public. They were sheltered. However, for black Haitian women to be in competition with the dominating males was a new development.

Fritz looked at the pile of photographs, and recalled that Crystal had wanted to be an architect. It had been her dream. Her father had discouraged her and advised her to pursue a career as a pediatrician. Fritz speculated about where she could be; Cap-Haitian, he guessed, but how did she make out, how would she react when she learned about the factory, his decision not to go back to Cap-Haitian? And with that, the weight of his own responsibilities reappeared. It was the day of his first visit to the factory.

He crawled out of bed, walked to the window, and opened it. The warm sun and crisp air engulfed the bedroom; the flame vacillated swiftly, then died. Fritz glanced at the clock. Its hands pointed at five forty-five. "Damn, I only slept for five hours!" he mumbled. He proceeded to the console with the solid intention of dumping the photographs back into

22

the suitcase, but he reached instead for the folder beside them. He smiled. On the binder was his new business card with the inscription:

Fabric Pro

Owner/Director, Fritz Jean Lucas

Addresse: Route de l'Aeroport

Port-au-Prince, Haiti

The cards were one more confirmation of his uncle's manifestation of enthusiasm for his project. His parents were his associates; their money had fueled the execution of his plan. He was the intellectual owner, entrusted to guide the vessel to a safe port. His new role pleased him. With zeal, he took the binder, laid it down on the bed, and flipped it open. He was absorbed, reviewing the information on his factory and jotting down notes on a pad, when the maid announced that the hot water for his bath was ready. On his way to the bathroom, he silently prayed, "God bless my efforts, make this workday productive, and bring happiness to my life." As if there were a link between his future and the photographs, he mumbled, "Make me discover the truth about the photographs."

By Kenscoff standards, the bath was just a tepid liquid obtained from a mixture of water from the boiled kettle diluted in a basin filled with cool well water. Fritz dumped the whole container on himself in two splashes after soaping his body. He walked out of the bathroom revived, rubbing the towel on his light skin in a vigorous semicircular motion. The friction warmed him.

He donned a café au lait-colored suit, carefully chosen the day before, and then glanced at his reflection in the mirror in the middle panel of the old armoire. "Ouch!" he exclaimed. "My mom is right. I look great." His six-foot-three frame adorned with 230 pounds of mostly muscle filled the mirror. He was resplendent. His toned bust empowered by years of regular swimming at the university bloomed above his long legs and reminded him of Coby, the English horse, parading in his parents' stable. His own stance transpired confidence, elegance, and a certain lavishness, once he had his shoes on and was holding his briefcase.

Fritz shrugged his shoulders. "No," he persuaded himself, "I don't want to look too bourgeois." He quickly got rid of the outfit and settled for a modest polo shirt and trousers. Abandoning the bedroom, he stopped in the dining room and drank a cup of black coffee, after savoring a slice of locally baked bread and butter.

He stepped outside. The dogs, to his great surprise, welcomed him and made him feel at home. He fed them, poured water in a bowl for them, went back inside and retrieved his briefcase.

First on his itinerary, he was to visit the factory, then would come the meetings, one in the late morning with the engineers, and one in the afternoon with the architect. He had questioned his uncle about the necessity for two meetings. Michael had not set them and to elude Fritz's probing he had answered, "You have to be ready to meet the architect."

The squealing sound of tires on the pavement outside his window signaled to Fritz that his uncle was curbing the car. Excited, Fritz joined him. They exchanged the usual morning greetings, and Fritz immediately remarked on his aunt's absence. "Is Aunt Martine all right?"

"She's fine; she just left earlier to open the store. I have to be at the custom-house today," replied Michael.

Fritz cast a puzzled glance at his uncle and asked, "Are you telling me that you won't be able to attend our meetings?"

"You got it, pal," joked Michael. Then in a serious tone he added, "I'm sorry. The chauffeur, Jean, will drive you around." As he started the car he touched Fritz's shoulder and murmured, "Don't worry, Fritz, you'll be fine. Now that I think about it, it's a good move for you to be taking over completely. I've already influenced your project too much. Welcome back."

Fritz blurted a hasty, "Thank you." His uncle always knew the right cord to touch. His confidence boosted, he braced himself for his first day as an entrepreneur in his home country. His family members had labeled him as "adventurous" in trying to start a manufacturing business.

———

This project had all started as the impulse to loosen his parents' grip on him. Two weeks before he had left for Paris and college, he had been in the dining room with his mother. She had prepared *kibbe* for him from scratch, his favorite meal, and was admiring him as he enjoyed the delicious rolls. It was an intimate moment for both of them.

Playfully, Arianne asked her son, "What are your plans for tonight?"

Fritz excitedly confided in her, "It's almost my last week in Cap-Haitian. I'm going to a dance with Crystal. I intend to spend all my free time with her."

Arianne's face had brightened with a contemptuous smile. She rose from her chair, moved to the window, and touched her chignon to make sure it was well sculpted—a bad habit of hers when she was worried. "Crystal is a very attractive, intelligent, black girl. She's a nice piece; it must be fun to amuse yourself so much."

Fritz indignantly pushed the plate of *kibbe* away and retorted, "I love her, Mom!"

Arianne's body jerked, her face reddened. In a cold, strong voice she said, "No, Fritz. This is summer fun. Remember, Crystal is Haitian and black. You are Haitian and Arab." She paused, examined her son, and pronounced with determination and finality, "Your father and I will choose the right wife for you. A wife that belongs to the same race as us."

Fritz pushed his chair back from the table, folded his arms across his chest, and with a challenging look in his eyes retorted, "Mom, I will marry the person I love. For me, complexion and race are not important. Only love, the kind of love that can break those barriers."

Arianne had examined her son with surprise. A frown appeared on her forehead, and her lips tightened. She strode over to him in a wild rage and slapped him as hard as she could. She turned her back on him, slumping in her chair with her face in her hands. She was trembling. By the time she had regained her composure, and was able to look up again, Fritz was gone, his empty chair and the unfinished plate of *kibbe* the only reminders of his recent presence. There was a loud bang and Arianne knew he had slammed his bedroom door.

Paris was what Fritz had expected: a city full of distractions. However, he concentrated on his studies. He knew he must bring not only the diploma back home, but also good grades to make his parents and Crystal proud of his achievements. He was in that spirit when Arianne, his mother, came to visit him during the Lent period of 1961. He thought she was on her way to Rome for the Easter celebrations. He was grossly wrong. One of the goals of her trip was to help her son move to the United States.

While in the States, Fritz's impulse was mixed with the desire to change the pattern of the family store. He wanted the black Haitian population to share part of the revenue of his enterprise, and the only way to achieve his goal was to create jobs. He had approached the subject with one of his university lecturers. Together they chose the idea of a factory. After many failed attempts, Fritz finally obtained a contract for manufacturing baseball caps and balls.

By then he was determined to settle in Port-au-Prince, away from his parents, and had contacted his uncle to convince him of the feasibility of the project. His parents rejected it at first, but agreed to take the risk when Michael assured them he would assist his nephew. It was only after obtaining their consent that Michael informed his sister and brother-in-law of the designated site for the factory: Port-au-Prince.

———

In the car with Fritz that Monday morning, Michael had remembered it was the first day of the state exams and that the main roads would be crowded with students, so he favored the earth-layered back road. After an easy ride they reached the new factory. Fritz thanked his uncle once more for his help, then exited the vehicle. He lingered, amazed, in front of the imposing structure that was his factory. He felt blessed and indebted toward his family. He admitted that for the Arab-Haitian community to stick together was a good practice, since it ensured their power.

As he entered the building, his nostrils were assaulted by the smell of burning iron, his ears deafened by the cacophonic clicking of instruments. He ambled around the property looking intensely, touching, experiencing the material. In the courtyard the workshop sprung up like a huge aquarium. Its brick walls dressed with numerous windows contrasted with the massive rock enclosure and conveyed a welcoming sensation. They stirred in Fritz an irresistible urge to explore their smooth design. He spread his hands on the flat surface. His body tightened as a reaction to the brick's cool contact, then progressively loosened to let the freshness penetrate his flesh.

His curiosity awakened, he peered through one of the windows and discovered a room inundated by daylight, with the sewing machines he had ordered parading in the center like miniature coral reefs. He glanced around and recognized the cutting tables in the corners. On them patiently waited the screens to cover the windows. Turning his head, he identified the source of the noise.

Two iron workers, their faces buried under protective gear, brandished a welding filament like a pistol. Their words and laughs mingled with the jet of electrical sparks. When they were busy measuring, the hammering noise controlled the space. Fritz noticed a lonely man in an adjacent room pounding a nail on a stool. "The worker's bench," he said aloud. He had copied the design from a tavern in the U.S., and mailed the sketch to his uncle months earlier.

His chest swelled with pride. The past year he had concentrated on the realization of his plan, entertaining with fervor anyone who would listen to the subject of building a factory in a third-world country. He had scoured the factories in Manhattan's Garment District and the warehouses in Chinatown, and had been distressed by their size. How could he afford such a big enterprise? Was it safe to begin on such a large scale with no prior experience?

On a trip to Pennsylvania, he fell in love with an Amish factory production unit and the way they functioned. A number of workers were assigned a dedicated task for a length of time. However, they were all cross-trained and could replace each other at different stations. Fritz had assumed that such an arrangement would guarantee that skilled and reliable relief was available. Those workers had also received a fair share of the factory profits, encouraging them to be more productive.

It was a revealing experience for him, and with it came the solution to his problems. He could invest in a factory for fifteen to twenty people, management included. He contacted his international trade professor who advised him on a product that suited his plan. Together they had decided on a non-perishable item, and ultimately he was blessed with the contract for manufacturing baseball caps and balls.

The difficulties encountered paled in comparison to the joy he felt on Monday morning. With a light step he continued his exploration. When he arrived in the workshop the workers sensed his presence and stopped working. Fritz presented himself under the curious and apprehensive gazes of the crew, then ordered them to continue. The hammering sound reappeared. Fritz settled in his office after a complete tour of the premises. He was pleased with the work being done; he just fancied some adjustments to be made, mostly to his office.

The chauffeur was back for him. On his way to New Spectrum Engineering, Fritz visited his aunt at her store, where they ate a light breakfast. He was not hungry but full of enthusiasm and anticipation. He left the store with bright, new ideas bursting, blasting his mind like popcorn in a microwave.

It was eleven sharp when the secretary announced him to the principals. The engineers were awaiting their client. They had expected a spoiled, rich, bourgeois kid walking in with a confident smile, a flashy outfit, and an exuberant conversation to prove the affluence of his exposure to the States.

With that conviction in mind they had prepared different subjects of conversation to impress their client. They browsed over advances in technology they had considered important to mention. The entertainment arena was not neglected; they had read feverishly about fashion trends, and were delighted at the prospect of discussing the miniskirt and its influence on women's liberation.

They started the meeting eagerly, undeterred by their client's casual appearance. However, after their presentation, their enthusiasm waned, and a sour surprise blended with a vague sense of panic hit them right in the gut. They were shocked by their young client's flurry of questions concerning the impact of the factory on the environment, and the consequences of the heavy traffic on the construction. In all, they had to justify every single alteration they had made to the original plan. What they assumed would not be noticed by most clients, figured on Fritz's list.

He handed them an exit door when he requested details about the final touches for his office. The engineers jumped on the opportunity, suggesting it was better to contact the architect since they had not yet received the final draft. Their boss, Engineer Alex Turnier, interpreted their setback as a signal to put an expeditious end to the meeting. He also proposed to introduce Fritz to the architect before their scheduled afternoon appointment, reasoning that she was more suited to answer and satisfy his poking than his engineers.

Crystal Dijon opened her lunch bag, turned her head and checked the time: 12:15 p.m. The cathedral's clock had struck the twelve beats to stamp the midday hour. The twelve impassive beats had echoed in the capital's down-town, infusing its residents with the knowledge of the implacable passage of time, and reminding them of their own limitations. They had resounded in her office as in years before, but she had not heard them. The veiled humming of the traffic was changed to a rumbling pierced by sporadic honks.

It was the signal of the public transportation in a hurry to dump its riders home and make extra rounds on Monday, June 14, the first day of the state exams. The noise did not reach her. The sun had caressed her window, flirting with her cactus that she had forgotten to water. Every Monday for the past two years she had paid special attention to her plant. It was a gift from her uncle, Engineer Turnier.

The pampering was one of the phases of her established routine. But she had not followed her ritual that morning. Instead she was immersed in the soft music spilling from the cassette that she had placed in the cassette player. Her office appeared the same to her; on her desk laid the "Fabric Pro" folder with the project she had worked on for the past 24 months.

However, today she could not concentrate on finishing her preparation for the meeting with the owner of the fac-tory she had designed. It was as if a delicate butterfly that was gliding, hanging by an invisible thread, suddenly flut-tered its wings. The faint movement disturbed a vast, still air that one thought was settled, stable, immutable. And the commotion woke up an array of partitions, as when a conductor signals an orchestra to begin playing.

The wind whistled, the birds sang, the flowers danced, the leaves trembled, and her own heartbeats joined the symphony, her mind waltzing in uncontrollable steps to carry her to places that were nonexistent to her. She could retrace her restlessness to the day before, Sunday; it was linked to her brother Gregory's visit. She had been ready to go to church when he showed up. After kissing her good morning he had asked how she was doing. She'd answered that she was fine. But it was an awkward moment, and she sensed that something was coming, that there was something in store for her.

Since when had her brother traveled after partying all night to catch up with his sister and enquire about how she was doing? To fill the silence, she bragged about her work at New Spectrum, then excused herself; it was time to leave, if not she would be late, and she hated being late for mass. Her brother offered to accompany her, which to her seemed so strange.

Back at home after mass, he stayed and asked her to fix lunch for them. Crystal, while changing in her bedroom, speculated on what was wrong for her brother to choose to have lunch with her on a Sunday. She had observed him and concluded that their father was not the person of interest, but guessed that her visitor was on some type of mission. She joined him in the dining room. While she officiated at the stove, dipping cut plantain into hot oil, a sporadic crinkling noise erupted to cover their seemingly forced casual conversation.

Gregory had stammered the word 'factory.' She was stunned by it, because all that interested her brother, a physician, had to do with the medical field. She assumed he needed some favor from her fiancé, Dr. Gerard Armand, and she teased him about the motive of his visit. But the word 'factory' kept bouncing back into their conversation. Then he insinuated that he had met the owner of Fabric Pro at the dance at La Chaumiére the previous night.

Crystal congratulated him on his new attitude, his aggressiveness. *Men*, she thought, *they are all the same; they consider business in every facet of their lives.* She assumed he was trying to secure a position, a job on a Saturday night, at the dance. She offered to assist him, to play his tune; if her brother was contemplating being the factory's physician, why not? She would team up with her uncle, Engineer Turnier, and approach Michael Kahlil. They would persuade their client to hire Gregory.

But it was not the case. There was no need to contact Mr. Kahlil, her brother assured her. He placed his hand on her shoulder, a gesture she wanted to laugh at because it was so serious and she was used to her brother being playful. Then he dropped the bomb.

"I met Fritz at La Chaumiére." He stopped and took a deep breath. "Crystal," he continued, his voice soft, the grip of his hand on her shoulder becoming ever more apparent, "he is the owner of Fabric Pro."

Her world succumbed, swallowed by those words. She knew why he hadn't bothered to say a last name. They both knew that for her there was only one Fritz, Fritz Jean Lucas. The man she had dated five years earlier, and from whom she had not heard a word, had not received a sign, for four-and-a-half years.

She revolted, enraged that she had been working all that time on a project without knowing who the owner was. She blamed the Arab-Haitian community for their closeness and their secretiveness. Then she blamed herself for her naiveté, for not inquiring. It was too late for her to withdraw; a meeting was already scheduled for the following day.

Greg had turned off the stove, the half-cooked plantain and the half-filled plates were abandoned on the table. For a moment, only her angry protestations roamed the room. A heavy silence erupted when she stopped. Gregory had waited patiently. She regained her composure, claimed that her pride was hurt, but that she was fine, she just needed time. Exiting the dining room, she let her body fall aloft a seat on the porch. Greg, who was trailing after her, sat across from her, waiting. There, she confessed that her vacation years earlier in Cap-Haitian had been the best time of her life. Greg just listened.

By the time he had left, she had decided to try to impress Fritz. Her brother had told her he had not informed Fritz about her being the architect for his factory. She had thanked Gregory with passion.

———

At 12:15 p.m. on Monday, one hour and forty-five minutes before her scheduled appointment with the owner of Fabric Pro in her office, she admitted to herself that she had dressed for him, for Fritz. Just so that she could create in him that turmoil, the same turmoil she had experienced during his absence.

When her fiancé had come in to give her a ride that morning, he became caught up with her elegance, and assumed it was for him. She resented it. And as a child protecting her favorite toy, she had kept the feeling with her. Gerard would be jealous; he would not understand the kind of intimacy she had shared with Fritz. Friend/lover, or just friend now.

Because without knowing it they had worked on the same project, exchanging ideas through Michael Kahlil for two years, her proposing, Fritz accepting. What excuses would Fritz come up with to justify his past behavior? An irresistible urge to discover what had happened four-and-a-half years earlier overcame her. Then she refrained from the temptation. She persuaded herself that she was in control; it no longer mattered. She had her fiancé.

It would be a flat, distant welcome for Mr. Lucas. She sat at her desk with the resolution of enjoying her lunch on her mind, since in her anxiety over the sudden reappearance of her former boyfriend, she hadn't eaten breakfast that morning.

Then, her office phone rang; it was a peculiar tone for an internal call. Somewhat annoyed, she answered dryly, but when she recognized Engineer Turnier's familiar voice requesting whether he could stop by, she replied, "Of course." She hung up, not waiting for more information. She was feeling vulnerable and needed someone in whom to confide the gossip she had learned from Greg the day before.

Together Fritz and Engineer Turnier crossed the hall separating the engineers' conference room from Crystal's office. A slight knock on the door announced his presence, then Turnier opened it.

Crystal's hand, holding a fork with a slice of mango perched on it halfway to her mouth, froze in midair. Her eyes dilated, her nostrils flared, her lips parted in anticipation for the food quivered, her body grew tense. At her door, beside her uncle, stood Fritz Jean Lucas.

As the door opened, Fritz could see Crystal seated at her desk. She was poised in wonder with a sensual look on her face, listening. Soft music clung in the air that Fritz identified as "their" music. He stopped in mid-sentence, blushing, his eyes fixed on her. His heart pounded faster and faster, his respiration quickened, his limbs were paralyzed, and cold sweat came out of every pore.

Alex was struck by their reactions. He became embarrassed, and moved hesitantly to Crystal's desk. "Crystal, this is Fritz Jean Lucas, the co-owner of Fabric Pro. He directed many questions to us that were more suited for you, the architect, to answer. This is why I stopped by to personally introduce him to you before the scheduled appointment later today."

Crystal slowly placed the fork back into the bowl and pleaded, "It's my lunchtime. I thought you were here to address some personal matter." At the sound of her voice Fritz inhaled deeply and blushed.

Alex suddenly realized that Fritz was the boyfriend Crystal had talked so much about in the past. He tiptoed to the door, closed it after him, and hurried back to his office.

Crystal and Fritz locked gazes. Images of the summer they had spent together five years earlier flashed through their minds. She remembered the afternoon when she had fallen from her bike and Fritz had offered his help. How gentle and caring he had been. She noticed that he was still the same, handsome and muscular. His yellow polo shirt hung loosely over his beige pants. She could see the same broad shoulders, the flat stomach, the narrow hips, and the long, muscular legs, but his hair was longer and he had lost his tan, which made his blushing even more pronounced.

Crystal could not help but burst out laughing, thinking Fritz never could hide his feelings. With surprise in her voice she said, "Good afternoon, Fritz." She eyed him pensively from head to toe, then added in a deferential tone, "You have appeared as you disappeared—unexpectedly." Pulling her chair back, she stood and moved toward the mantel mumbling, "Time to turn off that music."

Advancing swiftly, Fritz caught her arm. The contact made their bodies tremble. For a short time they faced each other in silence, measuring. Fritz tightened his grip on her arm and with a deep hoarse voice warned her, "Don't, Crystal. Don't do anything that would hurt the memories or hurt us." He moved closer and hugged her. For that moment everything around them disappeared; whatever difficulties they had faced dissolved in that embrace, as their hearts beat in harmony with the music.

Crystal had heard the surprise and shock in his voice. She also recognized her body's reaction to Fritz's touch, that flutter. For a split second a natural impulse spread over her; standing so close to Fritz she buried her head in his chest as she had five years earlier. She fought for control while pondering the weight of his assertion. "Us, us," played in her mind. She cast him an inquisitive stare, interpreting his insinuation with the use of "us." Her mouth dropped open in disbelief. She parted from him, moved away, and shouted, "Us! What us? What do you mean by 'us', Fritz Lucas?"

Despite herself, images of them strolling on the beach, laughing and kissing flocked to her mind. Fritz teaching her how to swim, Fritz parting her lips and teasing her with his tongue, touching her, caressing her tense body to make her relax. Fritz hugging her tight, then holding her chin while forcing her to open her eyes, so she could admit her love for him without embarrassment.

Deep inside she felt that since the forces of whatever circumstances created the gap that divided them had vanished, again they were to be close. And for a reason she could not describe, she was once again haunted. She was tantalized. The spirit that invaded her made her become bewildered. She breathed deeply while reasoning to calm herself.

Fritz was also possessed. Crystal's defiant stare and defensive pose had gotten to him. He remembered how she had always been a fighter. She was the only girl in her family, the younger sister of two domineering twin brothers. She was very smart but instead of being complimented for her achievements, she was made an outcast as a nerdy, bookish, pretentious girl.

Her father, a widower since her mother's death three months after her birth, had placed a heavy burden on Crystal. As Fritz judged her position now in New Spectrum Engineering, he realized Crystal was the only woman among the engineers. All the secrets she had confided to him about her struggles when they were lovers emerged in his mind. How she wanted to please her father by becoming a pediatrician, but felt she had no desire to work in healthcare; instead she was very interested in the architectural field. In a flash Fritz admitted to himself, *She stood up for herself! She made it! She is an architect and a good one.* He looked her straight in the eyes while extending his arm to turn down the music's volume. Then he murmured, "Good afternoon, Crystal. I'm happy to have you as my factory's architect."

They did not know how long they had been standing close to each other, listening to "their" music. She motioned him to the guest chair, sat, retrieved the Fabric Pro folder, opened it, and began flipping through the pages. The whole time Fritz sat in the chair across from her desk, he was admiring her. Crystal was again the one who interrupted the silence. "Welcome back, Fritz. It seems you asked the engineers many questions about the construction. What can I help you with?"

Fritz fumbled through his briefcase and soon his notepad materialized.

Crystal started again, "The last time I met with Mr. Kahlil, we discussed the changes to be made in the fence. What do you really want?"

Fritz now solicited her expertise. "What do you suggest, Crystal?" While talking he was observing her. She was taking notes and nodding her head in approval, or frowning.

She said, "Mr. Kahlil and I discussed some possibilities. Didn't he inform you? You do realize that the second entrance will increase the cost, not that I think money would be one of your concerns, but safety wise. Would you leave two watchmen, or not?"

"To tell you the truth I hadn't thought about that aspect," avowed Fritz. "Maybe I will keep the keys to that entrance." Then all of a sudden he began giving her information about his family members. "Michael Kahlil is my uncle, my mother's older brother."

"He's a fine client. I respect him for never questioning my presence, since architecture is considered to be a male's domain," snapped Crystal. She switched the subject back to business. "What else did you want to discuss with me about the architecture?"

Fritz did not answer, but instead moved his chair closer to Crystal's desk. He spied the sparkling diamond stud on her left ring finger and felt a sharp, stabbing pain in his chest. He told himself, *Crystal is not married, she's engaged. What happened? Has she been engaged this whole time? Or did she get divorced and is now engaged again? No, that couldn't have been it. Or maybe?* The creeping doubt came back to him. *Did my mother lie to destroy my relationship with Crystal? What more powerful motive could she have used than the military?* He glanced at the unfinished bowl of mango slices and requested, "May I have some of your mango?" The simplicity of his request stunned Crystal. She recalled that Fritz had always been direct. His solicitation made her feel at ease.

She pushed the bowl and fork toward Fritz, took a cup from her drawer and poured water for him. She shrugged her shoulders and with a faint smile on her face confessed, "It's Mango Baptiste from our farm in Cormier. My father spoils me. He always manages to send me these fruits. Since he lives by himself, every weekend he stays at our farm twenty minutes from Cap-Haitian."

Fritz smiled, engrossed by the remembrances. He took a bite of the mango slice, closing his eyes to savor it and absorb the music. Then he opened his eyes and confided, "Maybe this is why I came back. Things here did not change: the music, the mango."

Crystal was once more puzzled by Fritz's insinuation. What was he referring to? She realized what could happen if she was not careful. She scolded herself, *Crystal, this is the man who abandoned you. He just left you. Be firm, tell him you are engaged, that you made it past his treason.*

Crystal looked him straight in the eye and she saw softness, a desire that she knew, but also something more, a sort of sadness that was foreign to her. She drifted her eyes back to her notes. Concerned, she pondered what could have been the cause of that sorrow. She concluded that the melancholy displayed in Fritz's eyes was the result of suffering. *Fritz has gone through some rough times,* she convinced herself. She admitted that he was more cautious, less innocent, even the neat notes written about the factory were one more proof of his maturity.

She considered whether he was a complete stranger to her, or whether they were both strangers to each other. *No,* she thought, *like me he probably just matured.* A new feeling visited her, an urge to protect Fritz. She thought about

40

what happened to him during his absence, the difficulties that were encountered by all foreign students. She first eliminated money as a problem, since his family was rich. She considered the schoolwork, then remembered Fritz was more than an average student. She was guessing about the loneliness he experienced before making friends, and as thunder empowering a clear blue sky, the truth struck her. The sorrow in his eyes had something to do with them, with their relationship. He was as profoundly touched and destroyed as she was.

She recalled experiencing different reactions about them from different groups. In fact, the complexion of 95% of Cap-Haitian's population in the 1960s undulated from brown sugar to dark chocolate. The 4% light-skinned and the 1% Arab-Haitian swirled like a vanilla ribbon with legendary comfort around the darker majority to achieve a delicate mosaic.

Despite the seclusion of the Arab-Haitian folks in a hermetic group, the town exuded a sense of harmony. It was as if the different players had signed a pact. They had embraced the customs of the immigrants. They had accepted the fact that the Arab-Haitians married among themselves, and did not include foreigners in their business. The close relationship exhibited by Fritz and Crystal had shocked the Cap-Haitian pattern. The feelings awakened by the infringement sailed from amazement, to bewilderment, to denial. A common remark from all parties was, "They will never make it!"

Crystal praised herself. It was the only time that her loneliness paid off. No one could ask her information about her relationship with Fritz. The way she was perceived paid off too. She thought the townsfolk did not feel sorry for her

41

or pity her. Instead, they claimed that she liked to take risks and met her challenge, her measure.

Crystal reached across the desk for Fritz's arm, and with a soft voice and affection in her eyes murmured, "No, Fritz, things have changed. We are grown up now, real adults." In a way she had not expected, what she said touched both of them; she realized that she still cared about Fritz and wanted him to succeed. But also, the thought of him suffering or being exposed bothered her more than she cared to admit.

She continued, "I made it in the firm not without struggling. My father was right. Being a female architect in Haiti is not an easy path. Thank God I have Gerard's support." Fritz frowned at the mention of that name but did not ask any questions. It was only after the words had left her mouth that she realized she had confided in him, the way she used to years earlier.

Fritz was doing the same. He told her, "New York was not that easy of a stay. For one thing, I never quite liked the cold weather. The schooling was manageable. Writing English was one thing, but speaking it was a lot different. Too often, I was reminded that I was not trying hard enough, that my accent was too thick, that I would never fit into the North American or U.S. business world."

Crystal was intrigued and cornered him, "Why didn't you come back before? You had vacation, summertime, and those long recesses."

Fritz shrugged his shoulders, bit into a piece of mango, chewed slowly, and drank some water. Evading the question with a trailing voice and a dreamy air he said, "I missed the boulevard, the sea, the disco, the mountains, the people. When I decided to come back my parents wanted me to be with them in Cap-Haitian, but I refused and contacted my uncle instead to get the construction started."

Crystal's body jerked, and she exclaimed, "You decided to come back? What do you mean? I thought you left for Paris University to come back in four years, post graduation." Before he left for Europe they had planned to wait for each other, get married when reunited, and live happily ever after—the dream of all women in love. That was how she had viewed their relationship at the time.

How did he end up in an American university? What was that other mystery? When had he moved to the States? All this Crystal wondered. That some kind of constraint forced him to adopt a new stand surged in her mind. She paused, her eyes wet, her voice a whisper, and then enquired, "When did you change your mind?"

Fritz looked searchingly at her, and a hint of surprise blended with curiosity on her face tortured him. She was prettier than he'd remembered. Her thick, black hair reached down to her shoulders and softened her look to make her appear less severe than she would like.

He thought about her long, shapely legs and how she moved with grace. He wondered whether she still played volleyball. An image of the two of them playing on the beach flashed through his mind. He flinched and persuaded himself, *No, Crystal did not cheat on me. Something must have happened.* Out loud he said, "I needed to do something by myself from scratch, to come up with a new idea. For more than eight generations my family has been in the import-export business. It was time for a change."

Crystal fixed him with incredulous eyes. Her voice still a whisper, she probed, "Why didn't you build the factory in Cap-Haitian?"

That question forced Fritz to face the real reasons why he had refused to settle in his native town. He revealed to Crystal what she already knew. "I don't want to have my parents on my case every day, and be under their grip. You know, the concerns I shared with you before leaving, the whole Arab-Haitian thing; remember that I'm also their only child. Their attention is focused entirely on me."

He stopped, not wanting to pursue the subject, leaving a part unsaid. Crystal sensed that there was more to come. She crossed her arms and waited. Fritz drank some water and added, "I don't see myself in Cap-Haitian without you. It seems that I live with the memories." He glanced at the ring on her finger and inquired boldly, "Who is Gerard?"

Crystal forgot that she had mentioned her fiancé's name. She became tense, resentful. "How do you know about Gerard?" she stammered.

Fritz answered, "Didn't you say earlier, 'Thank God I have Gerard's support'?"

Relaxing, Crystal volunteered, "He is my fiancé."

Fritz, taking advantage of the situation, formulated the concern that was bugging him, and inquired, "Is he one of the engineers I just met?"

Crystal smiled. "No. He is a physician, Dr. Gerard Armand. He teaches at the university. He also has his own practice, he is a surgeon," she said simply, a veil of melancholy displayed in her eyes.

Fritz skimmed through his mind the faces that he had seen at the dance at La Chaumiére Saturday night and decided that none of them fit the description of Dr. Armand. With an unconvincing tone he congratulated her. He looked at the note in front of him, then added, "I hope Dr. Armand will make you happy."

44

Crystal felt a sharp pain in her chest. She was disturbed by the conversation, and thought, *What right has he to question my happiness?* She revolted and exclaimed, "I don't think he will abandon me, causing me as much pain as you did. He has been very good to me. He proposed and we are planning a July wedding."

Fritz blushed. The accusation struck a very sensitive cord. Arching his eyebrows and glaring at her through murderous eyes, he spat, "Crystal, it was not my choice!"

Crystal rolled her eyes, an exasperated look on her face. Then she twisted her mouth in a disdainful smirk and blurted, "Poor me, poor nerdy me! I waited three years for you, three years lost. I guess the townsfolk were right."

Fritz flinched as if stung by a bee, not registering the last part. He was flushed red, his heart racing. He fixed Crystal with bulging, searching eyes, then repeated slowly, "Three years," for the meaning to imprint in his mind. Then he moved deeper into the chair and burrowed his head in his cupped hands.

Shocked by his reaction, Crystal remained silent. They were each absorbed in their own assumptions, their own interpretations of the new development.

Fritz was astonished, astounded, curious, but at the same time embarrassed by Crystal's disclosure. He felt like a heavy weight had just been dropped on him and a menacing crater had opened its jaws, asphyxiating him with its intoxicating lava. His mind was blurred, as it had been years earlier when his mother presented to him the pictures of Crystal with a lieutenant. It was one of the most horrifying experiences of his life.

It was nothing to compare to the tales of werewolves or evil spirits roaming the city at night—one could fight those devilish hosts. It was why he carried a cross with him at all times, and his parents kept holy water in their house to annul the diabolic effect. Based on his mother's report, things had been getting worse, out of control, in Haiti. His parents had doubled the bribe they usually paid to the military, just so they could function in peace, but to no avail. They were constantly harassed. They had received anonymous letters accusing them of fraud in their business; the police chief provoked them by stating they occupied the best locations in the city.

The Arab-Haitian community felt they were the target of the military. There was no judiciary system to rely on. His parents used to say that if the police had a cold, the judge coughed, and the prefect had a high temperature. They joked all the time about the complicity of the authorities to control the city's affairs, and summarized the situation by agreeing that all of the authorities ate out of the same plate.

Armed with the pictures of Crystal in the company of a member of the dreaded military, Arianne had advised her son to end his relationship with her. She had never approved of his union with a woman of a different race, and had also always discouraged their long-distance relationship. She told him to leave Paris, abandon the university, because Crystal's intimate relationship with a military man could mean the end of their race's presence in town.

In Haiti's history, at many points, some governments had manifested the desire to expel the foreigners, meaning Arab-Haitians. The ones living in the countryside towns had never really felt the impact of the threat like those residing in the capital. However, they had to neutralize the military members to keep safe. One of the worst affronts one could commit against the feared group was to manifest some kind of interest in a woman they frequented.

It was the only case in which the close-knit Arab-Haitian community would not back up one of their own; in other words, the Lucas' would have to fend for themselves. Ultimately under pressure from their friends and relatives and the backlash from the offended military member, they would have to desert Cap-Haitian. After exposing the danger of the situation to Fritz, Arianne concluded her demonstration as follows: "You cannot offend the military rulers, you know that, son."

That was it. Fritz had gone to live with cousins in New York.

His chest now constricted tightly and he sensed that the suspense had grown to an explosive level. Now more than ever he felt compelled to solve the puzzle that had plagued his life for the past four-and-a-half years. A new vigor invaded him. He planned to go to his native town of Cap-Haitian the following day—the town where he had dated Crystal and where she was seen with that lieutenant. He wouldn't announce his visit. He would surprise and confront his parents.

Crystal was confused and dumbfounded by Fritz's reaction when he learned she had waited for him for so long. The man looked shaken, as if hit by thunder. The painful images of that sad period clicked in her mind. The hurt still lingered; it was the reason why she worked long hours, to forget. To be tired enough to just sink into her bed and not think. To ignore the reality of Fritz dumping her for no apparent reason or, worse, not even forging one.

In time, she had become enraged, conscious that her numerous letters pleading for an explanation remained unanswered. She was also ashamed by the acknowledgment that she had trusted Fritz so much and still he had betrayed her, proving the speculation of the townsfolk to be right.

Hadn't they presumed it would never work? There could be no such thing as an Arab-Haitian marrying a Black-Haitian—especially a wealthy one.

She broke the silence with, "What do you care for, Fritz? Tell me that you care."

What Crystal stammered hit him like a knockout. For a brief moment he had wished to disappear, because he realized she had suffered more than he had assumed in the ordeal, and that now she was frustrated and angry. It was the only justification he could arrive at for the boldness she showed. And, damn, he was embarrassed by the result of his actions; he had only considered his side of the coin. An only child, he was an egoist and now he admitted that his handling of the situation reflected the weakness of his personality.

How he wanted to pour out his heart and say, "I love you, Crystal." To have her believe him, as she had years earlier, to have her kiss him to let him know he didn't have to tell her so, because she knew how much he loved her. But, to gather the courage and present his feelings today would be like offering her an empty, broken vase. She would ask for facts and proof. He must clarify the situation, then approach her. He did not want her to assume he was a coward, or that he had abandoned her for no reason. He retorted, "Do you recall when I called you from Paris at the public telegraph in Cap-Haitian?"

"Of course I remember; it was Easter vacation, six months after you left. You asked me how I was doing, but did not tell me the real justification for an urgent call at the telegraph. It was the last time I heard from you. All my letters remain unanswered to this day."

They faced each other, Crystal trying to figure out why the man sitting across from her, who claimed he loved her, had disappeared with no explanation. Fritz admitted to himself that whatever motivated his past decision to break off his relationship with Crystal did not stand, no longer mattered. He needed time, time to learn about what happened. Who was the military man in the pictures? Fritz had acted impulsively. Could it be that jealousy was associated with the fear that propelled his rage? How could he question Crystal now? How could he present his torment? He was beginning to feel rather silly over what he had done; after all, he had acted without any rationality, and now found himself unable to speak truthfully to Crystal and tell her so.

Besides, in Haitian culture it was a manifestation of total disrespect to even think a woman could be unfaithful. Imagine the mess he had caused and was resolved to clean. He wanted her back, and to get her back he would have to repair all the damage he and his mother had so stupidly caused. For now, he felt close to her, too close to a woman with a fiancé. He repressed the thought and addressed her about the construction, "My office has to be changed. I would like a small garden in the front, windows on both walls, a sleeping area and a small kitchen."

"How big do you want the rooms? The size of a one-bedroom apartment or a studio?" Crystal asked.

He wanted her to talk, to give him advice like she had years earlier. Soliciting her help he asked, "What do you recommend?"

Crystal rebuffed him, "Come on, for how long did you live in the States? You know the difference better than I do."

Ignoring her sharp tone Fritz replied, "I would like a place where I can rest during the day, and my wife and children can do the same. That is why I want a private entrance, so the workers won't know everything about my private life. I hated it when as a young boy at my parents store I saw the employees witness all our moves, what we were eating, my parents' discussions."

Curiosity again stirred in Crystal. She wanted to know about Fritz, whether he was married or not. "The size of the apartment will depend on how many members you have in your family. Your wife, and how many children do you have? You know how noisy children can be."

Fritz looked at her sadly and said, "Wife? Children? I wish! There is only me, no one else." He laughed a nervous laugh that sent a chill through him, and Crystal. Then he added, "Whatever my mother tried did not work. She could not find someone to steal my heart."

Wonder illuminated both their gazes while their music still played in the background. He wanted to add, "My heart still belongs to you." But he kept quiet and just glanced tenderly at her. He did not want her to think he did not respect her making career advances while he did not clear the past. And, she was wearing an engagement ring. He had to justify his actions. He had to see his mother.

Crystal's heart melted. Flustered, she fumbled through the Fabric Pro folder. Fritz had avowed that he was free, that his mother had failed.

The atmosphere once again relaxed, and Crystal was rejoicing to learn that Fritz was available. She arranged her notes while they discussed the office, deciding on a one-bedroom apartment. They briefly mentioned the subject of the renovation at his home on the plantation. They agreed it would be better to deal with the updating needed the following day while at the premises.

Two hours later Fritz retreated from Crystal's office. On his way out, the secretary handed him an envelope, which he took and placed in his briefcase. Jean, the chauffeur, was waiting for him outside. Fritz climbed in the car and requested, "Do you know a nice florist?"

"Yes, Mr. Lucas, just one block down the road."

"Will you please stop there?"

Five minutes later, Fritz chose a bouquet of yellow roses on a bed of leafy fern mixed with baby's breath secured by a golden ribbon. The bundle was to be delivered in a beautiful vase the following day. A simple card with the note "Congratulations, Crystal, for a job well done. Fritz" was attached with clear tape at the vase's mouth.

———

Sitting around a rectangular table filling almost the entire room, Dr. Gerard Armand waited to present a summary of his demarches to a medical committee. Six of his peers shared his fate in the rector's office at Haiti State University. They had been glued to their chairs for the past hour, expecting the rector, whom they all eyed with high regard and envied his position.

But they secretly resented the fact that the rector must report to the president of the republic. The censorship machine operated from the presidential palace, and the president's aides selected the material to be presented to the students. The rector was summoned for an emergency meeting by the chief on that Monday morning; it was justification enough for them to wait for his return. No one would dare leave or criticize, since any proposition could be interpreted as a sign of rebellion against the established regime.

Today, the committee appeared gloomy, its members spiritless. Dr. Armand, the youngest among them, usually entertained the crew with his enthusiasm and knowledge of current medical news. He had recently returned from Florida, where he represented the department in their effort to obtain financial help to upgrade the university's library. The *Lancet Medical Journal* he always carried to the meetings was missing. His hands were clasped in a knot on the table, his lips were tied shut, his eyes were vague, and his face withdrawn.

Often, he checked his watch as if he were needed somewhere else, or had to participate in a more important event. The clock standing in the back corner of the room boomed a bang that startled the attendees; on the third one the cathedral's clock joined the jingle. The uproar marking noontime swelled in the room as the rector arrived, his long strides translating his uneasiness. He apologized, and then took a minute to address each one of his peers.

Dr. Armand was in agony. Time was passing, and with each minute his anguish escalated. He had to see Crystal. Early that morning, when he had gone to give his fiancée a ride to work, in the dining room at her house, something had happened; something he could not understand, could not touch. He described it as discomfort, like when your car skids on black ice and you lose control; you don't know where to put your feet, afraid of slamming down on the brake pedal, and terrified of accelerating.

That was the feeling his fiancée's attitude had aroused in him that morning. He had been in the kitchen, waiting for her, a steaming cup of coffee in front of him. When he saw Crystal, his face had brightened and his eyes had dilated in admiration. Slowly he had stood, walked over to her, and kissed her.

"How are you doing?" he'd asked, searching her eyes. "How was your weekend?" He'd looked at her closely and raised his eyebrows at her outfit. "You look marvelous this morning! Are you going to a conference today?"

"No, it's just another day of office work," she had replied dismissively. "How are you doing?"

Gerard released her, took three steps back, reached for his cup of coffee, took a sip, swallowed, and said, "Thank you, Crystal. Thanks for taking the time to make yourself pretty for my return. It shows me how much you miss me when I am out of town."

Crystal still had her handbag clasped in one hand, and realizing this, he grabbed it from her and placed it on a chair. Then he gave her another admiring glance and momentarily regretted that he did not have more time to spend with her. His specialty, surgery, was difficult, demanding, and even jealous, he reminded himself. But right then Gerard decided to make more time, if there was such a thing, to be with his sweetheart more often.

He pulled out a chair for Crystal across from his and inquired, "What are you going to have for breakfast?"

"Nothing. I am not in an eating mood." Crystal's tone was distant and vague, almost dismissive. Gerard could not understand why she did not flood him with questions. She did not even ask about the list of beauty products she asked him to buy in Miami. Watching her closely, Gerard sensed that she was absent-minded. Then the door from the back yard creaked and Maria, the maid, entered.

"Good morning."

"Good morning," they answered in unison.

"Miss, what would you like for breakfast?" Maria asked.

"Nothing, but could you prepare a mango for me, for lunch?"

Maria chose a firm, yellow mango from the fruit basket, took out a small plastic bowl from the cabinet, then left.

Gerard remembered that Crystal's cosmetic items were in the trunk of his car. He excused himself, then came back, and placed them on the table in front of her. She thanked him coldly as she distractedly shifted around the various items. Even the perfume Gerard had bought for her, which he had had specially wrapped, did not catch her attention. Gerard was baffled. His surprise gift lay meaningless on the table, lost among hair and skin products, creating no impact at all. Maria came back with the prepared lunch bag. Crystal took it from her, thanked her, and ordered her to bring the items on the table to her room.

The ride to the office did not help the situation. Gerard was irritated with so many cars on the road because of the state exams; congested roads were Gerard's worst nuisance. For about ten minutes the driving occupied his mind. He was tense, his hands gripped the steering wheel tightly, his heart pounded heavily, and his gut muscles were taut. He tried to concentrate on the road, but Crystal's attitude was really what bothered him. He would not ask the cause. Usually Crystal was the one to voice her concerns, the whimpering one. She was so sentimental.

Gerard gave her a quick glance. Her head was turned toward the sidewalk; she was absorbed in the students talking animatedly, walking to school. A reason flourished in his thoughts: *It's PMS! Women! Why did I not think about it before?* His body relaxed, his heartbeat was less intense, and for the first time his back touched the seat of the car. He parked the car in front of New Spectrum, took Crystal's left hand, and caressed it, an unusual act for him. Then he searched her eyes and, even more unusual, reached out for her lips and kissed her, almost a full mouth kiss in the early morning's bustling activity. Slowly he parted from her. Crystal hastily gathered her belongings, exited the car, waved goodbye, and entered her firm's building.

Crystal, his Crystal, had not been recognizable; she had been drifting in a world he could not identify. A world that was not theirs, that was not for sure the one he had built for them. She appeared distant, engaged in a fairytale. She was beautiful in her mint green suit. Her face sported a dreamy air with a mysterious note. He had forced himself to interpret the image she exuded. The result of his search frightened him. All he could relate it to was love, complicity. Jealous he was, jealous he became more and more. A jealous man anticipated some kind of collusion in all his partner's relationships. That trust was the ingredient missing in their union. But love, what kind of love can brighten, even metamorphose, a person in two days? He had last seen her on Friday.

No, it could not be, she had probably read some romance book. It was out of the question that she could have met someone during his absence, for Crystal would never attend a party or a social outing without him. No, he was wrong. She would, because months earlier, she had chosen to go to the upcoming New Spectrum anniversary party instead of accompanying him to a dinner conference offered for the physicians.

It was an exception, a rare occurrence for the festivities to fall on the same date. He had swallowed his pride, but intended to punish her. He would not attend her firm's anniversary party, which would start after the engineer's presentation, and close with a dinner/dance. He was not married yet, and so he still had to bend to her will. He did not see any harm in his fiancée being alone with her co-workers. Still, a tinge of panic lingered in his senses.

Gerard presented a poor account to the rector of his journey to Miami, declined the invitation to stay for some refreshments, and left the rector and his peers baffled. He drove his car toward his fiancée's workplace. The traffic was lighter on his side, and he passed the New Spectrum building, only realizing so when he was two blocks up the road.

Fuming, he made a U-turn, ignoring the protests of the other drivers, joined the opposite heavy lane, now going toward the building. After fifteen minutes, which to him seemed like an hour, he entered the building still wearing his university badge. He had forgotten to take it off. In the hall, he crossed paths with a tall Arab-Haitian who was leaving. He passed him like a storm, and flew up the stairs without taking the time to say hi to the secretary.

Dr. Armand reached Crystal's office door, knocked, and then opened it. Crystal was seated, her arms folded on her desk, her chin resting on them, a vague sensual look in her eyes. Gerard was stunned. "Are you okay, Crystal?"

"Yes," she muttered, "I will be fine."

"You appear so tired, drained. Are you working too much?"

"NO," said Crystal. "It was just a strange day." She stood, snatched her bag, and requested, "Will you please drop me at home? I need some rest."

She passed Gerard, who trotted after her like a zombie. The ride to her house was dull. Crystal's face was withdrawn and Gerard felt frustrated. As they neared their destination Gerard's beeper went off, and Crystal emitted a sigh of relief as he curbed the car. She gave him a slight peck on the cheek and was gone. Gerard had to leave; they were calling him *stat* to be at the hospital.

During the ride home Crystal had analyzed the situation: the factory construction was almost done, the renovation at Fritz's house would last at the most three months, there would be a few parties where she would be in Fritz's presence, and then it would be over.

———

She ate a light dinner with her aunt and cousins, then went to her bedroom. She turned on the radio, listened to the news, and switched the station to light music. She deliberately dug in her bottom drawer for Fritz's picture and took a long look at it.

She placed it back in the drawer, gathered a towel, went to the bathroom, showered, dried herself, returned to her room, closed the window, and crawled into bed. Fritz's profile surged and filled her mind. He was the same now, she observed, except that he had lost his tan. This was why she had laughed so hard seeing Fritz turn as crimson red as the pepper in her garden. A tender feeling encompassed her body. She weighed the effects of sharing the news with her best friend, but backed off. She was too confused to present the facts impartially.

But, speaking to Fritz after four-and-a-half years of silence, she was very unsettled, disturbed. She thought that Fritz still loved her and was hiding a secret.

Her thoughts drifted back to the afternoon she had met Fritz, Friday of the second weekend of July 1960, a time cherished by the teenagers in the provincial town of Cap-Haitian. It marked the end of the school year, and for her it was vacation time back in her native town. For the native twelfth-grade teenagers it signaled access to freedom or university life in the capital.

It was a special weekend in that it represented the shortest vacation span of their life: Friday, Saturday, and Sunday. Monday morning, they would travel to Port-au-Prince, where they would attend Prefac courses all summer long in preparation for the admission exam at the university. Fritz had double reason to take full advantage of those days. He was a high school graduate, but since he had been accepted to Paris University, he was going to be by himself for the summer in Cap-Haitian once his friends left for the capital.

Crystal remembered word for word the story Fritz had recounted to her all summer long about the day they met. Earlier that Friday afternoon he had fetched his bicycle, exited his house on the western side on Rue des Capuccines, walked while pulling his bike the block's length, and ended on the other side of his domain. He was then facing east and the sea.

Fritz cast an amused glance at the distance he had traveled and marveled at the size of his house. He compared it to a big cave and avoided the place as often as he could. He would have preferred a smaller house packed with brothers and sisters to bump on and fight with. But as his mother had put it, "It was God's will" that he was an only child. He lay the bike against his fence and advanced toward the sea, inhaling and deeply absorbing the salty air.

The sky was clear, a pale blue. The air was still, the palm trees parading on the sidewalk in front of the properties, dominating the landscape with their trunks erected high, their large leaves dropped around their tops like a pleated skirt. The deep blue of the Caribbean Sea stretched indefinitely, contrasting with the pale sky, inviting lovers to share their intimacy and friends to share their secrets. Fritz admired and appreciated the scenery. He liked the silence, that sort of full emptiness where nature reigned. This was why he always hit the boulevard early, before the afternoon *promeneurs* showed up. He mounted his bike and routinely rotated his head right then left to check the boulevard runway.

Usually the thoroughfare was empty, bleak, but that afternoon there was someone else biking, plunging toward the point where the concrete ended, with the seashore blooming a few yards down the road. A slender form directed the bike in a zigzag pattern. Fritz was a little annoyed by the intruder's presence. His curiosity awakened, he pedaled to see who the biker was.

As he neared the form he could tell it was a girl. He now rushed to identify her, but before reaching her Fritz witnessed how, when she was at the steep side of the last stretch of the boulevard, she fell. He hastened to help her. When at her level he kneeled down and discovered his twin friends' younger sister, Crystal Dijon. She was lying on the pavement, her right arm outstretched past her head, a bump on her forehead, her bicycle wheels still turning fast between her splayed legs.

She was panting, her hair disheveled, and she looked at Fritz with widened eyes. Then she closed them and tried unsuccessfully to sit up. Fritz moved the bike away from her, reached out his arms and offered her his hands for support, advising her, "Move slowly, Crystal!" He helped her to her feet and they stood facing each other, their hearts beating faster and faster, their heads spinning, their chests bursting. Crystal had her back to the sea, her head up and straight, the protruding bump garnishing her forehead disfiguring her face. She adopted a new stance and stared boldly at Fritz. Her eyes were flaming; she had a slight protrusion of her bottom lip, her shoulders were erected squarely above her swollen chest, rising and falling in rapid sequences.

Fritz was lost in admiration. For a second he thought Crystal was going to cry or explode, and that he would not know how to respond. But he rejected the idea, reasoning that Crystal was too proud for that. Interrupting the silence he asked, "Are you okay, Crystal?"

She nodded. "Yes."

"Come, Crystal, let's sit on the sidewalk for a few minutes."

Fritz grasped her hand and directed her to a bench. Then he advanced to the seashore, took off his shirt, plunged it in the blue liquid, soaked it, and made a ball with it. He returned to Crystal's side and said, "This is a good remedy. The salt will help make the bump go away." Fritz carefully dabbed the balm on Crystal's forehead. She had closed her eyes so that the dripping water would not get in them. She was thinking about how caring Fritz was and how beautiful were his eyes, his voice deep, resonant; his lips, and the blush, his skin a deep red.

During the same time Fritz was questioning himself. How could he have been so blind for so many years? What had kept him away from her? Was it because she attended school in the capital, or was he intimidated because he knew she was very smart? At the beginning of each vacation, her twin brothers always voiced their hope that for once Crystal would not be able to show off her A+ grades from the top religious high school she attended. But now, she was in Prefac while they still lingered in twelfth grade. Fritz felt embarrassed. They, him and the twins, had decided with a silent pact to shun her presence. *Maybe, it is why she was by herself this early on the boulevard,* thought Fritz. All he wished for now was to hold her in his arms.

At that instant the two of them were visited by the same thought, sharing the same feeling, the impulse to be together, to know each other, to share each other. Together they assessed the damage caused by Crystal's fall. A few scratches on her right arm and leg, dirty pants with spotted brown mud, and the head bump. "Thank God it's not that bad," said Crystal. "Thank you for your help, Fritz."

Fritz put his wet T-shirt back on and they sat side-by-side on the bench, the two bikes abandoned on the street. "It happens to all of us sooner or later," said Fritz. "This side of the boulevard is treacherous.

Crystal smiled sheepishly and admitted, "I should have known better. I have seen my brothers fall and criticized them for being too adventurous. We should have a sign placed there to remind people of the risk." She turned and faced him. "I guess this is what happens after nine months of being stuffed in a boarding school."

Looking back at her he asked, "When did you get back?"

"Yesterday. This is my first outing!" Crystal exclaimed.

"You like the sea that much?" Fritz asked with a dreamy look on his face.

"Well, I enjoy biking at this time of the day."

While talking to Crystal, Fritz kept thinking of how easygoing she was. In the past he and the town boys had assumed she was a smart, preppy, pretentious girl not worth their attention. But that afternoon all he wished for was to be with her.

A slight breeze woke up, balancing the palm leaves, making the crashing of the waves louder, animating the bicycles' wheels. Fritz laughed at the sight of himself with a wrinkled, crumpled, dripping shirt glued to his body and Crystal with her dirty clothes and the bump on her forehead.

The time had come when the boulevard received its habitual lovers and the flood of teenagers on that first vacation weekend. Fritz presumed the local teens would question the sight of them together, but most of all they would tease Crystal. She was considered a newcomer each vacation, a snob who preferred the tumultuous capital to simple town life. Fritz felt as though he had to protect her, so he proposed, "Why don't we go home? My house is only a block away."

Crystal agreed. They left, Fritz pulling the two bikes and Crystal strolling at his side, both remaining silent until they reached his house. Fritz had used all his charms to seduce her that afternoon. He first made Arab tea for her and served it in his mother's precious china. Then he retrieved his family album and exposed the story of his family to her.

When his school friends came to pick him up for their outing, Fritz flatly declined to join them. So they left with amused smiles on their faces, and the news spread, even before Crystal had gone back home, that she and Fritz were falling in love and had chosen to share intimate moments instead of participating in town events.

Fritz had accompanied her back to her house at sunset. They lingered for a while on the square outside Crystal's house. When Crystal's brothers showed up, it signaled to Fritz that it was time to put an end to his talk with Crystal. With regret he wished her a good night. He went home happier than he had ever been in his life. His mother, initially angry for her china being used for no valuable reason, was stunned to discover the cause of her son's excitement. She panicked, then she remembered Fritz was going to Paris at the end of the summer; she assumed he would forget about any casual relationship born during his vacation. She felt relieved.

Before Crystal could even explain to her father what had happened, her brothers informed him that Crystal was in love with Fritz and that everyone in town knew about it. Crystal dismissed their intrigue as small-town gossip, but they all agreed on one point: Fritz was a gentleman.

Crystal and Fritz spent the rest of the summer together, their love the subject of criticism among the townsfolk, who presumed the relationship wouldn't last. "It has never been done before. Imagine a white Arab-Haitian married to a Black Haitian." They were shocked by the couple's intimacy. The young couple looked so natural, so lost in their own world, that they were soon admired, respected by the citizens. Except Fritz's family members. Especially his mother.

Crystal painfully recalled how she had sat late at night in the small, cramped room back at the boarding school, writing letter after letter to Fritz in Paris. Letters that remained unanswered. She had not been able to think of any explanation for his attitude. He had stopped all communication after she'd last spoken to him at the telegraph in Cap-Haitian. It was an unusual conversation, and Fritz had appeared strange, as if he were worried or disturbed. He had asked her how she was, what she was doing. It was small talk, not the usual deep conversations they always had, and Crystal had been alarmed by his attitude.

At home, Crystal's father had informed her that Fritz's mother was abroad visiting Fritz in Paris. He had learned about the trip from Father Ignacio when he had noticed Mrs. Lucas' absence from the Lent ceremonies. That was all anyone knew, as the Arab-Haitian community was by nature secretive and when they felt to reinforce that side, no effort could breach their plot.

After some vain attempts directed at her brothers who were, like her, in the dark, she had abandoned all exertions for learning of the cause of Fritz's silence. But she had kept on writing to him. She did so for a year, then had stopped and waited for another two years, always keeping the hope that Fritz would never just abandon her for no good reason. She had wanted to blame the Arab-Haitian community, yet she finally reasoned that Fritz was an adult who had to assume some responsibility for his actions.

Still, she couldn't help but think that she and Gerard had never been as close as she and Fritz had been. Gerard had been persistent; he had chased her for two years and was patient with her. He was 35 years old, eleven years older than her, and she had assumed he was ready to settle down. He was working hard and planned on becoming dean of the faculty.

Gerard was handsome, ambitious, and always busy. In a way, Crystal suited him because she, too, was always busy. They did not spend a lot of time together: a ride home after work, dinner on the weekends, a show at the theater sometimes. Why had he proposed? Crystal could not figure it out. He was domineering, jealous, and very proud of himself.

He claimed he had always wanted "a Crystal," that she fit into his plans, but Crystal knew he secretly resented her zeal for work. However, he was good to her when she was discouraged by the obstacles she confronted at work as the only female. He boosted her confidence, admitting, "Women are as intelligent as men. You are a talented architect. I wouldn't hesitate to have you design my house." Smiling he added, "Not because you are my sweetheart, but because you are knowledgeable, motivated, responsible."

She had often relied on Gerard to help her navigate difficult paths. But this time, Gerard would not be able to assist her. She had to find the solution to her problem herself.

———

After ordering the bouquet, sitting in the car with the chauffeur on his way back to the factory, Fritz imagined Crystal's eyes glistening with pleasure, her lips molding into a delicious pout manifesting her surprise when she received his roses. He recalled how she used to appreciate even the simplest gift, a chocolate bar, a bunch of wildflowers, an unexpected card. That thought opened the window to the errands they had undertaken in the Cap-Haitian countryside and awoke a string of sensations increasing his present uneasiness and anxiety.

Many contradicting feelings tortured him. Love, a strong burning flame inside him, pushing him to revolt and feeding his will to fight. Fear, a sort of uncontrollable worry fueled by the probability that he could lose Crystal forever after finding her again. Anger boiling inside him and mingling with sadness accompanying the strange acknowledgment of playing the main character in an act where he ignored the outcome, because he was manipulated by the invisible strings of a harsh destiny that pulled him deeper and deeper into loneliness, regret, failure.

He was overwhelmed. He compared himself to a beast trapped in a tight net, unable to escape the smashing tornado destroying his retreat, annihilating his life. His head throbbed, a deep malaise that he never experienced before gagged him. He sensed he was being metamorphosed, his skin changing into a cuirass. He reasoned to elaborate, to come up with a justification to explain his mother's actions, because his talk with Crystal confirmed what he had suspected for years: that she had not been unfaithful.

He pondered, *Was it a mistake? Or did my mother pay someone to take the pictures?* He was fully aware that marriage remained the cornerstone of Arab-Haitian society, ensuring the repartition of wealth and also the vital element to produce the offspring carrying the families' names. He remembered how his grandfather had often broached the subject with him while he was still a young lad, enumerating his responsibilities: work hard, be a good provider for his family.

Marrying was a must, and his wife must be fertile. His parents never assumed he would cross the line, be interested in a woman of another race; it had never been done before in their family or their race. When his mother realized he was serious about his relationship with Crystal, she had panicked and had reminded him of their tradition, how Arab-Haitians kept to themselves, no foreigners admitted.

The assumption that his mother had deliberately accused Crystal of cheating appeared mean to him. He chuckled and rescinded, "No, my mom would never go that far. She would not be able to carry that load." That conclusion consoled him somewhat. But his misery deepened as he considered his reunion the previous Saturday with his former classmates, and childhood friends, the Dijon twins.

His first night back in Haiti, and like a fool he had divulged all his personal information, the most relevant being that he was the owner of Fabric Pro. They had not told him that their sister was the architect working on his project. They let him walk unprepared to discover the challenge that awaited him, to face his past. His gut tightened with remorse and guilt. What about Crystal? How devastated and hurt she must have been upon learning that for all that time she had been working for him.

Fritz guessed at how she must have reacted with disgust. Insecurity and a frightening despair drenched him. He reached his factory, his stomach churning, nauseated. After entering the building, he raced to his office's bathroom and poured cold water over his head. He regained some courage after shaking off the gloomy thoughts and convinced himself one more time that he must act fast.

He stayed in his office for hours and checked the progress of the work being done. He told the contractor to contact the architectural firm if he needed anything, because he would be unavailable.

His uncle and aunt dropped by the factory. "How was your meeting with the engineers?" asked his uncle.

"Everything went smoothly. The engineers were helpful," Fritz answered evasively.

"You met the architect, didn't you?" Michael Kahlil asked. "Isn't she something? To fight her way among the presumptuous men. She must be tough and smart. She is pretty, too."

"Yes, she is. Do you think I can join you for supper tonight?"

His aunt gave him a reproachful look and replied, "You are more than welcome, Fritz. Our house is your house. You know you don't have to ask. I will tell the maid to add another plate."

They climbed into Michael's car. As they crossed the Petion-Ville main road, his aunt addressed his uncle, "Will you please stop at the market? I want to buy some fresh bread."

Michael scoffed, "Always have to stop there, can't you have one of the maids go during the day? What do we pay them for?"

Fritz interrupted them by saying, "I'm going to Cap-Haitian tomorrow; maybe you can buy whatever you think my mother will need. I could bring it for her." Fritz's voice was a distant whisper when he solicited the purchase of items for his mother. If a stranger had been in the car, he would have registered some kind of hesitation in his tone; a feeling of apprehension in his bearing.

However, neither his aunt nor his uncle noticed the distress wafting from his posture. Instead, misinterpreting his feelings, they highlighted the concern that had gnawed on their conscience for the past two years, and they expressed their relief with encouraging gestures.

His aunt and uncle both turned to face him with surprise, affection, and approval in their glances. They both assumed Fritz had finally decided to be close to his parents again, to pay them a visit as a sign of his renewed affection for them. His uncle voiced his encouragement, "God bless you, Fritz! I knew you were going to visit your parents. They are so hurt by your distance, your coldness. Your stay in Cap-Haitian will bring them happiness, peace of mind. My sister is going to be thrilled."

"Fritz, remember to bring *cassava cocoyer*. How long are you staying?" asked his aunt.

Fritz, contrary to the good manners to which everyone was accustomed, became rude. His new preoccupation was quickly turning into an obsession, and he ignored his uncle's comment and did not offer an answer to his aunt's request. Pursuing his own line of thought he informed them, "I should be back by Wednesday afternoon."

"What's the rush? Stay and spend time with your parents; there is such contentment when sharing quality time among family members. I will take care of the factory and the house in your absence," Michael suggested.

The fact that Fritz did not bother to enter the store to choose an item for his mother, or worse, that he did not name one, did not catch the attention of Michael and his wife. They desperately wanted to believe in their nephew's happiness, and had concluded that his trip to Cap-Haitian would eliminate the strain in his relationship with his parents and reestablish the closeness of the past.

His aunt left to get her bread and came back with some things for Fritz. The atmosphere in the car changed after his aunt returned, and each of them remained silent during the ride to Kenscoff. Fritz was thinking about his uncle's assumption about his parents and realized his family members did not truly know him. He wished he were able to share what mattered most to him—starting a family with the woman he loved.

He reeled back to the afternoon gathering at his Kenscoff bungalow with his family members upon his return the previous Saturday. The car had passed through the gate that had been left open for his arrival, the vehicle's wheels screeching as it stopped abruptly in front of the bungalow. Fritz had exchanged a flurry of kisses and embraces with his aunt and cousins. He entered his house, toured the place and thanked his mother for the fresh, new curtains. Fritz acknowledged that she was the one who had replaced the curtains, fixing the bungalow to his taste.

The delicious smell of sizzling cabbage drifted in the air and filled Fritz with a sense of well-being. He felt empowered by the welcoming message carried by the aroma. That particular scent of *meshi*, an Arab-Haitian appetizer, stirred old, warm memories. He imagined his aunt carefully stuffing the cabbage leaves with spicy cooked ground meat, sculpting them into small balls that she dipped for a few seconds in boiling water. The odor betrayed that dinner was ready for the guests.

The celebratory dinner had been served, but the family just enjoyed the *meshi* and barely touched the rest of the flavorful dishes. Excitement had dampened everyone's appetite. By the time they were done with dessert it was 4 p.m., when Fritz got up from the table and invited his mother and aunts to join him on the porch. There, he disclosed his next reason for choosing Kenscoff. "I've always liked this bungalow; the silence, the trees, the flowers," he said, pacing. "I enjoy the fresh air as much as the fresh fruits. Don't forget, I have the disco at the corner, and Petion-Ville is just fifteen minutes away. I plan on partying and relaxing a lot."

His cousins had heard earlier talk between his mother and aunt about arrangements for his marriage. They were curious and asked him if he had met the woman chosen for him yet. Arianne cut in without giving Fritz a chance to answer. She coarsely reprimanded her nieces, reminding them marriage was an adult's subject, and that they should be interested in games and other such nonsense. She claimed she was tired after the end of her harangue and that she needed to rest, since she must assist the six o'clock mass before her trip back to Cap-Haitian. She had hurriedly packed some food for the trip and kissed her son goodbye.

As soon as the women and children had left, Michael confessed to Curtis, "It was a big surprise to us when you confirmed that Fritz would be living in Kenscoff."

Curtis, in an atypical move, turned to Michael and confided, "His decision has been the subject of many discussions between Arianne and I. Both of us would rather have him in Cap-Haitian. We deluded ourselves with that hope since his birth, until we learned about his plan two years ago. I accepted his wish, but his mother was devastated, she could not understand why. She thought he was running away from home."

Fritz shook his head. "I am not running away from home," he answered gravely. "I just think there is nothing in Cap-Haitian for me."

Curtis, taken aback by this harsh answer, again surprised them with an inquiry, "What brought you to that extreme conclusion? Was it your unhappy love experience?"

Fritz blushed and his eyes suddenly became somber. "I never really accepted what happened," he acknowledged. "It did not make sense and I never had the opportunity to investigate. A long time has passed now, and I want to make peace, peace with myself. I want to explore new territories and exploit new opportunities."

When Fritz got home from his uncle's Monday evening, it dawned on him that his quest to reunite with Crystal was not only going to affect his relationship with his mother, but with his entire family. His mother was originally from the capital and since Michael had been raised in the same house as Arianne, Fritz thought he might be as conservative as she. On their way home from the airport on Saturday, Michael had manifested a kind of admiration for the architect, but he had not been aware that Crystal was Fritz's ex-girlfriend. Would his attitude change once he learned about them?

Fritz was tired and fell into a deep sleep on his bunga-low's porch. When he awoke the sun was gone, the sky a deep navy blue studded with shining, twinkling stars. The air was crisp, the gentle dancing wind blowing, caressing the leaves and carrying a slight beat of *compas* music. Fritz abandoned the hammock, then stood and turned to face his bungalow. It was illuminated. The maid had turned on the house light before retiring to her room. It reminded Fritz of the lantern he had carried in town every Christmas Eve when he was a child.

He stretched his arms to touch the slanted portion of the ceiling. His grotesque shadow was displayed on the floor, and Fritz played with it as he had when he was a young boy. His grandfather's warnings flashed in his mind. "You know what happens to people who play with their shadow? Their past comes back to haunt them!"

Fritz wished his grandfather was still alive. He would confirm to him how true his anecdote was. His past was here: Crystal, the pictures, his mother, his town, all of them with full swing assailing him. He also remembered his grandfather used to say, "You cannot escape your destiny." Fritz sighed, admitting that he was ready to face his.

Fritz called the maid and instructed her that he would be leaving for Cap-Haitian the following day. Then he plunged into his bedroom, got out his suitcase, and pulled out a large brown envelope. He sat on the edge of the bed, frowning, and replayed the sequence in his mind: his love for Crystal, the controversy borne from their relationship, his mother's disapproval, and his original plan to come back after college to marry her.

How he had shared with Crystal the hope that their love would overcome the racial biases of their small community, the promises they made to one another before he left for Paris. Not one piece of the plan ever materialized. Instead, only six months after he'd left Crystal, while he was studying hard to obtain his degree, his mother had come to visit him with pictures of Crystal parading around with a handsome lieutenant right in front of her house, at the same spot where he and Crystal used to sit and talk. The memory of the shock and anger he had felt from seeing those pictures still unnerved him.

———

Fritz had become intrigued after learning that Crystal had waited three years for him. Now he asked himself what had happened. Who was the lieutenant? Only Crystal's father could help him. He couldn't ask Crystal. He would never have questioned her, because she was engaged now and he could only present the pictures with no proof, yet, to contradict the accusation they carried.

He imagined she would lose all respect for him if he told her straight out that he had taken his mother's word. How was he going to prove that he had doubted she was cheating on him, after which he broke off all communication? Fritz persuaded himself that he had to go to Crystal's father because he loved her and still wanted her.

Walking over to the closet, Fritz chose two sets of pants, t-shirts, and underwear, and flung them into his sports bag on the floor. He crossed the room to his bed, seized the envelope of photos, dropped it in his bag, and zipped it up. He proceeded to the bedroom door and locked it, looking at the bedroom displaying the chaos that echoed in his life.

———

TUESDAY

———

FRITZ AWOKE EARLY THE next morning, amazed that it had only been three days since he had been picked up at the airport. At 5 a.m. the rooster's crow had pulled him out of sleep. It was too early to leave for Cap-Haitian, so he went for a jog. He alternately walked and ran, watching the steam come out of his mouth, tracing his breathing pattern. He tapped the pavement until exhausted, then walked back home. He was ready to embark on his exploration. He showered hastily, dried his body quickly, dressed in a simple outfit, and waited for his ride to the airport.

His car was moving slowly down the curvy hill, making him rotate his head, absorbing the scenery. He gazed at the towering profile of the pine trees that dominated the landscape while their aroma tinged his nostrils. A steady drizzle had wet the area overnight, soaking the tree branches, making them heavy and bent, forcing them to drop the excess water onto the ground.

A light, low fog moved hastily, covering the area like a blanket, and a mystery took hold of the place. The habitation was located on the ridge of Kenscoff Mountains. It was a flat, outstretched, vast land, the size of four football fields surmounted by a gentle hill. Fritz's bungalow, a low ranch structure, nestled on the head of the hill like a crown. Fritz identified the bungalow's red tile roof sparkling like the dome of a crab shell.

While descending the slope, he admired the bungalow, sprung like a gigantic mushroom sleeping leisurely on a green carpet. In front of it stood a big wall inundated with pink and white hibiscus branches pointing out from a mass of deep green leaves. The venerable, numerous pine trees towered over the rest of the panorama giving it a transcending sense of mysticism.

This was the place Fritz had cherished since childhood, and where he wanted to ultimately settle. He drank it all in as he left it behind, thinking of his dream of living here with Crystal. He took deep breaths of the fresh Kenscoff Mountains, hoping they would give him strength for the journey on which he was about to embark.

It came as no surprise to him, or any of the other passengers going to Cap-Haitian that morning, that their flight had been cancelled. There was no explanation, no details as to why, just a simple apology. Fritz shrugged; this was the way things were in Haiti. You had to go with the flow; it was practically a cultural proverb. He had to wait for the eleven o'clock flight.

He dropped himself on a chair, picked up a magazine that lay forgotten on the seat next to him, and absentmindedly drifted through it. Again his mind wandered to before he had seen her, to the party he had attended with the Dijon brothers. He was sure that Crystal, at least for the past 48 hours, had known he was the owner of Fabric Pro. Still she was shaken when she saw him. What about the music she'd been listening to? She appeared trance-like, as if she'd been in a dream, once again enjoying those moments they had spent together.

Yes, thought Fritz, *I am glad I decided not to settle in Cap-Haitian. My mother will never accept my decision to investigate. Wait until she learns that I met Crystal!*

Fritz recalled that his spirits had been low after he left Paris for the United States. He attended the same university as his cousins, New York University, and they paid him great attention in an effort to ease his adaptation to Manhattan. However, Fritz had continued to be depressed. He lost a lot of weight, let his hair grow past his shoulders, and offered to explain his disgust for life to whoever would listen.

He obstinately refused medical help, but joined the university swimming team. He slowly began to regain his enthusiasm and to participate in various activities. He encountered many women that he found interesting; initially he was eager to go out with them, trying to fill the vast hole that presided over his life, but they all complained about his guarded manners, and when they learned he was from Haiti's deep northern town of Cap-Haitian and intended to settle down there, they thought it was wiser to dump him.

But he had developed a kind of mutual understanding with Carmelle. She was also from Haiti, from Port-au-Prince, and was the exact opposite of Crystal. With her, Fritz was always lost since he could not predict what she was aiming at. He was pleased with the situation; there was a challenge in the air and he predicted that his family would have their hands full. Carmelle was light-skinned; she could almost pass for a white person.

Fritz knew that his parents were aware of the relationship, but as they never broached the subject with him, he did not present it to them, either. As Fritz had started compiling information for the factory, he informed Carmelle of his plan to propose to her after the factory's inauguration. He received the biggest surprise of his life when she advised him that he was a good friend, but wouldn't be a good husband, because his mind was still possessed by Crystal's imprint.

Fritz fought the assumption, then from a common accord they decided to remain friends. Carmelle had chosen to be a flight attendant, pushing Fritz to admit that with that kind of career, she would have never suited him. Fritz had found himself back at square one, still guessing about what had really happened to Crystal and looking to find himself a wife. But Crystal, his Crystal, was the one who owned his heart. She was not only his lover, but also his friend.

She was the first and only person to whom Fritz had confided his worries, his failures, his fears, his achievements and his joys, and she had a way of listening, of understanding, that made Fritz feel relaxed, free, around her. She had offered him support, patience, affection. Fritz also had brought the same to her. She was seen as a strong, smart girl and she was under a lot of pressure from her father, who expected her to be the best in everything, and from her teachers who bounced her from competition to competition. Her life was centered on her studies and all arrangements to make her obtain perfect grades.

Fritz knew that no other woman had Crystal's impact on him. He had been searching for what he found in Crystal, but had found no match. When he thought about it, deep inside he was sure of only one thing: his heart belonged to Crystal Dijon. She was, and is, his only love. And maybe she was the reason—the sole reason—that he had come back to Haiti. To follow his heart.

Engrossed in his thoughts, Fritz jumped when the overhead announcer requested that the passengers traveling to Cap-Haitian line up at Gate 2. He joined the crowd ascending the ladder to the airplane. It was a beautiful, sunny day. There was no wind, and the flimsy plane made the trip in thirty minutes and landed smoothly. Every passenger exited with a smile on his or her face, glad to be off the rickety little aircraft and on safe ground, and searched for family members expecting their arrival.

Fritz, with a determined stance and a brisk gait, was the only one to cross the waiting room without stopping to hug and kiss an expectant relative or friend, instead walking straight to the main street. Alone with his one bag, he hailed a cab and told the driver, "Dr. Dijon's clinic, please." The man at the steering wheel twisted around to see his passenger and, with a look of surprise etching his features, said, "Welcome back, Mr. Lucas."

———

Crystal was drained on Tuesday morning. Her sleep had been restless. The events of the past 48 hours had turned her world upside down. She was now fully aware that Fritz cared more for her than she had assumed, and from his reaction she concluded that he had not abandoned her without a sound reason. She was going to see him again and she was anxious to discover how he was going to act. What would be his next move?

She was glad she did not have to see Gerard that morning. In fact, Tuesday was the day for her to do her survey work and for him to perform elective surgery. She was filled with enthusiasm for having the opportunity to work for her best friend, Fritz, but also was uncomfortable by the uncertainties of such an awkward situation.

Were Fritz's parents still in the capital? Was she prepared to meet them, knowing they were probably responsible for her breakup with him and if so, was it safe for her to be exposed to their unfair judgment and whims? She shifted her thoughts from those troubling worries, boosted her courage, and relied on Fritz's weakness: his honesty, which was often deplored by his former classmates, because they could not count on him to execute their scheme to beat the opposing team. She concluded that only an open discussion with Fritz would bring her peace of mind.

Her outfit was simple, the opposite of the day before: blue cotton slacks and a t-shirt. Her concerned face at the breakfast table caught her aunt's attention, who reassured Crystal by joking, "Girl, don't look so weary! Your Arab client will love you, love you a lot. That I can guarantee!"

The comment made Crystal shiver. She offered her aunt a timid smile in return, her heart pounding and her mind blurred. *What a woman, always bragging and supporting her relatives' efforts*, thought Crystal.

Her aunt noticed the New Spectrum vehicle parked outside, handed Crystal a thermos with iced water, and said, "Have a wonderful day!" Crystal swallowed the last drop of her coffee, grasped the thermos and her bag, and still shaken by her aunt's love allusion, left.

Crystal climbed into the car, saluted the chauffeur, and they set off for the ascending road from Musseau to Kenscoff. It was a beautiful morning, and the traffic was light. As they approached the countryside, Crystal admired the landscape. The sun was high in a cloudless blue sky, numerous chirping birds were flying from tree to tree, and tribes of butterflies drifted from flower to flower.

The car attacked the steep hill with difficulty and its motor emitted a protesting note. The far-off barking of a dog faded into the air, dying in the thick buzzing of an army of bees. A solitary goat munching on grass at the side of the road cast a fearful glance at the car, trotted away in zigzag, suddenly stopped, parted its hind legs, cocked its head to the sun, and bleated. It was as if the goat was announcing their arrival. They had arrived in front of Fritz's house. The gardener was watering the outside plants; he saw them and opened the gate. Crystal got out of the car and said, "Good morning! Could you please tell Mr. Lucas that the architect from New Spectrum is here?"

The old man took off his hat, bent his head in a curtsy, put his tool on the ground, and hailed, "Vonise, they are here." He preceded Crystal down the paved alley. Crystal waved goodbye to the chauffeur and entered Fritz's domain. She was admiring the old house's architecture when the gardener's voice brought her back to reality, "Mr. Lucas went to Cap-Haitian this morning; he left instructions with Vonise to show you the place."

Taken by surprise, Crystal inquired, "Is everything okay?" Then she remembered Fritz's bizarre attitude the day before and guessed that he probably went to take care of some familial affair. The maid presented herself and accompanied Crystal through the house, unable to give her all the information she needed. In fact, the owner of the premises must be present in order to specify the extent of the modification to be inflicted on the original structure.

To fill the time she explored the back yard, since she had dismissed the chauffeur. She discovered a shaded area with bunches of fern and wildflowers carpeting the ground. And as if it were her property she decided this lot should be preserved. She was lost in contemplation trying to sort out the diversity of the ferns when the New Spectrum vehicle came back for her. She chose to return home; her mind was too crowded to concentrate on work. She was worried for Fritz.

Dr. Armand always started his day earlier on Tuesday mornings. He was the only physician to hit the surgical block of the hospital at dawn. He allowed for extra time to review his patients' charts, and personally reassess them before their operations. Five hours later, after he was done with the surgeries, he left the operating block wearing his street clothes. He looked younger; the frown on his forehead had disappeared. His gait was sure and a proud smile brightened his face as he approached the reception area. He shook hands with his patients' relatives and informed them that everything went fine, that the three patients he had operated on would be able to see them soon.

He went to the nursing station, grabbed the charts, wrote new orders, tagged them, and placed them in the bin. Under the admiring glance of nurses and visitors he left after giving a quick salutation. He descended the stairs, entered another hall, and went to the physicians' reading room. There he reached for the phone and dialed Crystal's direct line. The phone rang indefinitely. He hung up in a pensive mood. Biting down on his bottom lip with his upper front teeth, his mind wondered madly.

Usually Crystal was back from her tour of houses to be remodeled before eleven. Where was she? He was annoyed and checked his watch. It was fifteen minutes past twelve. She must be at New Spectrum. Gerard convinced himself that Crystal was probably giving a report or talking to the engineers about Fabric Pro, the factory design she was working on. He decided to stop by her office on his way to the clinic to announce that he'd made a dinner reservation for them at Bambou.

The blazing midday sun welcomed Dr. Armand. Pedestrians swarmed the streets, hurrying to reach their houses and benefit from the shade. Gerard concentrated on

81

his driving and his new preoccupation: to find out where Crystal was. He was just parking his car in front of her office when a delivery man left a van carrying a bouquet in a big vase. He was handling his load with great care, like a prize, as he entered the office and ambled to the secretary's desk.

Gerard passed him, flew to Crystal's door, and knocked. There was no answer. He frowned, moving to the balcony with an anxious look on his face. After standing there for a while, he walked reluctantly to the secretary's desk to inquire about Crystal's schedule. The secretary was busy on the phone, giving information to a client. The delivery man was standing in front of him, also waiting for the secretary.

As Gerard joined the line, the smell of fresh flowers tinged his nostrils. He glanced evasively at the arrangement and concluded that it was a little extravagant, when his eyes fell on the card attached to the rim of the vase. It was addressed to his fiancée. His interest sharpened and he moved closer. He quickly blinked his eyes, trying to recall any special event. No, there was none that he could think of. He leaned closer, bent, and read the note. Blinded by jealousy, he acknowledged the signer: Fritz.

Gerard saw red. His head spun. He felt dizzy, as if he were falling down a big hole. He whirled around, his shoulders slumped, his head dipped down, and his body fell limp against the wall as he walked outside. Gerard felt his feet growing heavy as he painfully dragged himself to his car. He sunk into his seat, turned on the switch, and stared blankly in front of him. Confusing thoughts collided in his mind.

He mumbled to himself, "Yes! It was what I read. Fritz signed the card. The note said 'Congratulations, Crystal, for a job well done!' What job was he talking about? Was Fritz not out of the country? How did he know about Crystal's job? Had he ordered the bouquet from the States? Was Crystal in some kind of relationship with him? Or was it that Fritz was just another client?" Yes, that was probably it, he reasoned.

From what he knew, Fritz Jean Lucas had been Crystal's former boyfriend. She was not on good terms with him, as far as Gerard recalled. Or was he wrong? No, Gerard assured himself, if Crystal was in contact with Fritz Jean Lucas, why did she not bring up the subject? Why did she not discuss the situation? Was she hiding something? No, she was not that type! She usually confided her problems, her concerns, to him. What happened?

A sort of wild rage, then a deep worry, took hold of him. His heart was beating wildly and his breathing was heavy. All his muscles were taut and his body felt like a tight knot ready to unravel. His car was running, the engine emitting a persistent purring, the muffler puffing a cascading chain of coiled dense smoke. The suffocating smell made him gag. He angrily grasped the steering wheel, shot a furious glance at the oncoming traffic, and bounced the car full speed into the clear street. The car's screeching tires signaled his departure.

By routine, he drove the distance back to his clinic, and parked negligently, taking two spaces. He slammed the car door, then slowly climbed the three steps to the clinic. He nonchalantly unlatched the lock and pushed the door open. A burst of cold air assaulted him, and he raised his head. In front of him like an unfolding fan, he observed the crowded clinic waiting room where rows of patients were waiting for him.

He smiled at the sight; his face relaxed, he straightened his posture, waved to the new patients on the left, saluted the secretary, then on his way to the consultation room he purposely shook hands with his former patients on the right, identifying them by name and asking them, "How are you doing?" It was a habit he developed early in his practice and had stuck to it, realizing how pleased the patients were by the special attention. His chest was inflated with pride as he accessed his consultation room, readying himself to perform his duties.

It was what he liked best and had worked so hard to achieve. He thought, *This is my first priority. Everything else is secondary and if a woman really loves me she has to accept me with my practice, my obligations.*

In his consultation room he eased himself into the chair behind his desk and, swiftly analyzing the situation with Crystal, said aloud, "This is why I disagree with women working. They should stay home to take care of their husband and children. I don't understand why my wife should work. I'm making enough money to support a family. As soon as we are married, she must resign." His intercom buzzed. It was his secretary, asking, "Doctor, can I send in your first patient?"

"Sure," he answered. He realized that he had been in his office for a while, and admitted that never before had he made his patients wait so long. He acknowledged there was a change that had affected him and his relationship with Crystal. He must find a way to gain control of the situation.

He reached for the pile of neatly arranged charts on his desk and opened the top one. It was Mrs. David's, a patient he had operated on a month earlier. He had seen her in the waiting room and just by looking at her he knew that she was doing fine. He once again experienced that sort of satisfaction, a kind of contentment acting like a balm, freeing him from his worries, bringing him peace. He spent the rest of the afternoon doing what he enjoyed most: taking care of his patients.

After the last patient left, Gerard ordered his secretary not to accept any walk-ins, and reminded her he would be out of town the following day for a conference, but his partner would be available. Then he called his associate, Dr. Cassis, to review patient cases with him. When they were done, Dr. Cassis wished him an agreeable day at the conference.

With that, Gerard turned his attention back to his private life. He decided to write Crystal a note; he did not want to meet with her. He scrawled on his business notepad: *I was at your firm around 1 p.m. and spotted a delivery man with a bouquet for you. Could you explain to me what your client's intentions were? Will you still argue with me about how women are not exposed and manipulated at work? This is why the weaker sex should stay at home. You must resign from that position at once. -Gerard.*

He sealed the note in one of the clinic's envelopes, shoved it in his bag, and left the clinic.

The traffic was scant with a few vans leisurely trolling the downtown streets, their drivers offering their empty seats to tired, uninterested merchants. Gerard stopped at New Spectrum on his way home. The firm's concierge was playing dominoes on the sidewalk across from the building, and he reluctantly abandoned his game to open the door for Gerard. Gerard hesitated about giving Crystal's note to the disgruntled man, instead choosing to slide it under her office door himself. His precipitant steps resounded in the vacant hall like thunder announcing the torrential sky. But when done, for some reason he could not pinpoint, Gerard felt relieved. He thanked the concierge on his way out and rushed home. It was one of the few times he had admitted that he needed rest.

The taxi sailed through the Cap-Haitian streets while Fritz sat in the back figuring out how to approach Crystal's father, how to break the news that he had met Crystal and was there to question him about a man in photos with Crystal given to him by his mother. To tell Dr. Dijon that he had broken his only daughter's heart because he thought she'd been cheating on him. The sports bag grew heavier on his lap, his breathing became labored, and his eyelids fluttered, a sure sign of nervousness. The car stopped and the driver trumpeted, "Here we are."

Fritz paid him and went into the clinic on shaky legs. He addressed a timid salutation to the two patients waiting for the doctor, and opted for the seat in the far corner of the room. Dr. Dijon did not have a secretary, but came out of his office, and yelled "Next!" while inspecting his patients. Fritz was aware of this practice and dreaded the moment, that first reaction when Dr. Dijon would see him.

As he observed a lizard crawling slowly along the gutter, Fritz heard a grating noise. It was Dr. Dijon opening the door, standing in the doorway saying, "Next." The doctor's eyes widened as he moved aside to let his patient in. Then he tilted his head sideways, narrowing his eyes as if to take a better look, to convince himself of who he was seeing. He jammed his hands into his lab coat pockets, cautiously crossed the room, and planted himself in front of Fritz. Extending his right hand he said, "My goodness, since when have you been back, Fritz? Are you here to see me?"

Fritz blushed, raised his head, and looked straight into Dr. Dijon's eyes. He shook his head and with a searching gaze mumbled, "I need to talk to you."

"Well," said Dr. Dijon, "I will be done soon." Dr. Dijon tapped on a small bell on the wall. Josette, the maid, appeared. He ordered, "Fix some extra food. Fritz will be having lunch with me," then went back to his work.

Fritz became embarrassed, and a sort of remorse gripped him. *How could I be so blind? Why did I not think of this before? Is it too late, or will I be able to surmount all the difficulty awaiting me and make up for the mistakes I've made? I'm a man in love who made mistakes. So, I shall beg for forgiveness.*

The sun crept on the service stairs, bathing them in light. The air was still, thick, dense. A lizard limped on the wall, glared at the sun, then pulled his body toward the garden. Dr. Dijon came back to the porch. His stance appeared less severe than before, since he had gotten rid of the lab coat. He exuded an air of affection. His hands were still humid after being washed and he was shaking them lightly to dry them completely. He moved thoughtfully to Fritz's corner and said, "Pass me your bag; we can talk in the ping-pong room."

"Thank you for allowing me into your home," Fritz answered timidly. He handed his bag to Dr. Dijon and followed him.

Dr. Dijon placed Fritz's bag on the ping-pong table and offered, "Have a seat." He looked around. "You know, since the kids left, no one has used this room." He took a seat across from Fritz and tried to create conversation, saying awkwardly, "I am ready to listen. How can I help you?"

Fritz blushed, fidgeted in his chair, positioned himself, drew his thighs closer, took a deep breath, established eye contact and said, "I was with the twins the other night." Dr. Dijon's lips parted in a faint smile, his eyes brightened with pleasure, and he asked, "How are my twins doing? Where did you meet them?"

"At La Chaumiére, a club in Kenscoff. It's only two blocks from my house," answered Fritz.

"I thought they were studying for a test!" exclaimed the doctor.

Fritz shrugged. As if it were the same subject, with no introduction, in one gulp he revealed, "They seemed to be doing fine. I also saw Crystal."

Dr. Dijon's eyes widened with surprise but he said nothing. He crossed his arms over his chest and leaned back in his chair, staring steadily at Fritz. His smile disappeared as the meaning of Fritz's sentence sunk in.

Fritz acknowledged the marked change in Dr. Dijon's features, but was determined not to let any rebuff discourage him. He continued with what he assumed would please Dr. Dijon and place him in a better position, "Crystal did a good job designing my new factory. She is passionate about her work, and a great architect."

The doctor remained silent. His feigned passivity, instead of intimidating Fritz, catalyzed his resolution to bypass all obstacles in his pursuit of the truth.

"I'm returning to Port-au-Prince tomorrow. I only came here to show you something." Fritz reached for his bag, unzipped it, and pulled out the envelope of photos. He handed it to Dr. Dijon. The doctor took it from him, and looked at it curiously. Slowly, he opened it and took out the contents.

"I'm sorry, but I cannot wait anymore. I have to know the truth," blurted Fritz. He looked away from the doctor.

Dr. Dijon shook his head in confusion, flipping through the pictures as he spoke. "Know what, Fritz? Why are you showing me these pictures? Where did you get them, anyway?"

Fritz pushed his body forward to the edge of his seat. "My mother brought them to me in Paris almost five years ago. She told me they were proof that Crystal had moved on. That she was dating that lieutenant in the pictures."

Dr. Dijon looked stricken. "Fritz," he said, "if this is a joke, then it is a very bad one." He stood, dumping the pictures on his seat. He shook his head in disbelief and paced the room, his arms locked behind him. Finally he turned to face Fritz. "The man in those pictures is Alex Turnier, her uncle."

The words sliced through the air and fell like dead weight. Fritz blushed, growing uneasy and feeling stupid. A deep frown creased his forehead. His mind reeled in recollection. "You mean the one she works with at the factory?" He stood slowly.

"Yes," said the doctor. "Alex attended engineering school while in the military. He came to this town for one week four-and-a-half years ago. He ate dinner with us every afternoon. Crystal was here for Christmas vacation. They shared the same interests."

"I knew there was something wrong," said Fritz, emitting a loud sigh. "It's not in Crystal's nature to abandon someone like that. But my mother insisted she was only playing the safety card, convincing me of how risky and dangerous it was to antagonize a military man." He sat down again, agitated, not knowing what to do with himself, feeling unnatural in his own body.

Josette came with the salad and *griot*. Dr. Dijon addressed her, "Will you please bring a beer for me. I need to wash the bad news from my system. I'm not working this afternoon." He turned to Fritz and said, "I'm leaving tomorrow for the capital. I will stay there for the conference on laparoscopic surgery and for the weekend. Most surgeons across the country will be attending." Fritz searched Dr. Dijon's demeanor for a reaction or some kind of information. He suspected the doctor was going to contact Crystal and divulge all that had just passed between them. Instead, Dr. Dijon broached, "What did you do during those five years, Fritz?"

Fritz listed his actions in a bland tone, still dealing with the blow of his mother's lie, the wasted years he'd spent without Crystal. "I visited the Western world, frequented a renowned university, rewarded myself with a diploma: bachelor in business administration, international trade major." He stopped. Suddenly he said, "Come and visit the factory."

"What is this factory about?"

"Nothing complicated. Manufacturing baseball caps and balls."

"Won't you get bored, son? The routine can be tedious and make you disinterested. Will you be involved in some kind of design or just executing commands?"

Fritz stood, his face flashing a grin, "Crystal and I will probably invest in the construction business."

Dr. Dijon's mouth dropped open. He stared at Fritz, who had been but a boy the last time he'd seen him, wondering at his boldness. He retorted, "What bravado you show, Fritz Jean Lucas! How do you know Crystal wants you back? As a matter of fact, she is engaged."

Fritz placed a hand on Dr. Dijon's shoulder, locked his eyes on him, and murmured a soft, "I know Crystal still loves me."

Dr. Dijon looked closely at Fritz, examining him, and realized that the grown man facing him really believed in what he said. "Let's eat, Fritz, the food is getting cold." With a sudden move Dr. Dijon grabbed Fritz's shoulder, forcing him to gaze at him. He added in a cautious, spiritless voice, "Fritz, be careful. Our society has not changed. Why do you think your mother brought you those pictures? Why did she get them in the first place? Please don't hurt my daughter!"

Fritz thundered, "My parents don't know that I'm in Cap-Haitian today. I came here directly from the airport because I wanted to clarify a situation. Crystal and I will decide, not my mother." Fritz sat, crossing his legs. In a temperate but defiant tone he added, "Sorry. I'm leaving tomorrow for Port-au-Prince. Wish Crystal and me good luck."

Dr. Dijon was surprised by Fritz's reaction. He had interpreted Fritz's sudden, unannounced visit as a sign of rebellion against his parents that might alarm them and their tight community, and who knew what kind of repercussions that could have?

He gulped down his beer, but did not touch his food. Fritz ate some, then mentioned his desire to go to his parents' house. Dr. Dijon offered to give him a ride. Fritz got his bag and stuffed the pictures back in their place, hating them, wishing he had burned them the minute he had first set eyes on them. Together they left the Dijon house.

The square across from the Dijon house regained some animation at mid-afternoon, a time when the children from kindergarten to elementary school assaulted the space. It was one of the few areas where they could run, jump, and laugh without restraint. They formed teams to play their preferred sport, while the adults who accompanied them congregated to feed themselves on talk of merchandise prices, new items on the market, and gossip.

The sunlight caressed the mountaintop, darting off softer, gentler rays. A shy breeze appeared, shuffling the palm trees, smoothing the atmosphere. Cool air engulfed the town; relief translated itself in the form of smiles on adult faces, while the children, panting from their effort at their improvised games and tired after a day of schoolwork, rejoined their parents or maids. They knew it was almost time to go home.

The town's routine assailed Fritz. This was the city where he had spent the first eighteen years of his life. He lingered at the doctor's front door, amazed by the display in the square, then entered Dr. Dijon's car with a renewed sense of reassurance spreading over him.

The ride to his parents' house was short, as Cap-Haitian is a very small town. The murmur of the sea slowly invaded the air, followed by the crashing of the waves against the boulevard rail. The palm leaves wheezed softly, disturbed by the flapping noise of birds' wings. Fritz's senses awoke from the heavy smell of salt, his gaze lost in admiration for the vast, still sky competing with the infinite dancing sea.

Large houses adorned by deserted gardens bloomed in straight rows like cacti decorating a desert field. Fritz's body relaxed and his mind eased. The sea always had a mellowing effect on him. Images of Crystal visited his mind while Dr. Dijon drove along the boulevard and stopped in front of the Lucas family house.

"Thank you for the ride. Have a good time at the conference," said Fritz. They shook hands and the doctor drove off.

———

Dr. Dijon's scrutinizing eye followed Fritz as he entered his parents' courtyard. The doctor witnessed how Fritz was welcomed by one of the maids, and deep inside the doctor had been pleased. He now moved the car slowly from the Lucas compound without paying any attention to their well-manicured lawn or their modern architecture and that of their neighbor's house.

Suddenly his face grew tense and somber. He slammed on the brakes and pulled the car to an abrupt stop, slid the gear handle to park, and turned off the engine. He dismissively answered the warm greetings of the *promeneurs* invading the boulevard, got out and crossed the street and slumped on a bench. His haggard eyes focused on the horizon.

Dr. Dijon was confused, annoyed. Disturbing questions kept appearing in his mind. *Why did Fritz come all the way to Cap-Haitian to see me? What was his real motivation? What is Fritz going to do now that he knows the truth? What will happen to my daughter? Is she going to let Fritz convince her to break off her engagement to Gerard? No,* reasoned Dr. Dijon, *Crystal is too smart for that. She would never ditch Gerard.*

He began speaking to himself, "Crystal must stay with Gerard, he suits her." Dr. Dijon now had a headache. His temples were hurting, he felt embarrassed. How was he going to approach his daughter? He planned a scenario in his mind. "Don't get me wrong," he would say. "Fritz is a good guy, from a good family, but that is the problem. I have known the Lucas family forever. Years ago I repaired Curtis Lucas's hernia and sometime after that I extracted

Arianne's appendix. They are fine with casual exchanges in public and business relationships, but getting into their family is another thing."

While practicing his speech a new worry surged to the head of the list. Why had Arianne tried so hard to destroy Fritz and Crystal's relationship? What would she do to abort their alliance now? Dr. Dijon felt guilty that he was partly to blame for this mess. The townsfolk had condemned him as an irresponsible father for accepting, even encouraging, Fritz and Crystal's union.

He remembered some of the young couple's displays of affection, from the first time Fritz brought Crystal home, to the many dates they had afterwards. He recalled how they were deeply in love and how he had admired them. He was now tortured by the decision he had to make. *Will I be able to face Gerard?*

The boulevard was now noisy with laughter, wind, bicycles and the waves still crashing at his feet. Man and nature insensible to his torment, Dr. Dijon cast a reproachful glance to the horde, and his misery increased. He asked himself, *How far did they go? Is it too late?* The truth assailed him. Fritz and Crystal were very close and if they decided to be together, they could never be pulled apart.

One of Fritz's statements materialized in his mind: "If I face any opposition, I will leave the country." Dr. Dijon revolted. *Why? Why my daughter? First she did not have a mother, and now this ordeal. No, no. I cannot abandon my daughter. I know how stubborn she is; this is why she's an architect and not a pediatrician. I have to support her, no matter her decision.*

Dr. Dijon felt relieved. He thought about the conference while walking back to his car. *I won't attend. I will stay at my boys' house in Port-au-Prince, visit my daughter and see after her, see that she is fine and happy.* He drove back home and informed the maid that, as planned, he was leaving in the morning for Port-au-Prince.

———

Itsa, Fritz's old dog, was jumping and barking in the yard. The old maid, Justine, came to the gate and opened it cautiously. She saw Fritz, abandoned her grip on the handle, threw her arms wide, and bent her head toward the sky in a sign of gratitude. Fritz hugged her, then placed an affectionate kiss on her forehead. She patted him as if to make sure she was not dreaming, then mumbled, "Thank God, Fritz is okay."

Seizing Fritz's sports bag, she gave him a wicked look. She knew he was up to something. She had received Fritz the day he came from the hospital as a newborn and had always been there for him. "How are you doing, sir? I thought I was going to die without seeing you."

"Nope, I'm here and glad to see you. You look rested."

"After you left, there was not that much for me to do in the house. Now that I'm sure you are okay, I will resign in a few months—just in time to train a new attendant."

"No, Justine. I will take you with me to Kenscoff. I'm sure Crystal will appreciate your expertise."

Justine moved swiftly. Her body jerked. She now knew why Fritz had come. She predicted that turmoil would prevail later that evening. From the night five years earlier when she eavesdropped on a conversation about Fritz and Crystal's relationship, Crystal's name always brought confusion, discord in an otherwise peaceful household.

She could not feign it; she sided with the young couple. Mrs. Curtis had noticed her attitude and punished her by sending her on errands when such subjects arose. *I have to be here tonight*, she thought, since she considered herself part of the family.

She preceded Fritz to the porch and said, "I'm going to clean your room, then I will go to visit my sister." She hurried to begin her task and inquired, "Where do you want me to put your bag?"

"On my desk."

Itsa was yelping for Fritz's attention. He sat on the porch and caressed Itsa's neck while casting a scrutinizing look around. The garden appeared the same to him, with bougainvillea climbing the wall, large pots with roses dispersed among the chairs, and a grapevine with intertwined branches forming a tent-like sitting area.

When Justine was done, she passed by and wished Fritz a good evening, then made believe that she left the Lucas household.

———

Returning from Fritz's house, Crystal took refuge in her room, abandoning her handbag on the nightstand, beside Gerard's picture. She sagged to the window with her shoulders slumped, suddenly feeling overwhelmed by the morning's events. She replayed the different scenes: Fritz had gone to Cap-Haitian, but what intrigued her most was Fritz's reaction on Monday when she told him she had waited three years for him. Fritz was really shaken and had lost control, as if shocked by the revelation.

Why did he assume I dated someone else before Gerard? Why was he surprised to hear I had waited for him? What about his Kenscoff bedroom? It was as if Fritz had been angry; his clothes were flung all over the place, suitcases were left wide open, a kind of urgency exhaling from the area. She was confused, lost. She persuaded herself that she needed more time to sort out a sound, plausible explanation.

She had planned on addressing that subject with him while checking the repairs needed for his private house. But Fritz had not been there, leaving Crystal annoyed. She went to the kitchen and joined her aunt, who was checking out the table set by the maid before calling them for supper. Her aunt approached her and said, "How was your day at Kenscoff?"

"Fine. As you can imagine, full of surprises." She did not elaborate and her aunt, usually more perspicacious, did not question that one. She knew about Crystal's past relationship with an Arab-Haitian. She had even discussed it with her brother, Crystal's father, but she did not realize her niece's client was her former boyfriend. Crystal did not volunteer the information. At supper, everyone—her uncle, aunt, and cousins—remarked that Crystal seemed worried, more concerned than usual. They did not want to bother her and attributed her attitude to the stress of her job.

While at the table, Crystal thought over her short list of close friends. In reality, she had Amanda and Julie, who were both married with children. They had chosen the housewife path, quite the opposite of hers. Julie was the one she was going to visit after supper. Like Crystal, she was also from the countryside; they had attended the same boarding school in the capital.

Julie was often the subject of criticism and jokes from their former schoolmates who made fun of her reserved ways. Crystal defended her with passion and they had grown rather close, each one confiding their torment to the other. Julie knew about Fritz and the whole race dilemma.

As soon as she finished her meal, Crystal excused herself from the table, announcing that she was going to visit her friend, and would be back later that night. She left her house and used the back road to reach Julie's house. Her pace was brisk and her face gloomy. As she neared Julie's the front door unfolded, revealing her friend with a warm smile and an excited look on her face.

"Come on in, Crystal! What brings you here at this time, and on a weekday, too?" Then she noticed that Crystal was withdrawn, her eyes sad. She moved aside to let her enter, seized her arm and asked, "Is everything okay? You seem pretty concerned."

"Oh, where is Roger?" Crystal asked.

"My dear husband will be home soon. Don't worry, we will have enough time to talk. What is the problem?"

"You opened the door for me before I knocked. How did you know I was coming?" asked Crystal.

"My daughter. She was at the window and saw you. Now tell me what's wrong."

Crystal took a deep breath. "Guess. I had the surprise of my life."

"The firm, your work at New Spectrum, the constraints of Haitian society...don't let them bother you. It's time for you to relax and have a good time!" Julie said. "Did Gerard come back from Miami with a new contract?"

Crystal shook her head. "No, no, no. Not Gerard, Fritz Jean Lucas! He was at the firm yesterday and I was at his house today."

"What?" Julie exclaimed. "You're kidding! Tell me you're kidding. When did he come back? How did he find out where you were? Why did you go to his house?"

"He's the owner of Fabric Pro," Crystal explained. "I'm the architect for both the factory and his house."

Julie relaxed and a smile spread across her face. "How do you feel about working for him?"

Crystal recounted the whole situation for her, explaining Fritz's reaction to hearing she'd waited three years for him before dating Gerard.

"Well I told you, didn't I? Something grave must have happened for Fritz to just disappear the way he did."

Crystal measured her words, "I think he might still have feelings for me, I'm afraid."

"Why? I'm sure he does. You know those Arab-Haitians, they probably pressured him. What's the name of that big shot in charge of the factory?"

"Michael Kahlil," answered Crystal.

"Is he related to Fritz?" asked Julie.

"Yes, he is his uncle. Probably on his mother's side, since his name is Kahlil, not Lucas."

"Does he know about you and Fritz?" Julie inquired.

"I don't think so."

"Crystal, be careful. I won't ask you if you still love Fritz. I know you do. But if he wants you back he better come up with a good reason for his attitude and absence."

"It's like I'm waking up from a bad dream. Gerard is so jealous. He'll never stand for me even being friends with Fritz, and it is also a good occasion for him to remind me of the reasons why he disagrees with women working. Seeing Fritz again makes me question my relationship with Gerard." Crystal paused, "I'm closer to Fritz than I am to my fiancé."

Julie put a soothing hand on her shoulder, gave her a deep, understanding look and said, "Wait, Crystal. Time is the best healer. Let's get some *cremas*!"

———

Fritz entered his childhood house, and a strong mildew odor hit him. He frowned, reached for doors and windows, burst them open. Sunlight and fresh air engulfed the domain. Fritz checked the refrigerator and with dismay acknowledged that there were no beers. He walked to the phonograph, placed on one of his favorite local jazz disks and started the turntable on high volume. A blast of music invaded the property, bringing it to life. He proceeded to his bedroom. He smiled widely at the sight of his bed dressed up with his favorite cream sheet, his tan jersey and his shorts cradled in the middle. His ball was also placed on the side of the bed. It had been Justine's work, an invitation to play basketball like before. Fritz explored the room, and saw that everything was as he had left it, untamed, untouched. He showered, put on the jersey outfit, caught up the ball and started bouncing it as soon as he reached the porch. After awhile he was relaxed and had almost forgotten about his worries.

Fritz's mother and father were stunned by the boiling music and all the noise emanating from their house. As they neared it from the town side, Arianne proposed to her husband, "Stay in the car. I am going to enter on the boulevard side and turn off that phonograph."

She paused, observed her husband with a contented smile on her face then added, "Remember the days when our son was at home? All that commotion is from him! My sister-in-law the blabbermouth probably informed him about the woman we found for him. He is for sure pleased with our choice. See, Curtis, we will have to accelerate the arrangements for his marriage!"

She exited the car and entered the house. The phonograph came to an abrupt stop when Arianne executed her plan, leaving only dense air hanging quietly, pierced by Fritz's heavy breathing, the stomping of his feet on the porch floor, and the boom of the bouncing ball. Arianne moved to the dining room window and admired her son, her face beaming. She emitted a prolonged sigh while thinking, *At least I have my son back!* She could not resist anymore and plunged for the porch trumpeting, "Welcome back, stranger."

Fritz stopped. "How long have you been there, Mom?"

"Long enough to turn off the phonograph and watch you play. You are still good, you know." Fritz landed in his mother's embrace, and a tight hug followed. She disengaged herself and exclaimed, "Your dad is waiting for us outside."

She seized her son's arm and dragged him to the gate. With her free hand, she waved to her husband. They opened the gate, each of them standing at one pole to let the car in. Curtis was all smiles, pleased at the sight, as he parked the car and joined them. Father and son hugged. When they parted, Fritz led them in a single file until they reached the porch and sat in their respective seats. It was as if he had never left.

Arianne began the conversation by saying, "Fito, don't you realize your parents are old and cannot deal with any big surprises?"

Fritz laughed heartily and replied, "You did fine, Mom. I thought the phonograph stopped because of the blackout. You tricked me. By the way, let me turn it back on."

"With the volume down, please," requested Arianne.

Fritz walked over to the phonograph, placed the needle on the vinyl disk, and music once again spilled into the air. Regaining his seat, he adopted a careless posture with his legs crossed, his arms resting on the chair's arms, his neck reposing on the back of the chair, and his eyes fixing the ceiling with a distraught glare.

Arianne exclaimed, "Justine, please fix the dinner tray for us! We will eat on the porch, and you can leave after you finish fixing the meal."

Fritz lowered his glance and nonchalantly informed his mother, "Call someone else, Mom. Justine went to her sister's house after cleaning my room."

"*Helas!* Then I will have to do it myself," complained Arianne. She entered the dining room and returned pushing a wheeled table with three plates, three cups, and utensils thrown in disarray. Sighing she said, "Thank God you did not bring any visitors with you. I'm exhausted." Edging over to the porch corner she requested from Marie, the cook, "Bring the food and some cola and then you can leave."

Marie executed the order promptly and fled from the Lucas household, energized by the certainty that she would not have to wash the dishes that night. The Lucas household was then empty of strangers, as Arianne liked it, so they could discuss family matters freely. Arianne and Curtis filled their plates, preparing themselves to enjoy fried fish, plantain, and salad. Noticing that Fritz only grabbed a small piece of fried fish, Arianne asked, "Are you not hungry, Fito? When did you leave Kenscoff?"

"Around six-thirty this morning. The eight o'clock flight was cancelled so I left at eleven. By midday, I was in town."

"So that is why Justine disappeared. She overfed you and felt guilty. She was again playing the overzealous nanny."

"No," answered Fritz. "Justine did not offer me any food. I arrived here less than an hour ago."

Arianne directed a reproachful glance at Fritz and inquired, "You wandered around town and did not stop at the store?"

"No," said Fritz, putting down his fork and plate, folding his arms across his chest, and fixing his mother with a stare. "I was at Dr. Dijon's house. I had to wait for him to finish his consultations. I had lunch with him."

"What?" said Arianne. Her body sprang up like an unfastened spring, some of her food spilling on the floor. She turned toward her husband for help. But Curtis hung his head and continued chewing, tapping his foot gently to the rhythm of the music.

Arianne steadied herself, deliberately put her plate and fork down on the table, reached for her glass, poured some cola, sipped a little, and swallowed with difficulty. She deposited her glass among the spilled food, not looking at Fritz. Then, scrutinizing her son with panicky eyes, she exploded, "Fritz, you are an adult now! We cannot always protect you. Why do you have to look for trouble?"

Fritz felt his face grow hot; he jumped to his feet, his heart suddenly beating wildly. "No, Mom, I was not looking for trouble! I just wanted to know the truth!" He flung the words in her face, disgusted with her preoccupation with decorum and respectability.

"The truth?" Her voice was a screech now, climbing higher octaves in her desperation to keep Fritz from slipping further away from what she wanted for him. "What truth? Feed your mother, I've been working hard all day; I don't have time for gossip."

"Oh, of course not, Mom," Fritz bit back bitterly, "but you *do* have time to get pictures of my girlfriend with a military man, and bring them to me, all the way in *Paris!* All the while scheming to break us apart!" He glared at her, breathing hard, daring her to deny it.

Arianne blanched, her respiration halted. She grabbed her chair's arm for support, lowered her head, and whispered, "It was a mistake, Fritz. My mistake. I'm sorry. You are my only child; it was my responsibility to let you know."

Fritz blinked at her, thrown off balance by her sudden seeming fragility. But then she raised her head and with assurance and pride said, "It's over anyway. God has blessed my prayers. We have found the right wife for you."

His revulsion returning, Fritz retorted loudly, "The right wife for me? Mother, don't try to rule my life, you don't know me. How can you choose a wife for me when you don't understand me? You don't even know what I want."

"Please, Fritz. That's how it has been done in our family for generations."

"Well, many couples matched by our grandparents are not happy. They spend a life in misery. They have money, luxury, but they don't live, they exist. That is not the kind of life I want." He paused, then continued, "Mom, when did you find out that the lieutenant was not Crystal's boyfriend?"

"Two years later. When you were feeling better, getting over your depression. I did not think it was wise to bring up that subject again. I'm glad because you did fine."

"I met Crystal!" blurted Fritz.

Arianne's eyes bulged, and she twisted her mouth in a pout. She risked, "I told you before, Crystal is an intelligent, beautiful, young woman from a good family. I learned that she is engaged to a surgeon."

Fritz whirled and opened his arms, laughing at his mother's audacity. "Mom, didn't you just say that you aren't interested in gossip? I envy that fiancé. I still love Crystal."

"Son, your father and I have already decided. We should meet with your candidate wife's family soon."

Fritz examined his parents. They appeared cold and distant. He pinned his eyes on his mother and interrogated her. "Mom, didn't you always say that you cared about my well-being?"

"Of course, that is why we went through the trouble of finding you a good wife."

"Mom, do you know love? Did you ever experience true love, spontaneous love?"

"How dare you, Fritz! Watch your mouth, have respect for our tradition."

"Our tradition," repeated Fritz. "That's all you care about. Our tradition. What about me? Don't you think I can make my own decisions? Mom, I'm your son, your only son. I know you love me in your way. But what I'm asking is for you to love me for myself. Fritz Jean Lucas. Love me for who I am, what I stand for, what I have achieved; not what you have achieved for me. Don't consider me as a well-deserved prize, a trophy you want to expose to your friends."

"Exactly. We love you. That is why we made the sacrifice of going to that store every day, ensuring some territory for you. All we ask from you is to be thankful and give us satisfaction."

The word 'love' had a special meaning for Arianne. She took advantage of the situation to explore her passion in life, how she viewed or expressed her love all those years. "My grandfather said that one of our values as a people was to take care of each other, to take care of our children. And for me, being a good parent means taking care of your child."

"I don't see anything extraordinary or special about it, just the contrary, Mom. You just did your job as a parent."

"Fritz, you are tired. Get some rest and think again. You will agree with me that you cannot embarrass us."

"Embarrass! Mom, don't you get it? I love that woman and I intend to win her back. If you or my father have any objections to my decision, I will leave the country."

"Fritz, don't threaten us." She stopped in mid-sentence. Curtis was pressing hard, too hard, on her hand.

He cast her a glacial look, stood, and asked Fritz, "When are you leaving for Port-au-Prince, son?"

"The first flight tomorrow morning."

Curtis touched his son's shoulder and tried to reassure him. But Fritz was angry, his head throbbed, a haggard expression spread to his eyes. He did not feel like talking anymore. He excused himself and went to his bedroom. He lay on his bed, peered at his sports bag, and retrieved the pictures.

Then he saw the envelope the New Spectrum secretary had handed to him after the meeting with Crystal. He unsealed it, exposed the single-page memo, and read it. It was a reminder for the following day's party celebrating the firm's fifth anniversary. Fritz beamed as he absorbed the content. "Yes! All I need is an occasion to meet Crystal again and explain the situation to her!"

———

The evening hours glided by lazily. From his bedroom Gerard listened to the constant humming of cars and vans unfurling on the main road. It was one of the reasons why he'd bought the place. He'd claimed it was his alcove. The house was in the middle of everything, close to downtown, the hospital, and the suburbs so he could be in surgery whenever he was needed. He thought it was practical for his profession.

There was an empty lot behind the house where he planned to build a house for his family and transform his alcove into a clinic. He had told the plan to his parents, but his mother's remarks had displeased him. She'd complained at the time, "How can you decide for your wife-to-be? Who says she wants to live there, that the location will suit her? Why don't you wait, son?"

The advice had angered him. "Am I not the head of my family? I will provide. My income is more than enough to cover the expenses of a well-to-do family. And if my wife loves me, why could she not follow me? Marry me, my decisions, my career."

His mother had still been adamant. However, he had brushed aside her comments as those of a stubborn country woman. Tonight, even in these difficult periods, he still held fast to his principles. He took Crystal's picture off the bookcase, admired her posture, concluded that her stance revealed inquisitiveness, resolution, the aim to fight and win. In a sense she was like him: assiduous, spirited, successful. This was what attracted him the most to her. He had pursued her for two years, thinking what a great couple they would make, but having the secret intention to persuade Crystal to abandon her work, and be a housewife. Although he would accept her giving presentations at conferences from time to time.

He placed the picture back on the bookcase and decided he would do whatever necessary to dominate Crystal. That conviction calmed him. He grabbed a medical journal to review the new technique used for laparoscopic surgery, and fell asleep.

———

After the discussion with his mother he had felt overwhelmed and sad. He had come to solve a problem only to discover that his mother's actions were based on prejudice, and that he had made a grave mistake. Crystal had not been unfaithful, and now he was even distanced more than ever from his parents and maybe his people. His mother was right; Arab Haitians did not marry out of their tight-knit community.

Don't I owe it to myself to love the person I marry, with whom I will spend the rest of my life? Am I a traitor to my parents, my race, my heritage? No, I don't think so. I have not and will never deny my origin. But my mother, the one person forcing me into that arranged marriage, has taught me since childhood to fight for what I want, not to ever give up, to achieve fulfillment. This is what I am after!

However, Fritz knew nothing was more valuable than real love and this was how he viewed his relationship with Crystal. He was ready to face material uncertainty, which would mean fleeing the country, leaving the factory behind. All that mattered to him was Crystal, her love. His head grew heavier. He abandoned the porch and went inside. He asked his mother, "Do you have any aspirin? I have a headache."

"Yes. Are you okay, son?"

"I'm fine. Just tired, like you said earlier. I'm going to lie down."

Fritz went back to his room while Arianne rummaged in her room for the pills. She obtained a glass of water and headed for his room. After opening the door Arianne stood for a few seconds to let her eyes adapt to the darkness, since the room was pitch black. Fritz had drawn the curtains tight and she saw an immobile form crunched on the bed.

Arianne flinched. For the first time in her life she realized her son wasn't happy. A deep sorrow invaded her and she questioned herself, *Is Fritz crying? Or is he mad to the point that he wanted to remove himself from his surroundings?* She blinked. Whatever the answer, she was not satisfied with it. This was not what she had worked for, nor what she wanted for her son. She hoped he would feel better as time went by. She neared the form on the bed, placed the cup and pills on the nightstand, and gently touched her son's shoulder.

"Fito, I have the pills for you."

Slowly, Fritz turned to face his mother, surprised by her affectionate tone. Their gazes locked and for an instant they were again mother and son allied for the best and the worst.

———

———

FRITZ AWOKE RE-ENERGIZED. HE ate and readied himself for the airport. It was a gloomy ride. He sat in the back seat and kept his eyes wandering over the busy streets. His parents remained silent during the ride. At the airport they hugged him, wished him a safe trip, and promised they would be with him for the factory inauguration on Friday. Fritz thanked them and hastily joined the waiting line. The flight was full and on time.

Canadian sisters and a lieutenant boarded the plane. It was Fritz's luck that the lieutenant had no choice but to sit next to him. Fritz wriggled restlessly and grew uncomfortable. He was flipping nervously through the pages of a magazine when the lieutenant extended his right hand and with a warm, engaging smile presented himself, "I'm Josue Charles. I was assigned to Cap-Haitian twelve months ago. I did try to meet all the businessmen, but I did not see you."

Fritz was annoyed and thought, *It's Haiti. If you are light-skinned, you have to be a priest or a businessman.* He reluctantly volunteered, "I just visited my parents, the Lucas'. You probably met them."

The lieutenant continued, "Yes, they are very involved in the town's activities. I'm from the south, Les Cayes, but have been assigned here. Cap-Haitian is a beautiful town with nice people.

Fritz's mind was churning with contradictory thoughts. *Why does the man want to talk to me? Doesn't he know Arab-Haitians don't speak to strangers? And mostly, doesn't he know we don't trust anyone from the military?* Fritz eyed the man suspiciously and answered his few questions evasively.

Then he closed his eyes and pretended to fall asleep. He replayed the scenes of his youth and imagined his parents around the family table criticizing the authorities. He admitted he had just discriminated against Josue Charles. Just because he wore the military uniform did not imply he was a "bad guy."

Fritz had judged him and assumed he was dishonest. It was the way he was brought up. Fear was the emotion experienced in the presence of the military, but what was the real reason for that? Was it justified? Fear had paralyzed him. All those years he had been taught that you did not antagonize military subjects because they would retaliate. Now that he sat near a military man he considered him a gentleman and reasoned that not all of them could be dishonest or criminals. Lieutenant Charles had waited to board the plane last; he was courteous.

Fritz opened his eyes and addressed the lieutenant, "Would you not rather be in your hometown?"

"They won't accept me. They resent the fact that I'm giving them orders. Don't get me wrong. It's not that they don't like me. They do, and are proud of me. But as a representative of the laws, enforcing order..."

"Are you tough on them?"

"Yes, but I'm against physical abuse, torture. I do make mistakes, though. That is why I'm asking for everyone's help."

Fritz was pleased with the man's attitude and he scorned himself, *I am blind*. Then he realized his mother had played the right card, raising fear, and hoping that everyone would be on her side.

The plane circled the Port-au-Prince sky, then landed and everyone readied to disembark. Fritz saluted Lieutenant Josue Charles and cordially invited him to visit his workplace, "I'm the owner of Fabric Pro. Stop by when you sojourn in the capital. You are welcome."

"Thank you," said the lieutenant with a handshake. Soon his tall frame was engulfed in the sea of travelers.

Fritz hailed a cab and stopped at the factory to check the progress. Everything was fine. Then he went to Avis, rented a car, and headed for the New Spectrum party.

———

Wednesday morning had found Crystal exhausted. She had not slept well the night before. She had tried her relaxation methods: deep breathing, closed eyes, nice thoughts. It had not brought her any relief. She had turned the radio on to classical music, which had helped, but past midnight there was no such thing as entertainment on the radio in Haiti. She had pictured herself at the seashore, walking, singing. Fritz had materialized in her mind. She had given up, surrendering to the abyss engulfing her existence.

She duly executed her morning routine and readied herself for her firm's fifth anniversary party. She disregarded the hot breakfast prepared for her by her aunt, opting instead for just a few ounces of milk, and responding evasively to her relatives' inquiries. She progressed to the gallery and waited for her ride. Crystal spiritlessly climbed into New Spectrum's car for the ride to her office.

It was a beautiful morning, the air crisp and cool. Students strolled along the streets in small groups, talking animatedly, their faces blooming with warm smiles. The sky was blue, decorated with a chain of light clouds sailing aimlessly, scintillating like strings of pearls dispersed on a bride's headset or a queen's crown. The cars cruised smoothly, cascading through the stirring streets. A few vendors proudly displayed their merchandise on the street corners, trying to attract both walkers and drivers, but those events did not catch Crystal's attention.

She arrived at New Spectrum and hurried to her office. She opened the door and saw on her desk the vase holding the numerous beautiful yellow roses. Crystal's eyes widened, her face illuminated with wild curiosity. She rushed toward her desk and on the way her foot slipped on something. She looked down and saw an envelope.

Still admiring the bouquet, she squatted, fumbled to pick up the envelope, and headed to her desk, her eyes still riveted on the roses. She also noticed and opened the card attached to the mouth of the vase. She read Fritz's handwriting and her heart rose, her body melted. She snatched the card and read the entire message. It was simple. A calm sensation invaded her.

Fritz is capable of creating this feeling in me with just a few words. He had evoked his understanding, his support. Crystal looked at the card in her hand and remembered the first time they had met, when he had dabbed his t-shirt to her forehead. She drew the roses closer to her, closed her eyes, and inhaled the perfume deeply while imagining Fritz choosing the bouquet.

A resounding voice outside her office brought her back to reality, and she scolded herself, *Crystal Dijon, you have a fiancé, stop dreaming!* She became tense as the sight of the other envelope sliding under her foot re-materialized in her mind. She rummaged among the objects on her desk and scooped it up from under her handbag. It was Gerard's handwriting, firm, authoritative. Under her name Gerard had drawn a slash, a strong mark. Crystal held the envelope, thinking, *What happened?*

She figured Gerard was mad, but she could not justify the reaction. Then she realized she did not really know him well enough to interpret his emotions. With resignation, she placidly peeled open the envelope. She read Gerard's note a few times, trying to make sense of it. Then a sort of cold rage overtook her.

She first thought perhaps she had hurt him, but it was just his jealousy. *It is a client complimenting me. Don't I deserve some recognition, some appreciation, for my efforts? You are so self-centered, Gerard, that you don't see what is happening around you. All you care about is your surgery, your success.*

She rebelled for an instant and persisted, *Well, I have news for you, Dr. Armand. The frail, dependent woman has toughened and is ready to discover and enjoy the thrill of pride. I will not resign my position!*

She retrieved Fritz's card and the truth assailed her. *Fritz is not an ordinary client, he is my former boyfriend. But was it enough of an explanation for Gerard to act upon, or for me to be deprived of the rewards of my success? Doesn't Gerard trust me? Doesn't he know I love him?* Doubt surged in her mind, a doubt she had expressed many times before. *Do I really love Gerard or do I find in him my father, the devoted physician who I admire?*

Her fiancé's resemblance to her father always comforted her. She often compared them and counted on her deduction to ensure affection for Gerard. Since Fritz had come back, she was shaken. She knew she somewhat loved Gerard, and did not want to hurt him. But it was not the same exquisite feeling she had experienced with Fritz, of that she was sure. Fritz had warned her years earlier, "What we share, Crystal, is unique, strong, rare. It's called love! Few people experience it."

The recollection of Fritz's words churned in her mind. Then she revolted against his attitude. Tossing his card to the floor she voiced through clenched teeth, "Why did you abandon me, Fritz? Was it because of another woman?"

No, she convinced herself, *it was probably because of my origin!* Slowly the taboo subject unnerved her, and a lump caged in her throat. She swallowed painfully, took some deep breaths to calm herself, cleared her mind, and recapitulated, *Gerard will come back, the factory blessing is Thursday, the inauguration Friday, and this afternoon is the firm's anniversary party. They are all occasions where I will meet Fritz, and then I will go on with my life.*

A slight pang pinched her heart as she realized she would be lonely at the party. Gerard preferred to attend the medical conference as opposed to going with her to the party. Consoling herself she thought, *I will bring a book and my canvas, paints and brushes.* Then she grasped the vase of roses and placed it on the mantel.

———

After dropping Fritz off at the airport Curtis toured the boulevard twice with his wife, then went home. They were still shocked by Fritz's attitude but neither broached the subject. When they returned home, Arianne retrieved two cups and poured coffee, offering one to her husband. They were drained by the previous day's events and headed to their room to prepare to go to their store. Curtis, while sipping his coffee, remarked, "You know how stubborn Fritz can be, just like you."

"Yes, I know," Arianne answered with a trailing voice.

"He is not going to change his mind," was Curtis' next comment.

"Time will tell," said Arianne.

"We only have one son, we can't let him down," advised Curtis.

"Our race always respects the marriage tradition. It's one of our values."

"By tradition we also don't abandon our family members. I'm not ready to lose my son, or be deprived of my grandchildren's affection."

Arianne was touched; she murmured shyly, "Look who is talking. You are dreaming!"

"Arianne, Fritz is serious. Imagine when Crystal and Dr. Dijon learn about what you call 'your mistake,' what will their reaction be?" Lowering his voice, Curtis added through clenched teeth, "I told you to destroy those pictures, not to pursue the matter, or at least let Crystal be the one to inform Fritz herself, to let him know she was seeing someone else."

"We all make mistakes, we're only human. I did what I thought was necessary to protect my son," Arianne replied.

Curtis only lost his temper for an instant. He had regained his composure and suggested to his wife, "Then do the same now. Remember how happy Fritz was when he was dating Crystal? Everyone in town gossiped about their relationship, but all admitted they were deeply in love."

Arianne took the cup from him and placed it on the nightstand. After a brief silence she avowed, "Even I agree with that. By the way, where did they meet? Did Fritz wire someone to find out where Crystal lives, or what she is up to? Fritz has not even been in Haiti for a week. It's like a fairy tale."

Arianne had just acknowledged that her son had been deeply in love with Crystal. That fact contradicted her past assertion that their relationship had been a "summer fling." Curtis was startled, and he looked at his wife with a searching gaze. But no, she was not shaking or blushing. It was as if her disclosure was weightless, powerless, shiftless. With a hint of perplexity he invited her to continue the day's routine, "Let's go to work. I'm sure our visit to Port-au-Prince on Friday for the factory inauguration reserves some surprises for us."

The word 'surprises' had an unexpected effect on Arianne. *What if Crystal is there?* She would not know what to do. How to act? Her face turned red. She cleared her throat to dispel the growing panic that constricted her airways, then blurted, "Do you know something that you are keeping from me?"

Curtis kissed her and murmured, "You just have to experience love and remember, to know." He was quiet, thinking, then proposed, "Darling, isn't tomorrow the factory blessing? A small ceremony with Father Ignacio. Let's surprise our son and be there."

Arianne wrapped her arms around her husband's waist, leaned her head on his shoulder, and shut her eyelids tightly. She was appeased by her husband's declaration. With a calm voice she rephrased her husband's proposition, "You mean we are going to Port-au-Prince tomorrow?"

Curtis folded his arms around Arianne. They cuddled in the quiet morning like two teenagers reaffirming their love. He laid out the program for the next few days in Port-au-

Prince, "Yes. We will sojourn in the hotel across from the factory, spend some time where there will only be the two of us. No store, no clients, no merchandise to worry about. Then we will have lunch in the restaurant facing our son's factory, to get an idea of how he is doing. That will give us the opportunity to watch him while he gives directions, and then we will surprise him."

"That's a plan. I love you, and thank you for your patience and understanding." Arianne let go of her husband, breaking off their hug. She experienced a new peace brought to her by the fact that she was going to be close to her son.

And, since Curtis was in such good spirits she would convince him to pay another visit to the family of their future in-laws. She would try to compensate for Fritz's indifference by claiming her son was shy, but would be glad to present his demands when his wife-to-be was back in the country. The scheme gave her satisfaction that she would not be embarrassed now by facing Linda's parents. She just needed to act fast.

Their day at the store was different from their drab routine. Curtis and Arianne were excited. They could not focus on their tasks, and often interrupted the transactions to exchange comments about their impending trip. At the end of the day, they announced to their employees that the store would be closed from the following day throughout the weekend.

———

When he awoke Wednesday morning, Gerard took a shower and mused at the idea of winning the Health Ministry contest, which would allow him to participate in a two-year training program at a top Paris hospital. He tackled the road to the French Embassy before the rush hour congestion, arrived first at the address, and stationed his car across from the main entrance. He watched young couples with their children hurrying to downtown, and Crystal came to his mind.

On an ordinary day, he would have been on his way to give her a ride to New Spectrum, but this day was no ordinary day. The conference meant a lot to him; the entire country's surgeons would be there, and imagine if he won. Then he remembered it was also Crystal's firm's anniversary party that afternoon. In fact, she had refused to assist at the dinner offered after his conference, preferring instead to share more time with the engineers she worked with every day.

Gerard resented her choice, but Crystal did not budge. She had voiced her will firmly to him three months earlier, "I will be at the firm party." She had reinforced her decision by adding: "You are free to go to the medical conference, I would not want you to miss such an occasion; it is the same for me, I will attend my firm's party." Her determination was unshakable. The blatant way she lay down her final decision had shocked and silenced Gerard at the time. "That attitude must change after I'm married; she must obey," mumbled Gerard.

The embassy entrance opened, and Gerard joined the throng of surgeons that had accumulated. They exchanged greetings and proceeded to the waiting room. It had white walls and a high ceiling. In the front was a table with a projector and a microphone; on the wall facing the room stood a screen where the slides would be displayed.

The room was occupied by rows of chairs, each one with a protruding desk surface on the right for writing. On the right side of the room was a table holding pamphlets and pens. Every physician chose from the pile the materials that would best fit their district. A door opened to give way to the lecturer, Dr. Alvin, a French physician, accompanied by the Haitian Health Minister.

The presentation went without incident. At the end, Dr. Alvin announced that the embassy would like the doctors to vote for one of their colleagues to benefit from the two-year grant. The French consulate had already fixed all of the necessary arrangements. Only the name of the winner should be added and his family members if there were any. The physicians were stricken by the knowledge that they were the ones who had to vote. A heavy silence plagued the auditorium as each physician measured their colleagues.

Dr. Alvin left the stall to pass around the casting papers. A blur of talking arose, friends consulting friends, pondering the consequences of their decisions. Then a frigid stillness stole the room, a deep frown appeared on the doctors' foreheads while they dutifully inscribed on the piece of paper the name of the person they thought would be best qualified for the grant. Dr. Alvin collected the notes and the count began.

One by one Dr. Alvin stripped the pieces of paper and read the name, "Dr. Armand." The Health Minister, tired of slashing perpendicular marks on a notebook, stopped and nodded his head in approval. Dr. Armand had gotten 34 of the 35 votes; the one vote was for the Health Minister. The doctors applauded warmly and congratulated Gerard. After giving a shy thank you speech, he left the conference to attend the dinner party that followed.

After the embassy dinner, Gerard decided to go home, even though it was still early. He could have gone to Crystal's party but he rejected that possibility. It was his way of punishing Crystal, making her pay for her refusal to bend to his will.

He felt satisfied. He was going to make arrangements for his clinic coverage during his two-year absence. He parked his car in front of his empty house. The maid left early on Wednesdays since it was one of his free afternoons when he usually spent time with Crystal.

He entered his room and undressed, donning shorts and a t-shirt. It was warm, so he ambled to his back porch. The sun hit the mountaintop, and a light breeze cruised along the tall cornstalks, shifting their weight, creating a flowing, permanent murmur.

Gerard sat down comfortably on his rocker and marveled at the wild field sprawling in front of him. A large crow silently circled the cornfield. Gerard witnessed helplessly as the crow hung in one place then plunged, emitting a piercing cry and flapping its wings, escaping with a frantic, vacillating garden snake clenched in its beak.

Gerard drifted his head upwards, following the predator. He observed the sky, saw that the sun had disappeared. A chain of gray, woolen clouds drowsily rolled toward the mountain, as a flock of swallows hurriedly flew away from the hill. The wind had grown steady; the plants shuddered, tumbled expectedly, their crisp, thirsty leaves longing for rain. It was a particular happening during the June month, spotting rain in parts of the capital. Gerard wondered if it was also raining at the beach. "Probably not," he mumbled with regret.

Through his professional victory, Gerard experienced some uneasiness. He should have been thrilled, but the trip abroad came with new problems for him. He did not want to leave Crystal behind; he would like to travel with her. He knew she would refuse, giving precedence to her work. As he was toying with the idea of how to render Crystal more submissive, he remembered the note he had left under her office door. He repeated the name to himself, *Fritz Jean Lucas, Fritz Jean Lucas. Damn it!*

He began to move the rocker. The last name Lucas meant something to him. He remembered what his father had once told him when he began his practice, "Son, all Arab-Haitians are related; they are like members of a big family. Treat one well and it's like you have treated them all well."

Gerard tried to recall which one of his Arab-Haitian patients was a Lucas. After intense reflection he came to the conclusion that none of them were. Then he recalled the parties he had attended with the Arab-Haitian population. No, no Lucas was never presented to him. The sky grew darker as Gerard continued to think. He now browsed over the funerals he had attended, not too many of them, maybe five. But one of them had retained his attention—one of his patients, an old man in his late eighties, a Kahlil.

What intrigued him at that time was the large attendance of family and friends coming from the countryside, traveling all the way to the capital to pay their respects to the man. Gerard jumped to his feet. Yes! Now he recalled the Lucas' among them. They were family members, too; close relatives sitting in the first row just across from the coffin.

Gerard sat back, still, his heart pounding and his head throbbing. Kahlil, Lucas. Where was the link? He checked the names of the rich Arab-Haitians in Port-au-Prince in his mind. Kahlil was one of them, and he slowly recalled that Crystal had many times mentioned her Fabric Pro client's name: Michael Kahlil. Gerard's mouth grew dry and his hands shook as he repeated his father's words: "They marry among themselves."

Kahlil could be Fritz Jean Lucas' close relative on his mother's side. He reckoned that the man—Fritz—was the son of a Kahlil woman and a Lucas man. He bent his head, his eyes closed, feeling dumbfounded, destroyed. That explained Crystal's attitude, and the flowers. Fritz was for sure one of the associates of Fabric Pro, and Crystal had been the architect working all that time for him.

Gerard abandoned his seat, went to the kitchen and poured a glass of cold water that he drank in one gulp. He headed to his bedroom, overwhelmed. He planned to discuss the situation with Crystal the following day. He blamed himself. Was he so blind? No. He admitted to himself that sooner or later Crystal would have met Fritz.

The Arab-Haitian community had money. If your business prospered they had to be your client anyway. He knew Crystal was probably Fritz's friend. Crystal was not the type to cheat, but he could never accept her having any contact with that man. Maybe she would accept traveling with him to Paris. She had to! He was her fiancé. She could not bring that kind of scandal and embarrassment to her father. For both her father's pride and Gerard's were jeopardized.

———

The New Spectrum party celebrated every year was mostly a family affair, where the engineers in the first period exposed the firm's achievements for the past twelve months and presented the plan for the next several years. Most clients left around 4 p.m., while the firm's partners stayed to enjoy the rest of the evening with their relatives. This particular year, the site chosen for the party was the Orange Bay, a beach hotel. There was really cause for festivity, as the large Fabric Pro project had served as solid advertising for the firm, which now envisaged an expansion. Crystal and her indefatigable effort and assiduous work were credited for most of the firm's success.

Her partners and co-workers wanted to thank her and show her how much they appreciated her input. She had been liberated from the task of helping to plan the party; she just had to attend the feast. She was pleased with the outcome of Fabric Pro and intended to celebrate, saying, "I deserve it."

She pushed away her resentment against Gerard and his decision to go to the medical conference instead of joining her for the party. She would be there with her co-workers and friends. She wore a black bathing suit under her beige linen outfit, and fixed her beach bag with her painting materials thinking, *When the corporate presentation is over, I will find myself a spot on the shore to paint.*

She knew Fritz and his uncle had been invited. She became excited, feeling something awaken at the thought of Fritz being there. Then she rescinded, *Fritz will probably stay with his relatives for dinner tonight.* With that in mind Crystal boarded a co-worker's car bound for Orange Bay.

———

Fritz eased his body behind the steering wheel of the rented car. It was a small vehicle and while ascending the slope to get to his house Fritz compared it to a ladybug crawling on a lettuce leaf. The comparison brought a smile to his face. He envied the insect for its freedom.

He admitted that the car would allow him some degree of freedom. He could explore the country without his family members suspecting the destinations of his whereabouts. The party he was to attend that afternoon was an example.

He still thought the ladybug was luckier than him when he considered the dilemma he was trying to solve.

Ladybugs don't need to fight their parents for their approval, just so that they can marry their girlfriend. And with that he became preoccupied with what Crystal's reaction would be when he showed her the pictures. Would she refuse to have a relationship with him because of his mother's lie? How could he neutralize his mother to prevent her from hurting them even more? And what about his father? It was evident he did not approve of Arianne's actions, but he was not strong enough.

Fritz had been deceived by his parents' attitude, especially his mother's. But until their final dispute on the porch he had not realized how serious she was. Now he felt guilty for believing her and blamed himself. *How could I have been so blind? My judgment did not do justice to Crystal. How can I compensate for my mistake?* He prepared himself to meet her, to explain to her the cause of his silence.

He readied himself for the New Spectrum party by putting on a bathing suit under his pants. Then he placed the old pictures in his pants pocket, suddenly feeling just how heavy a burden they were to carry, and took some extra money in case he had to pay for drinks or stay out overnight.

All that mattered to him now was getting Crystal back. He informed Vonise he would be out for the rest of the day, had a light lunch, then hurried to his rented car. The driving was easy, the traffic light, but he arrived at Orange Bay to find a packed parking lot. He spotted a remote space to curb his car.

He decided to rent a room to avoid driving in case he got drunk, and went to the receptionist to inquire about the rooms available. She informed him that most were already taken; only a few bungalows were left. Fritz settled for one, thinking, *The loneliness will fit me.* Then he headed for the party.

It was easy to locate since there was a big banner hung in front of the auditorium. Fritz followed the arrows and arrived at the entrance. Entering the room, he saw there were about 100 guests. He chose a seat in the back. A group of engineers were finishing their presentation, to which there was a steady flow of applause. All Fritz had time to intercept was that the talk was about Crystal's performance at the firm and that her work was deeply appreciated. Engineer Turnier, the lieutenant in the pictures in Fritz's pocket and Crystal's uncle, went to the podium, thanked the firm's clients for their trust, and invited the guests to help themselves to the buffet. Fritz joined the crowd, found his way to Engineer Turnier, and presented his congratulations while taking a closer look at the man's features. Fritz reassured himself, *Yes, that's the man in the pictures.*

Fritz left him and scanned the crowd for Crystal. He saw her at the buffet stand. She was addressing a group of young women, reminding them that their work would translate their effort and that they would gain respect for it. *She is a living example of it,* thought Fritz. He was pleased by her assurance, her directness. His heart swelled with pride. His attraction to her had grown since his return. It was a new feeling, not the memories, which made him a little nervous in her presence. He waited for her to finish, for the crowd to thin and then approached her. He walked up behind her and murmured, "Good afternoon, Crystal, congratulations again."

She recognized his voice, turned with a surprised expression on her face, but was pleased to see him. She offered him a hand to shake, which he took. Then she offered her cheek and he kissed her lightly. "Thank you, Fritz, for the flowers and for coming. How long have you been here?"

"Long enough to hear you motivating the female graduates. I feel sorry for my gender."

Crystal, with concern in her voice, said, "Fritz, don't tell me that I put the men down!"

"No offense. I was just kidding."

They started walking to the sitting area where numbered tables were now arranged. Crystal inquired, "What is the number on your card?"

Fritz replied, "I don't know." He dug into one of his pockets and found the card with the number 4 on it.

"It's the table assigned to businessmen. Let me introduce you to them."

"I would rather be with you and your brothers."

"They are not here yet, and you need to know the capital businessmen." She introduced him to the table's occupants and left.

Fritz sat with them long enough to finish his meal and learn about their different occupations. Then he excused himself, abandoned their company, and perused the room to locate Crystal. She was not there. Fritz was concerned. Had Crystal left? Most of the guests had left, only a quarter of them were still present.

Fritz went to the receptionist and asked where his bungalow was located. She handed him a crude drawing of the area and fingered a spot with bungalows dispersed among palm trees. Fritz thanked her and walked along the path of the shore with the hope of seeing Crystal. Noisy children playing hide and seek and couples stretched out on their towels crowded the bank.

Fritz retreated to the back road, speculating on where Crystal could be. Had she gone back to town? Or was she with her fiancé? It would be normal for Crystal's fiancé to be there to celebrate her success. The assumption saddened Fritz. He wished Gerard would be impeached so he could be with Crystal.

Fritz arrived at the conglomeration of bungalows and searched for the one named Celeste. He found it, a cozy hut made of crude wood and beige stucco with crossing palm leaves for a ceiling, imitating the natives' habitat. It conveyed an impression of purity with a front space holding a couch, a small coffee table, and a wicker divider that separated the sleeping area.

The bedroom had a full-size bed posing like a cool marble slab brashly displaying its starched, chiseled white sheets. Fritz smiled at the thought that once again he had been fooled because of his complexion. The receptionist had assumed he would like it and that he could afford the high price. He checked the bathroom. It was as rudimentary as the bungalow, a bathtub set on cement, a sink held by four iron bars with a window at eye level on top of it. Walking over to the open window, Fritz admired the blooming seashore and the dancing sea.

On his way back to the bedroom, he noticed the pipe feeding the tub sleeping like a water snake, the wicker basket dotted with a stack of neatly folded white towels. In the bedroom, he discovered a trunk sitting at the end of the bed, lifted its cover, where there lay extra sheets, towels, a box of candles, and one of matches. He let go of the lid.

He surveyed the room, noticing the miniature night tables, the stocky armoire contrasting with a thin cross on the wall above it, a small table in the corner with wild fresh flowers decorating a vase. A small painting representing a couple with the inscription "bienvenue" decorated the feet of the container.

Fritz locked the front door, as he had decided to explore the shore. He ambled casually out of the hut after burying the key in his pocket. He chose to head north toward the wilderness. The visitors thinned as he progressed in his wandering. Finally, he was by himself. He continued his exploration, bending from time to time to collect a shell whose shape intrigued him or to throw a rock into the sea, judging the resulting splash and the disturbance caused to the inhabitants.

He compared the intrusion to the unfairness of life. Then, he admitted, *This is a rough area almost untouched by civilization.* He was attracted by a surface with large, grey rocks emerging out of the sand in a circular shape like a cone, their points shooting toward the sky. They sheltered an enclosure where peace exhaled, with the cosmos for its roof and the infinite sea for a friend. That kind of atmosphere was what Fritz was fond of. He plunged for the coveted spot.

As he neared the site, he sensed a near-imperceptible movement. He cautioned himself, *Was this hole the nest of some rare seabirds or turtle? I don't want to frighten them!* He slowed his pace, hardly moving his chest, and discreetly attained the rocks and inspected the patch. His eyes widened with surprise and pleasure. There in a corner facing the sea was Crystal, sitting with her legs crossed and holding her canvas. Her face was concentrated on the fabric, her left hand supporting the painting while she stroked a brush vividly with her right.

She had on a cap, the visor partially protecting her visage. Her beige outfit suited her complexion and made her blend with nature, confounding her with the trapped beast Fritz had opted to protect earlier. This was the same woman he had longed for the past five years, intact as if not touched by the turmoil that had swept her life. She appeared like a Madonna of the sea, calming the savage weather and protecting the sailors.

She was so immersed in her task that she was unaware of being observed. She bent toward the jars of watercolors. While she was choosing a shade, Fritz flung a small shell at her feet. She jumped, startled, her eyes bulging, her heart racing. She identified the intruder with his torso erected between two rocks. "FRITZ!" she exclaimed. She closed her eyes to swallow the delight.

She shook her head and burst out laughing, then opened her eyes and scolded him playfully, "You scared me to death, young fellow." She placed the brush in a saucer, uncrossed her legs, and watched as he circled the parcel, squeezed his body through the narrowest slit, mimicked the victimized child with profound affectation, and kneeled before her as if asking for her forgiveness. She surprised him with a gentle kiss on his forehead.

Fritz avowed without shame, "I was looking for my dulcinea!"

Crystal remembered the walks and explorations they had done in the past, and acknowledged his love of nature. With her eyes glowing she replied with a hint of mischief, "I won't buy that. Were you up for one of your solitary promenades?"

He chuckled, admitting to himself that she knew him better than he would concede. He reinforced his point, telling her the truth, "I have been looking for you since I left my table."

Crystal smiled, absorbing, appreciating the fact that Fritz was interested in her, searching out her company for something not related to her work. She confided, "This is my first time in this area; I brought my canvas for downtime."

Fritz was puzzled. He analyzed the downtime implication while crouched in front of her drawing. His hair brushed her face.

A slight shiver ran through her body; she inhaled deeply, exhaled slowly, then volunteered, "I was just trying to catch the sunset, my strokes are not what they used to be. I'm rusty, need to practice more."

Fritz eased himself up and sat at her side. "You said downtime. Is your fiancé not coming to the dance tonight?"

"No," she replied in a hurry. "Gerard stayed in town to attend the conference on laparoscopic surgery."

Fritz took a closer look at the painting and feigning some indifference, advanced, "Laparoscopic, that's how they pronounce it? Your father is very interested in the new technique."

Crystal, curiosity in her voice, questioned him, "My father? Are you kidding me? How do you know what my father is interested in? Did you meet with or see my father?"

Fritz reversed his attitude and manifested mystery in his tone. He murmured, "I went to Cap-Haitian yesterday morning."

Crystal, thinking he had missed his childhood home and had gone to visit his parents, teased him, "You could not resist. You missed your parents already. How is Father doing?"

Fritz, adopting an air of great importance said, "He is doing fine, we spent a nice afternoon together."

Remembering that the man sitting next to her was not on good terms with her father, because after all, he had seen what she had gone through after Fritz had disappeared, she panicked and ventured, "Fritz, where did you see my father?"

He answered flatly, "At his clinic. I went for a consultation."

She laid her hand on his shoulder and asked with concern, "Are you okay? Don't tell me that you are sick."

Fritz repressed a tender feeling, seeing how much she still cared about him, and rebuffed her with a sudden coarseness, "No, I'm in good shape, but I needed his expertise."

She withdrew her hand, paused for a moment, then said with a new kind of interest, "Is there something I can help you with?"

Taking the situation into hand, he proposed, "Let's go for a walk."

Crystal's head was spinning with colliding ideas trying to guess the reason Fritz had gone all the way to Cap-Haitian, just to see her father. She could not figure one out, and was afraid to ask. Instead, she told him, "I wandered around earlier. There is a source, a river or something, ending here in the sea about a quarter mile north."

Fritz was looking around, defining the area based on Crystal's description and concluded, "I know where we are now. This is a beautiful lot. Do you want me to carry your bag or leave it here? I will show you the Birds of Paradise Garden."

Crystal pondered the invitation, manifesting some concerns, "No one really knows where I am."

Fritz reassured her, "It's not that far, we should be back before the dance starts. I have to talk to you."

That sentence brought back painful memories, and she exclaimed, "What? The last time you said you had to talk to me was for the appointment at the telegraph company four-and-a-half years ago. You had me there hanging at the other end of the receiver and just kept asking me how I was doing over and over. It was the last time I heard from you. Fritz Jean Lucas, what are you up to?"

Fritz stood, trying his most charming smile to convince her, "Come, you won't regret it." The wind was playing with his hair, his eyes reflected an affectionate expression, and he stretched an inviting, irresistible hand to Crystal, which melted her last fiber of resistance.

She sprang to her feet, admonishing herself, *Is it loneliness or something else that I don't want to acknowledge that makes me gather my brushes, watercolors, and canvas and toss them in the bag and abandon them against a rock?* She sensed it was risky to follow Fritz into that beautiful garden, but remembered his reaction at the office when she told him she had waited three years for him. She decided that she was ready to learn what had happened.

They moved toward the stream she had noticed earlier. On their way, they inspected an abrupt slope that exhibited its wild, twining plants with dangling, beaded jade threads obstructing a vault at the foot of the mountain. Fritz remarked that the dome of the vault shielded the Birds of Paradise Garden from view.

He appraised the landscape and explained they could go around, cross the main road and the fisherman's village to end in the garden. He paused, then informed Crystal, "It will take us forty-five minutes to get there, but if we climb the hill like the natives, it will only be ten minutes."

They walked farther north, located a twisting dirt path, a result of the continuous friction of men's feet rubbing the ground. Pointing, Fritz said, "There is the trail."

Crystal carefully inspected the slant, and judged that it was accessible. She rolled her pants up above her ankles. Fritz, standing at her side, enjoyed a close view of her cleavage, and her tiny waist giving rise to her blooming hips. He blushed, resisting the urge to hold her in his arms. When Crystal straightened her torso, she brushed against him, and once again experienced that quiver, as she had years earlier. To fight the growing, pressing demand that invaded her body, she became aggressive and blurted, "Fritz, you better have something good to tell me!"

Fritz shied away and affirmed with a thick voice, "It's good!"

Passing in front of him, she began ascending the slope. Her pace was measured, creating a rhythm that harmoniously rocked her body. Fritz was excited by her voluptuousness. He thought she looked like a flower dancing with the wind that floated in front of him, caressing his senses. For an instant he forgot his worries, his miseries, admitting how lucky he was to have found Crystal.

Crystal could hear Fritz's every move, and recognized that he still had the same confident cadence. She spied their shadows moving, sometimes hers superimposed in front of his, but often blended, hers lost in his. The reality of their closeness made her insides grow taut and when she stood midway to catch her breath, she extended her arms horizontally, lying back on Fritz to rest. He hugged her tightly for a brief moment, as if to infuse her with courage for what was coming. Then he let go of her and they resumed climbing.

She stopped twice again, just to look around. Her third arrest lasted longer than the previous ones. She kept turning her head with her eyes widened, a smile parting her lips. In front of her was a narrow bed of clear, transparent water sliding on gray packed sand, sculpting small waves that curled on each other to form a soft current emitting a babbling murmur.

On each side of the source pullulated stretches of deep green ferns surrounded by a wall of luxurious bamboo canes with elongated emerald leaves lulled by the cool breeze. Behind the emerald wall emerged a thick row of Birds of Paradise, then palm trees with their bodies erect and their profuse branches covering the landscape, providing shade to protect the flowers at their feet, like a mother's womb protecting her baby.

Butterflies, dragonflies, and bees swarmed freely enjoying the sun. Crystal remarked that it was cool. She raised her head and discovered she was under a canopy formed by interlaced branches of two big oak trees parading on either bank of the stream. She pivoted to face Fritz, who was waiting patiently for her, as he had years earlier.

His shirt was unbuttoned at the top, exposing a V on his chest. He did not break a sweat climbing the stiff slant. He had rolled up his sleeves and his arm muscles protruded, glistening in the sun. His eyes revealed his love for nature and admiration for Crystal.

Crystal thought of him as an educated Arab-Haitian who had kept his countryside, boyish tendencies. She was lost in her thoughts when Fritz moved aside for her to see what was behind him. Crystal exclaimed, "Fritz! It's enchanting!"

At their feet, sprawled under the mountain, was the Caribbean Sea, like a turquoise dolly decorated with scintillating diamond studs serenely glittering in the sun.

Crystal decided, "Let's stay here."

They sat on the protruding root of the oak tree. Fritz asked, "What were you thinking about when you were drawing?"

She felt her insides jump at Fritz's voice and it brought her back to the present. "I wanted to somehow translate the contentment I experienced from the result of my work at the firm onto my canvas," she said, sighing "No, maybe another time."

"Contentment," Fritz repeated, then remained silent for a moment. *Contentment.* He was amazed by Crystal's reference. It was what he was after: contentment. And he knew that to have it he had to get her back. Without preamble, Fritz began, "Cap-Haitian is the same. Mr. Ambien spotted me at the airport, and greeted me with, "Welcome back, Mr. Lucas!"

Crystal saw mixed emotions in his eyes, some kind of deep concern and affection. She was touched and muttered carefully, "This doesn't explain why you went to see my father."

Fritz advanced closer to her, his body brushing hers. He looked at her intently and blurted, "I had to show him some pictures and ask him some questions."

Crystal, her face illuminated with curiosity, demanded, "Pictures! Pictures of what? My father's only interest is the medical field. In what regard did you see my father?"

Fritz avowed sheepishly, "He helped me solve a burden that I have been carrying for far too long."

A worried Crystal exclaimed, "Please, Fritz, don't get Dad involved in any detective work! What did you get into while you were in the U.S.?"

"My mother brought me this." He reached into his pants pocket and flashed the pictures at Crystal.

She took them apprehensively, examined them with interest, and handed them back to him. She stood, opened her arms, dramatically glanced at the sky as if soliciting some comfort, and then fixed Fritz with a questioning gaze.

Fritz grew embarrassed. He managed to whisper, "I did not know. She brought them to me in Paris, claiming that you were engaged to the military man in these pictures."

Crystal backed away from him, scandalized, her voice a raging thunder, "What?! I was engaged to the man in the pictures? Please! Don't you recognize him? He is my uncle, Engineer Alex Turnier. In those pictures we were discussing the possibility of opening the architectural firm after I graduated. He hated the military and was attending engineering school as a way out of it."

Fritz jumped to his feet and moved closer to her. In a confiding tone he started, "This is why I left Paris and went to the U.S. My parents feared retaliation from the military man; they just wanted to play it safe."

Crystal shook her head disapprovingly and reproached him, "So you agreed with your mother that I was seeing someone else just four months after you left?"

Fritz pleaded defensively, "I wouldn't say so. She was supposed to have the evidence."

Crystal was furious. Her whole body trembled as she stammered, "Evidence! Damn it! Evidence of me cheating on you? And you bought the lie."

Fritz answered timidly, "Not really! But with those pictures I could not defend you."

Through clenched teeth Crystal affirmed, "You did not have to defend me. It was a pure lie." Then with defiance in her tone she challenged him, "Do you love me, Fritz Jean Lucas? Or maybe I should ask *did* you love me? Ever?"

Fritz suddenly understood the dangerous path she was taking. Bewildered, he exclaimed, "Are you kidding, or are you nuts? I never expected once in my lifetime that you would doubt my love for you."

"Ha!" Crystal barked "But *you* doubted *my* love for you. I never dreamed you could be such a hypocrite."

Fritz paced the trail, stung by her words. He calmed himself and, fixing Crystal with supplicating eyes, avowed, "I love you, Crystal. You have to believe that."

"This is why you waited that long! Why didn't you discuss the problem with me, ask me what was going on? It's *me* in those pictures, you know? It's *my* life, it's *my* reputation!"

Fritz neared her, eyed her intently, grasped her arm and said, "You're right, it is your reputation. Remember Easter vacation when I sent a telegram requesting to talk to you at the telegraph office phone? I was enraged and intended to discuss the matter with you. But, when I heard your voice I could not bear to expose our difference to the town gossip."

Silence plagued the atmosphere, stillness reigned while they stood measuring each other and the consequences, and all the while Crystal couldn't help thinking that maybe that would have been better than having her heart broken.

Fritz continued, "You know that whatever conversation took place at the telegraph office, the subject was discussed the same night in every household. I did not want to trash your name or our relationship. I reasoned that if there was to be a scandal, let them guess. They would never know the truth."

Crystal wrenched her arm out of his grasp and spat, "Why didn't you write or answer my letters?"

Fritz informed her, "I left Paris, I had a new address and never received your letters. Now, I must admit I was jealous and afraid and did not make arrangements to have my mail forwarded to me. I went through some difficult periods, you can imagine, trying to reconcile those pictures, their meaning and our relationship. It was torture."

"You wouldn't have had to go through those difficult periods if you had given notice of your forwarding address, because you would have received my letters." Her voice was cold, hard. Remembering the pain she'd seen in Fritz's eyes when he was in her office, she softened, realizing they had both suffered in their own way. "Your mother was wrong. Her zeal has caused us so much pain. Does she know who the man in the pictures is?"

Fritz mumbled a shy, "Yes, she does." He rushed on, needing her to hear what he had gone through. "I lost sixty-five pounds in seven months. I was referred to the school psychologist, but refused their help. I dealt with the situation my own way, which endangered my body and mental health. It was a blessing when I joined the swimming team. That move helped me regain confidence, and slowly I recuperated."

Crystal, intrigued, asked him, "Why did you keep those pictures?"

With a sarcastic smile, Fritz avowed, "My life was ruled by them. I had to know. Now, I can destroy them." He grasped the stack of photographs and tore them into small pieces, the wind scattering the bits sparingly, eliminating the possibility of them ever being assembled again, relegating their effect to a past forgotten, and tracing the path to a new future.

As she watched him, Crystal was once again taunted by the uncontrollable pain she experienced years earlier, and she could not refrain herself from questioning him "Did you ever believe I was unfaithful?"

Fritz, who was standing just in front of her, bent his torso so his eyes came to the same level as Crystal's. He replied with certainty, "Not for a second!" He shrugged his shoulders, and with a convincing smile continued, "I knew that you would never walk out on me like that." He pursued her with an emblazing tone, "As I told you before, what we share is unique. I kept quiet because I did not have the tools to fight the lie, now I do. I have a diploma and I am not dependent on my parents or my family heritage. I can work, provide for myself and my family."

Crystal had turned her head toward the sea, away from Fritz. Around them, the pieces of the destroyed pictures were drifting farther away in the wind, meaningless. Fritz moved closer to her, searching her gaze. Crystal had a dreamy air that made her appear solemn, beautiful like a rare piece of jewelry. Fritz held his breath for a split second as if to let her beauty impregnate him. Feeling his loins begin to stir, he imagined what it would be like to spend the night with Crystal.

She surprised him by taking his hands in hers. She too, was wondering about Fritz, *What kind of man does it take to go through so many difficulties and persist? What could be his motivation?* She felt the warmth of his hands, and dreamed of what it would be like to have him touch her. Just that thought made her take a deep breath, and she sensed her nipples begin to tingle, her heart pound faster, her legs weaken.

She realized that something had changed between them since being on that hill. She tried to pinpoint the exact time or cause. *Was it Fritz's trip to see her father to investigate about the pictures? Was it the acknowledgment of the pain he went through? Was it the courage to face his family members, or the fact that he chose to live with torment instead of exposing their problem, their dilemma, on the phone to the townsfolk's gossip?*

Crystal remembered that Fritz had always been very protective of her, since the first day when he kneeled to nurse her wounds and invited her to his house so she would not be teased by the town's teenagers. She experienced a deep fondness for him while holding his hands as they climbed down the hill. She knew she had fallen in love with Fritz Jean Lucas again, and that as her friend warned her, she had never stopped loving him.

The sky glowed like a giant fireplace, the sunset flashing a sheet of orange streaks that reflected their flickering flames in the sea. The leaves rustled, constantly trembling under the touch of the breeze. Their humming joined the mini-jazz spilling a soft music among the palm trees. As they reached the shore, Fritz proposed, "Do you mind going for a plunge?"

Crystal, an amused look on her face, teased him, "Naked?"

Fritz raised his eyebrows, narrowed his eyes, feigning indignity, and reminded her of the old Capois habit. "Did you abandon the practice? Always wear a bathing suit under your street clothes when going near the shore!"

Crystal burst out laughing and mumbled, "You remember the days!"

Fritz, in a dreamy air, whispered, "I can recount every one of them to you."

They were approaching the spot where they had left Crystal's bag on the beach. Fritz suggested they first get the bag and check into the bungalow he'd rented.

They were at ease with each other just like five years earlier. Fritz recovered the bag, and they proceeded to hunt for his bungalow. They were holding hands, but Fritz was baffled by the view as he approached the landscape where all the huts where illuminated like lilies sailing on a swamp. He sheepishly avowed, "I don't recognize my cabana. They all look alike. Mine should be dark."

Crystal informed him, "No, they service them during the guest's absence!"

Fritz complained, "This justifies the hefty price I paid. There it is: Celeste!"

They were in front of the hut. Fritz retrieved his key and opened the front door. There was a candle placed in the middle of the table shooting amber light and dissolving the darkness. The table was arranged with two place settings and a card with the mention of room service at 7 p.m. There was also a wine bottle sitting in an ice bucket. Crystal entered with glittering eyes; she explored the bedroom, then the bathroom, and came back to the sitting area. "This is cozy."

Fritz agreed with her and affirmed, "It's beautiful and discreet. Would you like some wine or the local *cremas*?"

Crystal eased herself onto the couch and crossed her legs. She ignored Fritz's offer but kept watching him with interest. Fritz was standing close to the table and the light was playing on his features. The shadow of his broad shoulders was disproportionately displayed on the wall above his narrow hips, making him appear like a giant ice cream cone.

The movement he made to uncork the wine revealed his ripe muscles, and he tilted his head to the side with his hair hanging, floating loosely, sweeping the air with each attempt. He raised his head and caught a glimpse of Crystal observing him with admiration. He blushed, as a sudden desire grasped him. He lowered his eyelids and cast a shy glance on the glasses he now held in his hand. While moving toward her he said, "You made no noise sitting down; I thought you were at the window, since you didn't answer my question."

Crystal, with a malicious grin that made him want to kiss her at once, teased him, "You were not supposed to know I was watching you." She had seen his reaction and hint at what he was thinking about.

"How long have you been sitting there?" he asked her.

"Long enough to witness your struggle with the rustic corkscrew."

He smiled, acknowledging how handy she was, and playfully reproached her, "And Miss didn't offer to help!" He kept moving toward her thinking, *Damn, Crystal looks good!* She still had her eyes pinned on him and the way he was looking at her made her feel the way she had years earlier, and she sensed the old instincts emerge, take over.

He handed her one of the glasses. She took it, thanking him as he sat by her side.

Crystal and Fritz were close now, their bodies brushing with each movement. Fritz watched her chest rise as she breathed in deeply, as if trying to repress an urge, exhaled, and brought the glass slowly to her mouth as if steadying herself. She was quiet for a moment, then said, "Do you remember how we used to sit across the rail on the far end of the boulevard with our legs dangling, the surf wetting our pants?"

"Of course! How could I forget? They are memories from the most precious time in my life."

Crystal pursued, as if addressing herself, "I often think about it, we were the only couple to turn our back to the street and face the sea. We were lost in our own world."

Fritz shared other people's reactions to their attitude, "They considered us nuts. I did try to convince you to change the position because of their derogatory comments. But you protested and justified our unconventional seating, bragging that it provided you with more time to see me and me only."

Crystal took another sip of wine, placed her free hand on his, and her voice filled the space. "I remember how we stayed for hours together, talking about the sea, the trees, the flowers, the wind, discussing our feelings, the understanding we offered to each other, how we cared about each other's happiness. I realize now that in that regard you are the same. Do you think I have changed much?"

Her hand lingered on his, and she kept passing her index finger in slow, light strokes, drawing small circles that communicated her deep feelings for him.

Fritz revealed in a confident tone, "I don't think so. You seem the way I left you. I have found the same understanding, caring. Your eyes betrayed you, your profound affection for me lingers in them." He paused, trying to recoup his line of thought, to find the right words. He continued with his eyebrows drawn together, his voice warm and tender, "You were not like anyone else I had known. With you, I experienced love, true love." He stopped, then asked her, "What about you? What else do you remember?"

She murmured slowly, her voice like a mother cradling her baby, singing to make him fall asleep. "I remember harmony, great harmony, a kind of completeness like the river ending in the sea. You were my first." Her timid confession, which to Fritz was a repetition of a beloved refrain played over and over, made him shiver. He sipped some of his wine, mesmerized by the time spent with Crystal.

With the same tender tone she avowed, "I was afraid that day, and, like when you taught me to swim, I was trembling. You didn't make fun of my insecurity. Instead you were gentle, taking the time to make me feel comfortable, confident, ready."

Fritz blushed and his voice was thick when he answered her with a simple, "Hmm."

"Were you that slow because of some kind of apprehension?"

He shrugged his shoulders, looked at her with affection and revealed, "I did not want to hurt you, to hurt your feelings, to make you feel inadequate. I wanted it to be delightful for you and to be an act of togetherness that we would keep for a lifetime."

She squeezed his hand while letting his words penetrate her senses. She put her head on his shoulder, closed her eyes. Fritz could smell her, the scent of paint clung to her clothing, but it was a clean, inviting, fresh smell.

Crystal disrupted the silence that had been established when she inquired, "Do you recall when I asked you how it was after our first time, you just nodded your head, then you noticed the despair displayed in my eyes and you kissed me?"

Fritz smiled at the memory and nodded his head again. Then he said, "I still have the sensation with me."

Crystal lifted her head from his shoulder and with innocence, like a child admitting to a mistake, she avowed, "I almost cried when you nodded your head; I assumed I was unskilled, but when you kissed me I felt your passion, your desire, your love. I have tried to forget that urge, that passion, but it remains with me."

Fritz admitted, "You, too, made an impression on me. In every woman I met I tried to find you, with no success!" He paused, collecting his thoughts, then continued, "I didn't want to ever lose what we shared, the way I knew you. This was in part the reason I accepted going to New York, to begin a new life. But as you see, it didn't work."

It was Crystal's turn to recall the painful stage. She murmured, "After living with the memories for three years, I finally admitted that you were gone for good. I always rejected the possibility of you loving someone else. I wanted to remember us the way we were that summer. This was why I never discussed the subject with anyone. I would talk about you sometimes, but never mention your desertion. Also, I took refuge in my books and my work."

Her voice was just a whisper at the end. Fritz was touched by her honesty. She snuggled against him and felt how wonderful it was to touch him. They remained silent for a moment. Fritz put his glass on the coffee table, then hers, too.

The sunset's orange glow had faded, leaving a shy amber streak that plunged through the window to sit on the wall behind them. The wind gathered force, speeding its course whistling through the thick foliage. The waves crashed with ardor on the bank, spitting angry droplets and bubbling foam in protest against the disrupting elements.

Crystal held Fritz tighter, as if to protect herself from the change in atmospheric pressure, and his warmth invaded her. It was not just the alcohol's effect on her, but all they had talked about. She was slow to admit it. All the repressed feelings from all those years emerged intact, as if preserved in a sanctuary, erupting that night and making her body yearn for Fritz.

She rubbed her hand lightly across his chest, searching, exploring, rediscovering the form that she knew well. Then she rested her head on his chest. Fritz murmured in her ear, "This is how we were once."

She kept moving her hand. She could feel Fritz's body growing tense, turgescent. He turned, passed his arm around her. Their bodies became pressed against each other; the heat of desire steamed between them. Her body began to tremble like the first time, but this night a profound desire was the cause, not some remote fear. Their tenacity, their honesty, their love, had brought them back together. The years apart dissipated like magic, the race difference buried in a sea of faith and courage.

Crystal lifted her head from Fritz's chest and looked at him with intense fondness in her eyes, a shy smile on her lips. Fritz kissed her softly on her cheeks, her forehead, while his hands caressed her back. She poised one hand on the back of his neck, brushing softly with her fingers, the other rested on Fritz's chest. He licked her lips, she bent backward, her neck extended, her eyes closed, her nose flaring with an intense desire.

She parted her lips as Fritz invaded her mouth with his tongue in a slow, tender kiss while their bodies mingled. Fritz ran his fingers up and down her legs like a feather. Patiently, he trailed his mouth on the same spot previously explored, awakening deeper, ancient responses, the ardor of their previous love spreading to her senses, her body soliciting their past intimacy. She whimpered a soft, muffled sound, and directed his hands to her breasts as she pulled back from him. He cupped her breasts, caressed them lightly and through the linen fabric teased them until he located her hard nipples. He nibbled them gently one after the other. Her whole body pulsated, trembling with expectation.

The sky vibrated with numerous scintillating stars. The vacillating candlelight appeared vulnerable with its dancing flame following the breeze's fantasy. Fritz murmured in Crystal's ear with a thick voice, "It's time to close the window." He withdrew from her embrace, eased out, and headed to the rectangular hole. As he closed the window, he spotted the maid coming to their hut with a basket. He pulled open the door to take it.

Crystal disapproved of the intrusion and demanded, "Why are you opening the door?"

Fritz answered, "The food is here." He took the basket from the maid, closed the door, and placed it on the table behind the candle. The hut was now cozier than before. The shy light provided an atmosphere of intimacy. Fritz walked back to the seat and planted himself in front of Crystal. She was sitting with her thighs joined. Fritz, playing with his legs, parted them, and began caressing her head, her neck.

She reached for Fritz's hips, sliding her hands down his thighs, molding his bulging muscles as if just discovering them. She threw her arms around his waist and poised her head sideways on his loin, feeling his turgid, palpitating penis. She closed her eyes, kissed his crotch then, reached for his buttons and began to undo them. Fritz was tracing slow circles on her arms. The pants liberated, they glided to the floor.

He stood with his shirt hanging over his bathing suit, excitement tingling in every cell of his body. She raised her head, absorbing the form in front of her from head to toe. Fritz moved her hand away, stepped out of his pants, and kicked them aside. Then he passed one arm under her knees, the other under her trunk, lifted her up, and carried her to the bedroom. She dangled her feet on the way, the clashing noise made them both laugh, relaxed.

Fritz deposited her gently on the bed, kneeled on the floor and kissed her. She grabbed his hands and directed them to the buttons of her shirt. Then she caressed Fritz's neck, his back, and played with his hair. He snapped open the top button, reaching for the freshly exposed area with his lips. He caressed her lightly, kissing her at the same time. His free hand lingered down her legs, defining her shape through the thin fabric. Crystal sensed a new feeling, an urge she had not experienced since Fritz had left. Her body was quivering with anticipation and thirst, like dry land expecting the rain.

She untied her pants and slid them down; Fritz pulled them off her legs. Reaching for his shirt, she unbuttoned it, startling him with her grace, her simplicity, her determination.

She stripped him of the shirt. He appeared gorgeous, almost vulnerable. She touched him lightly on his back, then his front, then tried to put order into his disheveled hair. Her eyes were shining with rays of longing and desire. She shifted her body to the other half of the bed, creating an inviting space for her man.

Fritz joined her, lay close by her side, put his arms around her body, and kissed her mouth slowly searching, demanding. Both of their bodies grew excited, enthralled. Crystal pushed Fritz's bathing suit down; he got rid of it. Then he freed Crystal of her shirt and bathing suit.

Fritz caressed her neck, her back, sending waves of passion animating her. His breathing was heavy but he wanted Crystal to desire him. He kept teasing her, licking her belly, rubbing his hair on her chest, cupping her breasts, nibbling her nipples. She whimpered, passing her arms under Fritz as if pushing him above her.

She parted her legs, closed her eyes. He was on all fours above her, his knees astride her hips. She ran her hands through his hair, curled her arms around his torso, pulling her body closer to him. Fritz kept nibbling her nipples, leaving one to catch the other while his hand caressed her thigh, massaging the warmth between her legs until she could not take it anymore, and his resistance faded.

Their bodies joined, fastened by an unfurling blast of passion. Rhythmically, they moved to the tango of their hearts, their shared desire seeking satisfaction and making up for lost time. Crystal held Fritz tight, like she did not want to lose him again, following him, his every move, with her body. She felt him deep inside her, felt his courage, his audacity, his strength, his passion, his gentleness, his urge. Then she lost control in an exploding sensation spilling over her senses, her body. She arched high while she was swept by a powerful wind. She cried aloud, her body shaken by spasms as she tightened her embrace to Fritz's and buried her face, panting, in the groove of his neck. She stayed there, her eyes shut, lost. She was startled by her body's reaction. Fritz, too, was panting, haggard. They observed each other when she reopened her eyes and they both smiled. Fritz kissed her again and she said, "I love you so much. You are the only one."

They started over, their bodies still yearning but their senses partly calmed, not satisfied, giving them the chance to go slower. They took the time to explore, to caress every inch of each other's skin. Their rapture was growing like the rising tide only to burst out in a gushing, vibrating stream. When their bodies could not wait anymore, they joined in an act of shared love, comprehension, where their avid passion climbed to attain the stage of paroxysm and elation.

They exploded together in a climax with their muffling, panting sounds orchestrated in a sublime symphony engulfed in nature's expression. It was as if they were never going to stop, for each time one performance was accomplished, their senses and bodies rewired for the execution of another one more blissful, more delightful, more revealing. Finally content, they lay in each other's arms, their desire appeased, beads of sweat mingling from their tangled bodies, and fell asleep.

When they awoke the moon was disguised as a yellow balloon and splashed down a domineering flood of radiance that dimmed the stars' glitters. Fritz pointed to the fact that the sea had always been their partner. It was the invitation to go outdoors. He took Crystal's hand in his, and they exited Celeste. The whole bungalow area was illuminated by the brightness of the incandescent satellite, while the surroundings reposed as a large onyx mass.

It was calm, silent, the air still. Crystal was startled by the beauty of the night. Since Fritz had left her she had not had the chance to enjoy that sort of environment: the kind that enveloped you with its beauty. Gerard was very attached to his laboratory and books, and did not have a great inclination or free time for outdoor exploration.

She moved closer to Fritz, snuggling her slim body against his. Together they advanced to the shore, their bare feet contracting when they touched the cool sand. They discovered small creatures crawling on the beach and Fritz explained to her they were crabs washed in by the tide. He anticipated that the surf and the river course were warm, too. With no more fussing they progressed to enjoy the inviting waves.

After relishing a good immersion they deserted the saltwater. With their dripping bodies, their blended respiration coupled to their muffled steps, they ran to the river for a wash. Their stay at the river was short. They did not talk much on their way back. They were each engulfed by so many remembrances, but also they both sensed that the time for them to be parted was approaching. They knew for certain they would have to face and determine their fate.

When finally they were in the bungalow's bedroom getting ready to leave, Fritz's good sense of humor prevailed.

He teased Crystal about her hair, "Your hair always grows thicker when you don't wear a shower cap."

Crystal smiled at Fritz's remark. Attributing his observation to ignorance, she informed him, "The hot press effect is gone from them; nature claimed back its place with revenge. You better get used to my nappy, spongy hair."

Fritz had a smirk of amusement on his face and presented to her a congratulatory avowal, "You are still beautiful and desirable." He advanced toward her, passed his hands over the unruly mound, kissed her on her hair, then selected a strand for her to fasten to the lump in a ponytail. Crystal was exasperated by the exertion, and with much application subdued the lump into a decent coiffure. Fritz made her laugh this time with his remark, "Yours looks better than mine, plastered on my scalp like twisted vermicelli."

It was Crystal's turn to respond and she observed, "Your hair is lighter when wet." Thinking awhile as she went around the room getting herself dressed, she added, "For most people their hair is darker when wet."

Fritz replied, "I'm unique in a lot of ways."

She smacked him playfully on the chest, protesting, "Mr. Pride, or rather, Mr. Unique, let's keep moving; we must be in town soon, so we can sleep enough hours to be ready for tomorrow's events."

Fritz preceded her to the sitting area and out of curiosity checked the food delivered earlier. It was grilled conch, salad, bread and lemonade. Fritz fixed a plate for himself with plenty of conch and a pinch of salad. For Crystal he arranged a large pile of salad with just a slice of mollusk. Feeling compelled to justify his discrimination he proclaimed, "I go by the custom, the saying is that conch is an aphrodisiac and is better suited for men to empower their sexual prowess." Crystal cast him a deceitful regard. He felt embarrassed and added, "It would not do for a woman, do you agree?"

Now Crystal, enraged by his comments, fumed, "I thought your stay in the States had exposed you to more acceptable affirmation of the female gender in general. But no, it seems to me in that matter you are close to Gerard. That Haitian belief that all women should be puritans, angels." She caught her breath and admonished him, "We are prudish, sincere, and do appreciate our men's support. Please don't force us to be hypocrites."

Unable to offer a plausible excuse, Fritz transferred meat from his plate to hers, making sure their share of conch was equal.

Crystal acquiesced and manifested her satisfaction. "That will do. I know how you detest vegetables, but it's good for your health."

As Fritz pulled up a chair Crystal proposed, "Let's go outside; the steps are clean enough to serve as benches." She seized the two plates and strolled outside, followed by Fritz clutching two full glasses of lemonade and the paper bag protecting the bread. After depositing the glasses on the balustrade, Fritz swept the steps with the empty paper bag.

The moon was bathing the sea with soft rays, frequent audacious trifling clouds crossing its vibrancy. As a result of this new disposition, the bungalow was plunged in semi-obscurity. A steady breeze joined the elements, awakening the palm tree leaves. Soon, their whistling was combined with the *compas* music that flooded out from the hotel.

Fritz and Crystal, comfortably installed on the steps, attacked their food hungrily. Crystal did not regret her intervention; she enjoyed the dish as much as her companion. She pondered the reasons why women in her country should be forbidden the right to pleasure or contentment, but could not register any. She persuaded herself to get rid of those conflicting thoughts jamming her reasoning. For now she resolved to relish what was left of the evening.

Sipping her lemonade she noted Fritz's legs shaking incessantly, a sign of nervousness on his part. She was going to ask him about his concern when he surprised her with a blunt question, "What are you going to tell him?"

Crystal was not on the same line of thinking as Fritz, and inquired, "Who? Who are you talking about?"

Like a dissonant note dropped in the middle of a harmonious symphony, Fritz whispered, "Gerard."

Taken aback by the request, Crystal replied with some hesitation, "I don't know." Then firmly she said, "I don't really know."

Fritz gave her an arched, deep glance. While hammering every single syllable he pronounced, "What do you mean by 'I don't really know'?"

Crystal placed her glass by her side. Looking back at Fritz she repeated with a flat equal tone, "I don't know what I'm going to do." Turning her head she tried to explain, "It happened so suddenly, I don't know how to view, to interpret, our reunion, how to make sense of it all."

Fritz stood and began to pace the length of the bungalow, then, as if chasing a bad dream, he shook his hand frantically in front of his face and said, "I will tell you how to make sense of it all: you, Crystal Dijon, are in love with Fritz Jean Lucas." He stopped, then added, "What do you have to say? Will you contradict me?"

Crystal said, "I must not, but I will avow that I was also in love with you during the four-and-a-half years of your silence."

Fritz said, "Are you taking revenge now by destroying what we have, to make me suffer?"

Crystal answered pleadingly, "I'm suffering, too. Why don't you learn to give someplace in your consideration to my feelings? Take my place in the game, or for a matter of fact, take Gerard's spot. Remember, I'm engaged to him." She lowered her voice and said decisively, "No, no, Fritz, I gave my word to Gerard."

It was now Fritz's turn to insist, "This whole situation does not make sense." But he added with determination and firmness one of his mottos, "True love will win."

If Fritz was troubled, Crystal was overwhelmed by the weight of her impending decision. She was in love with Fritz, she wanted him. But Gerard Armand, her fiancé, was the man to whom she had given her consent. Fritz's question resounded in her ears, *"What are you going to tell him?"*

Knowing Gerard, Crystal would never declare her recent escapade; it would pain the man too much, he would never understand. While tortured by her present position, it occurred to Crystal that a man as intelligent and well connected as Gerard must be aware of Fritz's return to the country.

There was no more guessing. Crystal realized Gerard knew she had met Fritz. As a matter of fact, her change in attitude toward him even before she was with Fritz had probably given him reason to doubt. Gerard and all his rhetoric about women and his code of conduct for the proper spouse crossed her mind. She admitted how despicable Gerard would find her, and reasoned that maybe it was for the better. But she resented Gerard's repulsion of her.

Fritz, during the time of her meditation, had run inside the bungalow. He had gathered her bag with her materials and come back outside. He drew Crystal out of her reflection by saying, "It's time to go." He offered her his hand and together they walked along the shore where now furious, noisy waves were crashing on the sand.

A solitary form standing on the back porch of the hotel became animated upon spotting them. He was moving in their direction, and when he was close enough they identified Gregory, one of Crystal's older twin brothers. He had been waiting for his sister.

Gregory played the gentleman that he was and met the couple mid-way. He welcomed them and proposed to Crystal to stay with him at the New Spectrum ball. Fritz thanked Gregory for his solicitude and reminded him that he expected his and his brother's presence at the factory blessing the following day, then walked to his car with Crystal's beach bag clutched under his arm. He felt as though he had to leave the party, the beach, the bungalow behind. He couldn't reconcile what had just happened with Crystal's *"I don't know."* Then, *"No, no, Fritz, I gave my word to Gerard."*

Brother and sister exchanged a glance of complicity. They waited until Fritz's car's rumbling noise was completely abated by the music, then Gregory entered the ballroom with his sister. He did not ask Crystal any questions, nor for an explanation, but instead invited her to dance. Gregory made sure Crystal was exposed to every one of their acquaintances and encouraged her to flash a bright smile and assume a relaxed stance.

When Gregory was satisfied with the result of his plan, which was to make everyone believe Crystal had been in his company, he went over to the table where all the members of their family were seated, except their father. They had arrived late due to their activities in town. Their impressive presence confirmed their support for Crystal. Gregory announced to his aunt, uncle, brother and friends that he was taking his sister home. During the drive home he informed Crystal that their father was in the capital, but had not attended the physician's conference.

———

On the porch, Gerard had experienced the appalling shock of discovering that Fritz was in the capital, and that Crystal had been working for him. When the paralyzing effect of that reality subsided, he conscientiously eliminated some of the implications of the situation, such as that Crystal could have been in contact with Fritz during the years he had pursued her.

No, he convinced himself one more time, *it cannot be.* However, even as that certitude sunk in, he was slowly transferred to a state of embarrassment. He could not help himself, he felt vulnerable. Vulnerable because Fritz's presence in the capital not only implied he would meet his fiancée, but that his weak spots, Gerard's weak spots, would be unveiled to the world.

He considered contacting one of his friends; the one he trusted most: Henry. Just the thought of talking about his ordeal made him sick. How could he explain that sort of dilemma to a friend? If his suspicions proved to be right, meaning his fiancée was not faithful, he had exposed his shame while he was not in control. But, the worst scenario would be for him to be wrong; that would be solid evidence of his fear.

He had revealed his insecurity and in the future could not pretend to handle the weaker sex. For a brief moment he contemplated confiding in his parents. He could travel to Leogane and open his heart to the old man, his father.

But no, his father would as always solicit his wife's advice. Gerard knew in advance the result of his demarche; his mother would downplay his worries, and warn him that his jealousy would destroy his relationship with Crystal.

The waves of indignity melted away with that last consideration and were replaced by a slow, rising anger. Gerard's head was throbbing, his heart aching, his eyes riveted on a spot on the horizon he did not see. He was looking inward, analyzing his past. His hands balled in tight fists, he admitted his previous judgment had sold him.

He had always assumed Fritz would settle in Cap-Haitian with his parents, that he would not represent an immediate threat. At that point, the wind picked up speed and was whistling through the cornstalks, the sky was low, dark with the heavy swollen clouds; he uncurled his fingers, abandoned the porch, and entered his house.

Lying in bed with his eyes wide open, his hands clasped under his head, his legs crossed, he was facing Crystal's picture on his dresser. He was startled to register that nothing had changed. Everything was where he had left them. But he knew it was a perception, his mind playing tricks on him. There were new elements in the game; he had won the grant for the two-year training in Paris. To confirm his assertion, he directed his gaze to the package with the contract and all the information for his installation reposing beside Crystal's picture. That setting calmed him, the contract bound to Crystal on his dresser. He mouthed silently as if to remind himself: *Yes, Fritz is in the capital.* Then aloud he voiced, "But I am the betrothed."

He rejected the menace carried by his rival's presence and concentrated on the fact that he was engaged to Crystal. He convinced himself that he must retreat, to gather force, gather momentum. He compared the situation to a hurricane and his position as the eye. The turmoil swirled around him, yet he was calm, intent at a distance.

He would challenge Fritz and Crystal, whom he considered to be in the twirling. He smiled. One of his strongholds was to remain cool in difficult situations. It was why he had been chosen as Chief Resident in Surgery. He was smart, but he was faced with valuable competitors. Except in great crisis, when everyone else was shaky and indecisive, he was always the one to take the lead and offer a rational solution to the problem. His perspicacity had ensured his promotion.

And that night, in his private life, he intended to apply the same tool that had propelled him to the head of the Department of Surgery. He reasoned about where his advantages lay. On top of the list, he placed his engagement to Crystal. He recalled how his friends had criticized him for proposing only six months after dating Crystal. They had also discouraged him during the two previous years when he had pursued her relentlessly. His friend had warned him that Crystal was waiting for the Arab-Haitian. But, their advice did not influence him.

He had wanted Crystal that much; she was the perfect fit for his projects. He reviewed the situation like a lawyer preparing the statements to defend a case, a difficult and delicate one because he did not opt to lose Crystal. Still a situation where one's heart, reputation and pride were jeopardized could be unsettling. One could be negligent or even irrational at times, he concluded, as he pushed away the repulsing temptation of elopement.

He laughed. How ridiculous he would look if he were to take that path! No, instead he would use the surprise factor as his second tool. Surprise was the powerful weapon to start his war. However, he conceded that weapons alone did not ensure victory. Strategy, good strategy, was an indispensable ally. Now came his contract, the third weapon.

Gerard planned to visit the following day, Thursday, the capital's governmental offices to check the regulations for an expedited marriage and make arrangements for his trip to Paris with Crystal. Fatigue progressively claimed his body. Before he slumped in sleep, his conscience pricked him. His behavior would hurt Crystal. But he refused the call to forgiveness. He felt satisfied. It was his revenge. Crystal deserved the lesson for keeping that full-time job at New Spectrum, and for imposing her will to attend her firm's fifth anniversary party rather than accompany him to the conference.

———

THURSDAY

WHETHER IT WAS THE wine, the cool weather, or the fact that Curtis and Arianne had decided the solution to their common problem meant traveling to Port-au-Prince to surprise their son at the factory's blessing, they experienced a good, sound sleep, with Arianne's body pressed tightly against her husband's. They awoke earlier than usual and started the day by disrupting the routine they had performed every morning for the past twenty-seven years before leaving their house for their store.

Arianne was exuberant, thrilled by her husband's proposition to shy away from the store and spend their free time in a hotel. That was what was missing in her marriage, she thought—great vacation time to indulge in intimacy and the ambiance of the capital with her life partner. She hastily dumped three sets of clothing and underwear for herself and her husband into a carry-on bag. Then she went to the porch on the boulevard side where she knew her husband was lying on the couch in the sunrise, one of his bad habits.

She kissed him good morning and summoned him to shower, telling him, "You better get going so we hit Route #1 before the commercial trucks get to it."

"Thank you for reminding me. I must hurry. You know how much I resent driving with those monsters tailgating my car."

Arianne gave him an understanding glance, not wanting to remind him that he was just a slow driver with a less-than-tolerable performance on unfamiliar roads. She offered him a hand to get off the couch and together they re-entered their home. Arianne locked the door behind him and proceeded to the maid's room and knocked gently.

Justine was already up. She answered promptly and appeared fully dressed, concern on her face. On a regular morning she was the one to knock on her patrons' bedroom door with a tray of steaming coffee. But since Fritz's return nothing had been the same, everything was changing.

Justine prepared herself for some harsh reprimand, but to her great surprise Mrs. Curtis was gentler toward her than she had been since Fritz came out of the hospital and was placed in her care. With some mystery her boss informed her that she and her husband were leaving for the capital that morning and that Justine was to be in charge. Arianne ordered Justine to prepare breakfast and lunch for them, then joined her husband, who was already warming up the car.

After trusting their house keys to their old maid, they left. It was still early by Cap-Haitian standards. Their neighbors were all awake in bed waiting for their coffee, and were annoyed by the unusual noises that upset their routine. Grumbling, they abandoned their beds to peer through doors and windows, eager to learn the activities of the Lucas'. Their curiosity not satisfied, they rescinded to obtain from their maids the destination of the early travelers, as the Lucas car wormed through the empty streets like a ghost haunted by sunlight.

The couple spent almost the entire four-hour drive in morbid silence. Arianne watched her husband maneuver the car with a deep furrow creased in his forehead. She decided Curtis was preoccupied not only by the driving, but also by something else that she hoped not to learn.

She enjoyed the landscape, addressing him only when she wanted him to stop so she could buy fresh fruits from the small village markets they passed.

After an easy ride, they arrived at the hotel where they were to stay. It was just across from Fabric Pro, and close to the main thruway, Delmas, the airport and downtown. Curtis had made the reservation for a room on the second floor at the corner, facing the private entrance of the factory and Fritz's office.

His wife had already spotted an acquaintance, another Arab-Haitian woman about her age, to whom she was animatedly explaining that the building across the street, Fabric Pro, was their family property, and that her son had come up with that bright project to innovate and enrich Haitian industry, and that she was here with her husband to surprise Fritz at the firm's blessing ceremony.

Arianne then acknowledged her husband's presence and proudly introduced him. Curtis gallantly shook his wife's friend's hand, then excused himself, pretending he was tired. His wife always reproached him for his shyness, blaming the country lifestyle for his lack of interest in gossip or socializing.

An attendant waiting in the hall gave instructions to Curtis on how to locate his suite. It was easy. "Just turn right at the top of the stairs, your door has '11' inscribed on it." Curtis found his nest with no problem. He marveled at the luxury of the bedroom and concluded that the décor was almost like the hotels in Florida. He sighed, recalling that his hometown, Cap-Haitian, offered hotel rooms shining with cleanliness and simplicity, but nothing fancy.

He proceeded to the private balcony adjacent to his suite and from there was able to observe the factory and all its surroundings. He spied on the activities performed at his son's business, but could not find Fritz. Curtis wondered about where Fritz was that Thursday midday. Fritz was not the type to ditch his workday for fantasy, so his father concluded he probably had gone to the bank or the seaport for serious transactions. Curtis regretted that they had not announced their visit, at least to his brother-in-law.

While driving, he had been speculating about what effect their scheme would produce, and even now he was not sure of what sort of result they would obtain. *Will Fritz be happy, or will he think we are trying to control him?*

Curtis returned to his room, and after a restorative shower he laid in bed musing about his son and how he would react to the surprise. Fatigue slowly took hold of him and what he disliked the most, a midday nap, was his recourse that day.

During that time Arianne was in the hotel reception room with her former classmate. They maintained an excited conversation where they perused the events missed during their years apart. Arianne complained of the boring Cap-Haitian life, while Magdala complained of the bustling, exhausting capital trends. They tried to surpass each other in courage, tribulations, happiness, and when their minds grew dry in inventions, Arianne beat her friend, giving her the final blow by inviting her to the afternoon's event, her son's factory blessing.

Magdala kindly rejected the invitation, feigning another commitment, and adding that her calendar was full for the month ahead. They exchanged phone numbers, and separated with the promise to keep in touch, a typical Arab-Haitian meeting of women. Arianne, satisfied with the outcome, thanked her friend for her time, then rushed to her husband's side. She found him snoring in their hotel room. She did not immediately wake him; instead she repeated the same moves made by Curtis earlier.

She went to the balcony and peered into the building across the street. As her husband had observed before, she saw no trace of Fritz. The same looming question crossed her mind, *Where is Fritz?* She was sure Fritz had safely returned to Kenscoff on Wednesday, as there was no accident mentioned. It was not in Fritz's nature not to be at his workplace on a Thursday. Her worry faded after she persuaded herself her son was probably having lunch with her brother, Michael.

A deep sorrow took the place of her previous worrying feeling. She wished she were closer to her son, that she could understand him, or better accept him with all his will and choices. Then another facet of the problem surged into Arianne's thoughts. She had to find a way to eliminate Crystal, her menacing presence, before it was too late.

She praised herself, *Crystal and Fritz won't meet that often. Crystal is a very reserved woman and she is engaged. All those cards play in my favor.* Then her husband's position flashed in her mind, *What about Curtis's promise to side with Fritz? No! He loves me too much; he will never obstruct my real desire. I can handle him. And what about Fritz? I just have to set an unplanned meeting where Fritz will meet Linda, the woman we chose for him, and I will play the ignorant, innocent mother.*

I'm sure my son will be pleased with her charm and youth. She is only seventeen. Before going back to Cap-Haitian I will persuade my husband to pay an official visit to Linda's parents with me. She paced the balcony, checking every corner of the factory her sight could reach, then abandoned her quest. She went back to the room and stirred Curtis out of his sleep with a kiss.

At 2 p.m. the large entrance to Fabric Pro was opened, giving access to a vehicle with the inscription, "New Spectrum." It was the architectural firm's car, from which exited two men wearing tailored suits, pads in hand, taking notes.

For the past thirty minutes Arianne and Curtis had been posted on the balcony after Arianne had aroused her husband out of his nap. Arianne informed Curtis, "They are the engineers. We will thank and congratulate them later. They did a good job, don't you think?"

Curtis, his eyes still riveted on the factory, disinterestedly answered, "I do." Then, as if reanimated by a new surge he said louder, while pointing in front of him, "There is Fritz."

From their spot his mother and father spied all his moves; how he curbed his rented car, exited, talked to the engineers, the workers, before entering his office. Curtis proposed to his wife, "Should we go now and let him know about our presence?"

Wanting to take full advantage of the situation, Arianne suppressed her husband with a downward gesture of her hand and said, "No, wait until Father Ignacio and my brother are there. It will be a true surprise, and also the proof of our desire as parents to support our son." While she was talking, the church vehicle dropped off Father Ignacio, who was warmly welcomed by Fritz.

As Fritz was touring the factory back yard with Father Ignacio, the New Spectrum vehicle once again entered the factory. This time, it contained four occupants, three men and one woman. Each absorbed in their own thoughts, Curtis and Arianne witnessed Fritz shaking hands with each of the men that had just arrived, then kissing the woman lightly on the cheek. Arianne shrugged at that occurrence, but now applied more attention to what was happening. Fritz was introducing Father Ignacio to the group. When the woman's turn came there was a long talk, and all the while Fritz was holding her hand. The woman had her back to Ariannne and Curtis.

After observing their conversation with Father Ignacio, Arianne turned to her husband and said, "Fritz for sure is close to that woman."

To which Curtis answered, "Be patient. It's only a few minutes until the ceremony begins. I presume the woman is the architect your brother has such a high esteem for."

———

Arianne, at her husband's side on the hotel balcony, observed with great interest the activities in the factory's back yard and grew restless. She felt empowered. She assumed she and her husband as parents had a point to prove: their dedication to their son. She concluded that the best way for them to demonstrate it that day was to show up late. So she cajoled her husband, then made the proposition, "Curtis, let's wait a few minutes to give enough time for the guests to be installed. We will join them just after the ceremony starts, to create a full impact."

Curtis just nodded. Arianne interpreted the gesture as full agreement with her scheme. She could see Curtis was eager to be with Fritz. His eyes were pinned across the street, his attention focused on the factory. She followed his attitude, turning a steady gaze toward the area of interest.

The last time Father Ignacio had met with Fritz was during the summer of 1960 before Fritz's trip to Paris. However, in the Fabric Pro courtyard five years later, he acted as if Fritz were one of his regular parishioners. It was because Arianne had kept him informed of her son's whereabouts, at the same time taking precaution to avert the sore subject of the pending match for Fritz's marriage.

Dr. Dijon was also one of Father Ignacio's fervent church-goers and was proud of Crystal's achievements. Since Crystal had left Cap-Haitian for her studies in Port-au-Prince, Dr. Dijon had always kept Father Ignacio aware of his daughter's progress in the capital. Father Ignacio congratulated her warmly, and hinted that he would use her services in the future. The allusion served as an incentive to Engineer Turnier's intervention.

Engineer Turnier led the group, speaking with great gestures and providing information on his work and expertise, trying to impress Father Ignacio, and hoping to secure a new client. When they reached Fritz's office and the guests were seated, one of the iron workers cautiously requested Fritz's attention. Fritz excused himself, left, and came back not too long after, signaling for Crystal to join him to check the worker's concern.

Crystal and Fritz crossed the factory, approved of the finished look of the iron rails, then circled the factory outside to examine the effect. Before they turned the corner to re-enter the office, Arianne and Curtis watched Fritz as he stood in front of the woman, talking. They appeared to be discussing a matter unrelated to the construction, because during that time Fritz caught the woman's chin and forced her to look at him straight in the eyes for a long time, and then there was more talking between them.

Arianne leaned on the balcony rails and stared at them with unblinking eyes. Her mouth dropped open and she addressed her husband dryly, "Have you seen them?"

Curtis's face presented a surprised and amused look. His eyes bright with dilated pupils and a pleasant smile parting his lips, he was absorbed by the scene and its significance. He replied in a whisper, "Yes."

Arianne was not satisfied with her husband's reaction and pondered in an angry tone, "Did you recognize her?"

Curtis, with a timid, not-so-encouraging stance, confirmed Arianne's doubt with the affirmation, "Yes, she is the architect, Crystal Dijon."

Arianne was astonished and at the same time annoyed that Curtis did not show any signs of anger or revolt. She leapt back, tumbled to her chair, sat to find support, and manifested her discord by asking fiercely, "When are we leaving?"

Curtis, engrossed in admiring the couple, a faint smile illuminating his face, answered, "Right now. It's time for us to go. Our son is going to be really happy to see us."

When his proposition met with glacial silence he turned toward Arianne, then quickly changed his eyes' direction to avoid his wife's murderous glare. Curtis reconsidered his wife's request: "When are we leaving?" He suddenly got a hint of the scheme and was baffled by it. "You mean you are not going to attend the ceremony? You want to go back to Cap-Haitian? What about the inauguration tomorrow?"

Arianne vociferated decidedly, "No. I can't go. It's too much for me to handle." Sensing that maybe Curtis would defy her and go, she tried to persuade him by playing the social and religious cards. She whispered, "Can you imagine what just happened? Fritz presented Crystal to Father Ignacio. Fritz is a traitor." Then she complained, "How can I go to church now?"

Curtis, knowing how sensitive his wife was about religion and how she was respected by the church members and priests, tried to comfort her and handed her a solution, "Come, Arianne. This meeting is like a buffer, a good occasion for all of us to be with Crystal, to amend with no embarrassment for past evil. Do you want a drink before we leave?"

Arianne said sarcastically, "No drink can give me my son back."

Curtis, still courting the prospect that he could coax Arianne into cooperating, convincingly proposed, "Today you have the occasion to win Fritz back by showing him your complaisance, your understanding."

Arianne was becoming increasingly disturbed by her husband's allusion, and manifested her irritation in those terms as she exploded, "Curtis, never, never! It will never do!" Not waiting for an answer, she continued, "Curtis, let's teach Fritz a lesson, prove to him that we won't budge, but will follow our Arab-Haitian tradition. What better way to show our point of view? We must let them all learn that we were at the hotel across from the factory, ready to attend the blessing ceremony. But, because of Crystal's presence we chose to abstain. We are going back to Cap-Haitian."

Curtis was startled by his wife's violence and lost all hope of persuading her. He checked his watch and determinedly announced, "I will be at the factory. If you need something, you know where to find me." He left, closing the door noiselessly behind him. It was the first time in their married life where by choice they were not to attend a familial reunion together.

Arianne was flabbergasted by Curtis's decision to go without her, but she could not find an answer to give him. She waited long enough for Curtis to arrive at the factory, then went back into the room, closed the door, and moved the curtain just enough to see the factory. She observed her husband conversing animatedly with her brother, who had just arrived in the factory back yard. Fritz came out of his office, saw his father, ran to him and hugged him, then did the same to his uncle and aunt. He went back inside and came out with Crystal. She extended her hand to Curtis, which he took, then opened his arms to embrace her. It was a chain of hugging, laughing and talking.

Arianne was lost, angry, dumbfounded. She sat back in the chair trying to make sense of what she had just witnessed. She recalled now her brother's reference on their way to Kenscoff the day of Fritz's arrival. His description of the woman architect had been flattering. No wonder he was all smiles and jubilant for Crystal's introduction; he already had good intentions toward the woman, even before learning she was Fritz's former girlfriend.

And from what Arianne had just seen she resolved not to discuss the subject with her brother, but she sure was going to challenge Curtis. How could he be so rude? She had been on the verge of crying, and he did not even offer his solace, as a good husband should.

Even Fritz would have been more sensitive than his father on such an occasion. Fritz, my only son, appeared so happy, so sure of himself, content. But how could he be? How could he live with a stranger that knows nothing about our traditions? A bright, new idea germinated in her mind: *Crystal could be Fritz's mistress. Fritz will marry Linda, Crystal would have the second bed after Fritz's wife. She would be devoted to him and he would satisfy his yearning. I will settle for that, but Crystal has to learn to be less social and spend only private, exclusive time with my son.* I will encourage Fritz to have an affair with that naive woman named Crystal.

The church was an obstacle to her scheme. She imagined parishioners reporting to Father Ignacio every gossip they fetched when they visited the capital. Every family in the countryside had a relative with some acquaintances in the capital to feed them on social and political happenings; it was called tele-mouth.

Those blabbermouths would insinuate that she was the instigator of the arrangement. Besides, Crystal's father would disapprove of the situation. It would be viewed as an insult to the Dijon family, undoubtedly giving rise to great resentment, even hatred. *I can live with that,* concluded Arianne. *My real problem is the church.* She paused in her scheming, looking for her next step. *I will provide a much larger contribution for charity, I will sponsor the canteen every week to bail out my soul and merit Father Ignacio's good graces.*

Pleased with that new picture, she curled up in the chair and relaxed. *Let me feign great discontent and complete disapproval so I can disarm my husband and brother, then drop the bomb: my new proposition.* She convinced herself that in Haitian society most rich men have a mistress. Curtis and Michael approved of Fritz's relationship, and anyway weren't they the family's older men? *It's fair enough for me to expect them to guide Fritz in setting the terms of that position.*

Arianne was now completely engrossed in her project. She ordered a late lunch to be delivered to her room with half a bottle of wine. She only ate half of her sandwich, but drank heavily.

When Curtis and Michael returned, they found her very talkative. The men exchanged a knowing glance at the sight of the empty bottle, but were reassured when she addressed them with a steady voice, her language sure. She was not slurring. "Hello, my dears. What good news did you come with for me?"

Curtis was taken aback by her question, certain that a change had taken place during his absence; since he was unsure on what grounds to approach his wife, he volunteered, "It was a nice ceremony. You should have come. Our son missed you."

Arianne gingerly asked, "Did you tell him I'm here?"

Curtis replied prudently, "No, but he knows you are in the capital."

Arianne pressed further with a more determined tone, "That was not my question. Did you tell him that I am here in this hotel?"

Michael intervened, "Why didn't you come, Arianne? Then you would have been as informed as we."

Arianne reproachfully addressed her brother, "Please. I watched how you enjoyed the company."

Michael responded by boasting about his nephew's achievement. "Fritz is an accomplished businessman, well formed, very courteous; he knew how to treat his guests. I'm sure Father Ignacio was proud of his performance. The whole project came from Fritz."

Putting a hand on his wife's shoulder to reassure her Curtis said, "To calm your worries, I don't think Fritz realized I crossed the street from the hotel to the factory; remember he was busy with the engineers. There is still time to make amends. We came to get you so you can meet Crystal."

Arianne cast both men a challenging glance and said contemptuously, "Who told you I changed my stance in less than two hours?"

Curtis replied cautiously, "Arianne, my dear wife, don't you understand, if you miss this occasion it will be very hard for you to make up for it?"

Arianne was sure of her plan and dismissed her husband's plea with, "Thank you, my husband. Now you are thinking about my future well-being. I did the same during your absence, after registering your abandonment."

Curtis defended himself, "It was a matter of duty and respect for me to be there, but for you it was a choice."

Arianne, with haughty regard and a defiant tone said, "Either way, I'm forgiving you, my son, and my brother. As a sensitive, responsible mother I acknowledged my son's happiness in the company of that woman. I also noticed your attitude toward her, so I must give way and accept the present situation."

Curtis kissed his wife, smiled brightly, turned to his brother-in-law, and said, "I told you, Michael, your sister is a woman of great understanding. I knew my wife was going to switch gears once she witnessed her son's happiness."

Arianne went to the window and observed, "Fritz's office is open. He must still be there." She paused, addressing the men with squinted eyes and furrowed eyebrows, and hammered out in an incisive tone, "In fact, I have switched gears. I see nothing wrong with Fritz having an extramarital affair with Crystal. She will be his mistress. It's a far more reasonable approach. Fritz will marry Linda, and keep Crystal on the side."

Silence plagued the room as each man, panic in his eyes, searched for the other's regard, then fixed Arianne with an unbelieving gaze. She continued, "Yes, see how flexible I can be? So you guys find a way to warn that stubborn man, my son, Fritz. After you do so, I will be ready to meet Fritz and Crystal."

Curtis fumbled about, finding the proper terms. "Wait a minute, what do you want us to do? Did you say affair? Mistress?" He sounded incredulous. "Are you out of your mind? Don't you know how much of an insult it is to a young woman to tell her and her family she doesn't deserve a ring, but only the second bed? And with Crystal being an only daughter, and so successful in her career?!" He shook his head in disbelief. "Come on now, be reasonable."

Arianne was unperturbed by Curtis's outburst. She crossed her legs, folded her arms across her chest, and tilted her head to one side, as if amused by what he'd just said. "Warn them, let them know we will not detour from our Arab-Haitian tradition, but since we want to accommodate our son, in this case we have agreed for him to have Crystal as a mistress."

Michael slowly walked over to Arianne's side and non-chalantly asked, "What Arab-Haitian tradition are you talking about?"

Arianne flashed a victorious grin and cited with force, "I'm sure you know, we choose our offspring's partner and arrange for their marriage."

Michael, jumping back in surprise, exclaimed, "Who chose your husband? I thought you did. I'm sure my friend Curtis was presented to you for an arranged marriage, but you wanted him. How many suitors did you refuse before accepting Curtis? We family members felt sorry for him. We thought he was going to benefit from your derision like the three that preceded him, but to our great surprise you even lied to meet him at the theater."

Arianne, wonder in her eyes, replied, "You were aware of my sneaking out to see him?"

Michael, with some malice responded, "Come on, how stupid do you think we are? We knew it all, but we just wanted to protect you, protect your dignity."

Arianne said, "I never would have married someone I didn't love. Curtis was so gentle that I was immediately attracted to him. Didn't I follow him to the countryside?" Suddenly, the truth appeared to Arianne. She had not really followed the Arab-Haitian tradition after all. She had chosen her husband herself. She requested for both men to leave her alone.

Curtis was startled to learn that he had been the fourth contender. He had never imagined that his wife had gone out with other men before him. Then, the first moment of surprise fading, he was pleased to discover that he had been chosen. He affectionately asked his wife, "What do you want me to buy for dinner tonight?"

"I will order from the hotel and stay here tonight," Arianne answered, renouncing their previous plans to stay in Kenscoff with Michael and Martine.

Before leaving to spend the night at his brother-in-law's house, Curtis teased his wife, "Should I oppose or reject your request? Arab-Haitian women by tradition don't stay alone in a hotel overnight."

Michael reinforced, "Sister, Arab-Haitian women by tradition have no say in decision-making; they just follow orders." He kindly added, "You can stay here. We'll see you in the morning."

Arianne retaliated by throwing a pillow at Michael. He caught it and placed it back on the bed. Both men kissed her good evening and left.

As soon as the men had left, Arianne was tortured by something close to remorse. She regretted her absence from the family reunion. She would have enjoyed it so much, and she condemned her son's stubbornness one more time. Her emotions were so confused and rattled that she soon forgave him, then condemned him again.

He had not chosen to meet with Crystal, she reasoned. *It was just that that class of people is very studious and ambi-*

tiou*s. I mean, Dr. Dijon is a physician, and he pressed his daughter into being an accomplished architect at such a young age. Who would have thought so? She can't be over twenty-four years old, only a year younger than her brothers.* Arianne paused in her thoughts. *And Fritz.*

She went back to the window and witnessed Crystal leaving the factory with the engineers. Arianne became tempted by Crystal's life, her whereabouts. *Where does she live?* She continued to peer down at Crystal as the thoughts rushed into her head. *How did she obtain that position, and at such a prestigious firm, too? What else was she doing in the capital?* Arianne grabbed the phone book and flipped to D. She was looking for Crystal's address, and thankfully there was only one Dijon noted in the book. Unfortunately it was not Crystal.

Arianne then remembered that Crystal, being an engaged woman, would never live in a house by herself. Haitian society would never allow for those kinds of liberties. It was considered too liberal, not appropriate for the general public to acknowledge a man, even an engaged one, going to see a woman with no restraint to hold him back. Arianne now recalled that Dr. Dijon had an older sister who he had many times mentioned in conversation.

Arianne convinced herself that it was the same Dijon as the one in the phone book. Dr. Dijon's older sister was a well-known seamstress, and that justified her name being in the phone book. Arianne pondered calling one of her former friends to collect information. Instead, she purposefully dialed the number in front of her and asked for Ms. Crystal Dijon. The maid answered.

"Miss Crystal is not home. She's at work, but you can leave a message for her."

Arianne was amazed by her finding. She hurriedly replied, "No, thank you," and hung up. Arianne was like a child who had just received a Christmas present and was wondering about discovering its secrets, what would be inside the box. She carefully wrote down the address and phone number. A bright idea surged into her mind. She would pay Crystal a visit.

She pleaded with herself, analyzing the risks involved. *Was it a safe action? How would the woman react?* Then she remembered that Crystal was reserved, one of her strong points. That was why Fritz had ended up being her first boyfriend. She was also well brought up and educated. *She will be nice to me,* thought Arianne. *She will be obedient, the way Haitian women are expected to be.*

———

The warm air slapped Michael and Curtis's deeply flushed faces as they retired from the cool hotel room. They walked deliberately to a shaded area at the other end of the balcony, where they stood and searched each other's gazes to unveil the magnitude of their altercation with Arianne.

Michael avowed, "I'm still shocked by her attitude. What she proposed was pure nonsense. Can you imagine Fritz having a mistress? First of all, it is not in his character to maintain an extramarital affair. My sister must be desperate to even consider that option."

Curtis agreed. "You found the right term to describe her fear. Only despair can justify her attempt."

Michael confirmed their position by stating, "Now she is fully aware that we don't agree with her. She will be depressed for a while, but I assume she won't let her mind travel and come up with another scheme."

Curtis remarked, "It's a very tough situation for Arianne. Not only has Fritz rejected our invitation to settle in Cap-Haitian, but I'm sure he's not going to change his mind about who it is he wants to marry. He told us that he loves her. So Arianne is just going to have to learn to respect her son's choice."

"And the way he was looking at her, too," said Michael, "it was as if they were passing secret messages among themselves. And what about when they came back to the room after the tour outside? Fritz was flushed and Crystal had an excited air about her. It was then that it struck me they are lovers; that Crystal was the woman Fritz dated before leaving for Paris."

Michael shrugged his shoulders, adding in a lower voice, "If Fritz had placed the factory in Port-au-Prince to run away from his past, he has not succeeded. It's just the contrary. Thank God I did not know Crystal before, for Arianne would have accused me of deceiving her."

Curtis let out a deep laugh. "She won't be able to blame me, either. I'm sure Father Ignacio had the same experience as we did. He knew about the couple in Cap-Haitian. Did you note the warm manner with which he welcomed Crystal? And he didn't even ask after Arianne. It's a clear message that he approves of their relationship. Trust me, these priests are very involved in their parishioners' lives."

Michael nodded. "I know. Martine is on Fritz's side, too. That's why she offered to help after the blessing. She is proving to both Fritz and Crystal that she welcomes them into the family. What about you, Curtis?"

Curtis pondered the question, and then answered, "Me? What kind of a question is that? I have no problem with my son marrying the woman he loves. What is important is his happiness. In my twenty-seven years of marriage, this is the first time I have ever really opposed my wife. I will stand by my son."

He paused and looked out onto the city, with all its glimmering buildings. "My father is laughing in his grave," he said suddenly. "He had predicted from the day Fritz was born that he would be a leader who would carry out new ideas and be successful. I guess marrying Crystal could be viewed as a new idea. Arianne's pride will suffer a blow, but time will cure her of any resentment."

Michael and Curtis stopped at the hotel reception desk on their way out and informed the secretary about where they could be reached in case of an emergency. They grew excited at the opportunity of being alone together for a whole evening. Curtis rejoiced at not having to convince his wife of the unfairness of her intransigence, Michael for having the occasion to settle an old feud.

Curtis always won at the card table, and his brother-in-law had carried that vexation with him for years. He never understood how a country man like Curtis could be so clever with a hand of cards. Now that he could identify all the cards he purposefully saved at home for the event, he proposed, "Brother, you are not too tired to play?"

Curtis's activities that day were what he termed leisure time, nothing to compare with the tumult of his store. He had planned to check out new plants for his back yard in Cap-Haitian. Also, he did not want to hurt Michael's pride further. So he kindly declined, saying with indifference, "I need some adjustment time; the capital with the heat and all the commotion is choking me."

Michael, who had assumed his trick would work and that he would crush his opponent, protested with a hint of contempt, "Don't chicken out of our game! Are you afraid of losing?" A rapid spark empowered his mind and made him back off. He buffered the impact of his accusation by adding, "Kenscoff is cool, man, you will have fun."

Curtis, his fighting instinct awakened, suggested with an amused smirk on his face, "What makes you so sure you will win? Whatever the challenge, I accept it. Buy us some drink."

Michael grinned, his face beaming with the conviction that he would wash away the past indignation he had suffered. He bought the strongest rum, Cadence 20% alcohol, the one he liked. He promised himself not to touch it. They continued talking about the weather, and improvised techniques to save water during the summer drought.

When they arrived at Kenscoff, Michael took pains to set the game table on the porch. At the bar, he mixed the drinks. He poured a touch of rum and a large amount of cola for himself. In Curtis' glass, he did the contrary—plenty of rum with a touch of soda. Thrilled, he waited with anticipation for the results of his scheme. He placed the glasses in front of their designated player and entered the house to fetch the cards.

As soon as Michael had his back to the table, Curtis switched the glasses. Michael returned to the porch and observed with great satisfaction his guest sipping his drink, and addressed him with an encouraging smile. He flipped the cards, sliced the pile, and handed Curtis his fate. He attacked his drink, wrinkling his nose.

One big gulp, followed by an even bigger one, then he placed his glass down in a precipitated move. His stomach was drenched by fire, his eyes welled; he cleared his throat, "Ouah! That rum is strong." He almost regretted what he had done to Curtis, but reminded himself that he must win. He lashed his first card with ardor.

Michael lost miserably, and he did not dare mention his head was spinning like a carousel. It was a complete disaster. The *griot* served by the maid did not help; his stomach was churning, his mind was blurry but he did not retreat, he could not accept his failure.

He emitted a sigh of relief when he recognized Fritz's brisk steps coming in their direction. Both men felt liberated at the approach of the subject of their common affection. Michael closed the game with some dignity, bragging that he considered his game not in the best shape, but vowed to beat Curtis the next time.

Right at that moment, Fritz passed the front gate, and they focused their attention on him. He waved to them, entered the house, checked to see what his aunt was up to, then joined the men on the porch. Michael hurriedly began the conversation, as he did not want his nephew to inquire about the game, and approached him on a topic of interest to all of them, "Well, the blessing ceremony was a success, everyone had a good time! Don't you think?"

Fritz was fidgety, and he remained silent, but looked at them with eyes reverberating a sea of concern. His father, to ease the culminating pressure, volunteered with great warmth, "Tomorrow, for the inauguration, you will need a lot of ice. The capital is like a hot oven puffing gas around 4 p.m."

His remark met with the same obstinate silence. Fritz stared at them steadily, his eyes flashing rays of anger, his face tightened in a bow of dissatisfaction. The former game opponents grew weary; they glanced at each other searching for support, united by the same dilemma: How were they going to handle Fritz? Each regretted that Arianne was not present. They believed her presence would have simplified their role, shifting the weight onto her, the perpetrator.

Fritz advanced swiftly to the edge of the porch. With his back to them, he was facing the wall and the flowers, lost in his own world. He pivoted, walked slowly toward them, and spat with an incisive tone the dreaded question, "Where is my mother?"

Curtis, reinforcing his role as head of the family, did not delegate his responsibilities to others, nor did he apologize for his wife's absence. He eluded Fritz's question by replying, "Oh, be patient, son, expect her at the inauguration tomorrow."

Fritz paced the porch, his chest inflated, his skin flushed, deep furrows in his forehead. He toyed with a dangling hibiscus flower to calm his temper. A few minutes passed before he asked, "Why did she not attend the ceremony today? Is she not in the capital?"

Michael, sensing that the question was a disguised reproach to Curtis for his weakness toward his spouse, intervened, "She is, but she will be the one to explain why she was not there."

Fritz planted his body in the middle of the porch, his stature towering above them. He exploded, his bitter laugh bouncing against the wall and filling the space. He presented in a voice blended with sarcasm the fact that she had embarrassed his family members earlier, "She probably discovered that Crystal is the factory's architect. Tell me if I'm wrong."

A veil of uncertainty crossed Curtis's face. He knotted his hands, pressed them on the table, then turned a limpid gaze on his son. He spoke with a deep reassurance, "Son, you are right, we are all aware of the situation."

Fritz's regard traveled from his uncle to his father. He advanced, pulled up a chair, sat, and inquired, "Where is she now? Why is she not with you guys? I checked every place on the plantation, no trace of her."

Not giving him the time to finish his probing, his father obliged, "She stayed in town for the night, to get adjusted to the new development. I'm sure she will feel better by tomorrow."

Fritz repeated his father's comment slowly, "Feel better by tomorrow, she stayed in town." He remained thoughtful for an instant, the photos of Crystal in the company of Alex Turnier resurfacing in his mind. He warned them, "It was a big mistake to leave Mom by herself on a night like this one."

His insinuation hit the men like a pebble dropped with force on the surface of a placid lake, creating tumultuous ripples that spun in an uncontrollable rhythm. They were paralyzed by Fritz's lucidity. Curtis regretted that his son had to carry such a burden, and invited him to spend the night with them. Fritz kindly rejected his offer, claiming that he needed time alone to think. Curtis renewed his affection for his son, reminding him of his unconditional approval of his union with Crystal.

Fritz thanked him for his support and, with a hint of humor, advised him to keep an eye on his wife.

———

FRIDAY

———

ARIANNE HAD BEEN THRILLED at the idea of meeting Crystal in private, and rejoiced at the fact that she was going to surprise her, which would give her the upper hand. When Friday morning dawned, long before the day's activities were to begin at Fabric Pro, Arianne hailed a cab in front of the hotel and requested to be dropped at Crystal's address. She had memorized everything she wrote down on that little slip of paper: Crystal's address and phone number.

She ignored the inquisitive glances from the nosy cabdriver and concentrated on her duty. Arianne's eagerness had been steadily rising, and as she arrived in front of the house, her excitement prevented her from noticing a car curbed just behind the taxi. After her persistent knock on the front door, Arianne had the satisfaction of identifying the voice of the person she had spoken to on the phone. The maid stood with her body crushed in the slit of the entrance she had just opened, her eyes pinned on Arianne, who repeated the same request she had on the previous day.

"Miss Crystal Dijon?" Maria repeated in a low voice. Her nervousness because of the early time of the morning showed. "Miss Crystal is not awake yet. She is sleeping."

"Go wake her up! I must speak to her immediately." Maria recalled the short phone call from the day before, simply curtsied, and hurried to Crystal's bedroom.

On the way there, she noticed that her boss, Crystal's aunt, had flung her husband's shoes in disarray in the hall, assuming the early caller was the old shoe polisher on one of his errands. Maria observed that her boss' door was tightly shut.

Crystal was not surprised when Maria told her that her presence was being solicited so early. Crystal expected Gerard to show up at the strangest times. Tired and disheartened by the situation with Fritz, Crystal had spent most of the night trying to figure out what to do and how to handle Gerard, and the accusations she knew would be coming from him: How she did not respect herself, how she was a weak woman, how she had brought shame to him and her family, how he should have known she could not be trusted.

Just thinking about it made her feel like breaking down in tears. But Crystal had braced herself for what she presumed would be her punishment for being in love, because true love was almost banished for a woman her age in Haitian society. She had decided to astound Gerard with the will to cooperate, follow his orders with no protest. Crystal threw on a bathrobe and headed groggily to the living room.

She stopped abruptly at the sight that met her. Standing in front of her, her lips pursed and her eyes cold, was Fritz's mother. There was no way to mistake her. She identified the woman she had caught a glimpse of a few times five years earlier. Mother and son both had the same features: the same light skin, the same full lips, the same dark eyes. The only difference was that Fritz's hair was darker, a trait he inherited from his father.

Crystal was so shocked that it took her a moment to register the situation. She hastily wrapped her arms around herself and mumbled an apology about her presentation. She was about to retreat to her room in mortification to change, but Arianne simply shook her head and assured Crystal that she looked just fine, and that she was not offended.

Crystal offered Arianne a seat, and for a second she thought she saw a shadow move across the porch. She looked at the spot for a moment, but as there was no sign of anything, she thought she must have imagined it.

After Arianne was seated on the sofa, Crystal took a seat across from her and immediately realized her mistake. They were right across from each other, and this created a tension between them, as if they were measuring each other. Arianne introduced herself in a haughty tone, "I am Fritz's mother." She paused to let that fact sink in.

Crystal did not answer, just fixed her with unblinking eyes. She was expecting Arianne to accost her with an accusation about trying to steal her son away from her, and Crystal was determined to keep her temper. She was surprised when Arianne asked in a friendly tone, "How was the Fabric Pro blessing?"

Crystal eyed the older woman with weary eyes and replied, "Nice."

Arianne did not really care much for a reply. She pursued, "You met my husband."

Crystal was not sure how to respond. What was she here for? What did the woman want? "Yes. He is a very nice man." She felt safe sticking with the word nice.

Arianne continued, "Yes, I know. All Arab-Haitians are nice people. Good people."

She's up to something, thought Crystal.

Suddenly changing the subject, Arianne said, "I must congratulate you on your work. From what I've heard, they are very pleased with your performance."

"Thank you," said Crystal. "I appreciate your recognition."

Arianne arched an eyebrow and said abruptly, "I did not come here to congratulate you for any achievements you might think you've made."

So she's showing her true colors now, thought Crystal. "I beg your pardon?" was the only polite reply she could come up with. The others would have been much too offensive. *What work was she referring to? Was she implying my seeing her son and the impact it had created on her family? Did she have a discussion with her relatives about my relationship with Fritz and what happened years ago and she is here to admit her wrongdoing? Was she upset about her mistake and the embarrassing position she faced in her family?* Assumptions swirled in Crystal's mind as she looked at Arianne.

Arianne was sitting erect at the edge of the sofa, and to create an overbearing impression she looked Crystal straight in the eye. She wanted to make sure Crystal understood every word that was about to leave her mouth. "I watched you two yesterday, you and Fritz. I saw you when you were talking in the back yard of the factory."

Crystal raised her eyebrows and shrugged her shoulders to show she was not at all surprised. "So you were spying again, were you?"

"What do you mean 'spying'?" Arianne asked sharply. She had expected Crystal to simply sit and listen, not to give any smart remarks. What right had she to accuse her of something like that, anyway?

188

Crystal spotted the shadow again, moving closer to them, and this time she was certain she had not imagined it. Maybe it was Arianne's chauffeur. She turned her attention back to Arianne, and the distaste she felt just from looking at her made her want to shout at the woman. "Spying," she spat out, "running around in other people's business like you did years ago when you got pictures of me and an officer. That officer was my uncle, Mrs. Lucas, not my lover. But you didn't care about the truth; you only wanted to get rid of me. You-"

"You watch what you are say-"

Crystal raised her voice over Arianne's and continued. She had waited to vent to the woman who had been the root of so much pain, and now that she had started she found she could not stop. "You took those pictures without even bothering to find out who I was talking to, and you showed them to Fritz. You lied to him and told him I was engaged. Engaged! That man in the picture? He wasn't my fiancé; he's my uncle, Engineer Turnier, and we both now work at New Spectrum. Fritz has met him. What are you going to tell him now that he knows what you did?" Crystal shouted the last few words. She was sitting forward in her seat, her hands gripping the fabric on the chair. Her chest was heaving and her eyes were blazing.

Arianne pushed her body back in alarm. This was not what she had expected at all. She was dumbfounded, and more than a little scared. She was torn between yelling back at Crystal and defending herself, and picking up her purse and leaving. But she couldn't leave now. She had come to do something and she was determined to go through with it. "How do you know about the pictures? Are you trying to tell me that the officer in them is an engineer at New Spectrum?"

"Fritz showed them to me, not that it's any of your business," Crystal answered coolly.

Arianne decided to ignore that last part. She took a good look at Crystal and decided that if she were ever going to get her to calm down, she would have to choose her words carefully. "I'm glad he showed them to you, because it's now all in the past. It does not matter anymore," she paused.

"Of course you would say that. I'm the one who has to deal with the consequences of your actions. I'm the one who got hurt, I'm the one who..."

"I know now that Fritz loves you." She waited for the effect of the fact she just admitted, which for her was like giving the young couple her seal of approval. Undisturbed by whatever reaction it might have caused in Crystal, she thought, *Good, I've got her now.* She continued her quest, enunciating the next affirmation, "I know you have a fiancé, Crystal."

Crystal nodded and stared at the gleaming ring on her finger, feeling as though it were an anchor weighing her down rather than a symbol of love. "I'm going to marry him," she said mournfully.

Arianne frowned at her. She had not expected Crystal to stay with her fiancé. "What about my son?" she demanded.

Crystal looked at her, her gaze steady and cool. "I'm following your plan, Mrs. Lucas. You did not want me for your son, and here I am, letting him go. He's all yours now." Crystal felt she had nothing more to say, and that Arianne could not possibly have the audacity to say anything more to her, so she stood up to leave.

Arianne winced and grabbed her arm. "Where do you think you're going? I'm not done talking to you."

Crystal gave her a cold look and wrenched her arm out of her grasp. "I'm going to my room. You know where the door is."

Arianne could see Crystal was serious. As she watched the girl turning her back and walking away, she played her last card. "Do you know what I can do to you? I'm going to tell the whole world that while you were engaged to someone else you flirted with my son. You were betrothed to another and yet you had your eyes on my son. Do you deny it?"

Crystal slowly turned around and fixed Arianne with an icy glare. "You're the kind of person who finds joy in being disappointed, aren't you? You wanted Fritz to be with someone else, and now you know that he can't be with me. Isn't that what you wanted? Now Fritz can marry a pretty, white girl and you can continue your damned 'tradition'. Can't you handle your own success?"

Arianne was startled by Crystal's coldness. She took a deep breath and said, "Sit down, Crystal. Flying into hysterics isn't going to help us. We have to talk like two grown women."

Flying into hysterics, Crystal thought, *I should really hit her for that.* She took a seat. "What do you want to talk about?"

Arianne cleared her throat. "I have been thinking about...you and Fritz. Your relationship," she began.

"Oh, you've been thinking, have you? That's surprising," Crystal snapped.

"Don't get me wrong," Arianne continued, as if Crystal hadn't said a thing, "We've already chosen Linda for Fritz. It is a fixed matter, and I refuse to yield in that respect. But, after seeing you two together, it has become clear to me that Fritz will not be happy unless he is with you."

Crystal frowned. "Let me get this straight. You think Fritz will never be happy unless he is with me, but you won't let him be with me?" she asked incredulously. *What kind of a mother are you?* she added to herself.

"I never said that," Arianne replied sharply. She took a deep breath. "I have a solution. My proposal is that you become Fritz's mistress. Fritz would have an Arab-Haitian wife; you would have the second bed."

Crystal took an audible sharp breath.

Arianne hurried on, "That way you two could be together, and Fritz would be happy. Everyone would be satisfied with the situation."

Crystal was shaking with rage and indignation. *Who did this woman think she was?* She pointed a trembling finger at the door. "Get out." Her voice was barely a whisper, every syllable strained with anger, and it was clear she was close to losing control. Crystal was so angry she did not even notice the shadow now pacing back and forth in the foyer.

Arianne did not move. She sat and stared defiantly at Crystal. She was not about to leave. She had come here on a mission and had no intention of leaving until she had it fulfilled. Crystal stood up quickly, knocking over her chair, and strode out of the room, but then she stopped herself. *No,* she said to herself firmly, *I've taken too much crap from this woman!* She turned around and faced Arianne.

"Who do you think you are? What right do you have to come over to my house at this ungodly hour and tell me that you want me to prostitute myself for the benefit of your narrow-minded, self-centered, conceited mind?" Crystal felt a heavy weight being lifted off her shoulders. "And how could you possibly think I would agree to such a ridiculously stupid idea? Do you have no respect for me? For yourself?"

Arianne was furious. "I'm doing this for you, you selfish girl! And don't you dare judge me! You have no idea what it's like to have your son stolen from you by an insipid child!"

"Don't fool yourself into believing you're doing anything for anyone except yourself. And don't talk to me about stealing. Fritz is a person, not a piece of property. You don't own him. He has a mind, and he uses it to make his own decisions. He chose to defy you, and you know it."

"I...I...you...I'll..." Arianne stammered.

"You'll what? Expose me to society? You know what, I don't care. I'll expose you for the vile creature you really are. Everyone thinks you are charitable and devout, but I see you for what you really are: a sad woman with nothing but lies and deceit to keep her company. I never had a mother, and I always thought that somehow, with her alive, my life would have been better. I'd always envied Fritz and other children because of that, but now I see there was no need for that. If having a mother means having a crow over my shoulder, telling me she loves me when she really has her own selfish agenda, when really all she cares about is what other people think, not what I think or what I have to say, then I don't want a mother. I don't want to deal with your stupidity and narrow vision. I don't want anything from you." Crystal was breathing hard. "I believe I told you to get out."

Arianne rose, trembling. Everything Crystal had just said came rushing through her ears and filled her mind, stealing her of her assurance that she was right. She felt she had to defend herself, to say something that would erase all she had just heard, say something that would justify her actions. But she couldn't even lift her head to look Crystal in the eye. "I..." she began.

"I don't want to hear it. Just leave." She turned her back on Arianne, waiting for her to do as she had said.

Crystal heard the latch kiss the expectant lips buried in the door frame with a thud. Arianne's heels hammered the pavement; their monotony echoed in the living room and startled Crystal. She slumped in a chair and covered her face with her cupped hands until the pounding faded. When she assumed Arianne's venom could not touch her anymore, she set her face free.

She came to her feet, and as an automaton directed herself to the door. As she lifted the sheer curtain, her mouth dropped open, her eyes popped out, her heart fluttered. She laid her forehead on the door for support. But the immediate result was that the glass magnified the quavering hunchback's shadow ambulating down the sidewalk. Crystal stood motionless, recording the slow progress of the haunted form to the corner.

Her heart skipped a beat when, before turning the curb, her visitor pivoted hesitantly and glanced in her direction. Crystal had the time to notice that Arianne was still deeply colored, that her face was withdrawn, her handbag jammed negligently in the hole of an armpit, her arms hanging limply to her side. Crystal was struck; gone was the arrogance displayed by her interlocutor a few minutes before. All she could identify was remorse mixed with a hint of sorrow. She restrained herself from opening the door and running to hug Arianne, to reassure her, tell her that they would be fine. Regret gnawed her for the way she had treated Fritz's mother.

She swirled away from the door and threw herself back into the chair. For a reason she could not pinpoint she felt gloomy; the sight of Arianne's devastation did not provide her with the relief she expected. She was irritated, doomed by a sense of uncertainty. As she sat in the chair, her gaze drifted to the balcony. Furrowing her brow, she walked to the porch. No one was there. Yet, who had been there during her confrontation with Arianne? Maybe she had been right before, maybe it had been Arianne's chauffeur. But why had the man stood outside instead of next to his employer, as was the custom?

Her mind began to race. Why hadn't Gerard visited her this morning or the day before? *Oh my God!* What if it had been Gerard on the balcony? What if he'd heard the whole conversation? And, what if he'd heard the part about her flirting with Fritz? Crystal got a sick feeling in her stomach. She shook her head. Holding her stomach, she pushed herself off the railing and returned to the living room, pacing, until finally she decided to go to her room.

Thoughts whirled around in her head. Gerard, and the scandal she was threatened with, resounded in her mind, but she rejected that possibility. But those were not the only things that bothered her. Something else, something more ominous, was causing her to feel uneasy. She persuaded herself that because her father was the Lucas family's physician in Cap-Haitian, and that Fritz's mother and father would not trust anyone else with their ailments and their lives, Arianne would never materialize her threats.

Fritz was her prime concern. Crystal fidgeted with the dark ideas that crowded her mind like heavy, gray clouds rolling in the sky with turbulent winds announcing a hurricane. What if Fritz was in danger? What if his mother had menaced him and driven him to the brink of desperation? Arianne had not been at the factory blessing but she must have been in the capital since her husband had been at the blessing, proudly assisting his son.

Had Arianne committed a fatal mistake that could not be repaired? Could it be that she confronted her son with the sore subject of his arranged marriage? Had Arianne caused so much grief to Fritz that he had done something irreparable to himself? Would Fritz attempt to destroy his life to prove he was serious? No, Crystal rejected that odious alternative firmly. The chaos exuded from his bedroom Tuesday when she had visited the plantation popped into Crystal's mind and made her settle for a more comfortable outcome: Fritz would probably leave the country.

The shadow moving restlessly on the porch flashed in her recollection. What? What if? She was affected, like a child fumbling with its ball of thread, watching his kite wandering in the limpid Easter cosmos, all chance of securing the treasure lost. She kneeled down and prayed with fervor. Her mother appeared to her, smiling, holding her, and singing to her. The bedroom was illuminated by her presence. Crystal felt refreshed, reenergized, appeased.

She hurried to shower and prepare herself for the day. She pushed to the back of her mind the factory opening ceremony she must attend, where she would meet Fritz and probably his mother. She concentrated on the orders she must give for the finishing touches of the Fabric Pro workshop and Fritz's office and one-bedroom apartment.

She shied her austere office outfit for a skirt and short-sleeve top. She smiled as she tied her hair into a chignon, remembering Fritz's comment at the bungalow about its texture. She picked up her bag and a book, and crossed the hall to the dining room.

She recalled her father's presence and how he had declined a ride to the twin's house after having supper with her and her aunt the night before, and wished he had not heard the morning turmoil. He would never intervene, but would bear the weight of secrecy, looking forward to assisting his progeny. Unlike any other morning, she was the first one in the dining room. She ignored Maria's frequent glimpses, instead disarming her curiosity by engaging in an unexpected conversation, "Maria, may I please have a cup of strong coffee?"

The maid forgot her reason to be in the house without her boss' persistent calling, and offered, "Sure, Miss, I got some ready for your father." Maria poured the black liquid into Crystal's cup, added two spoons of sugar, and slid the container sitting on the saucer to crystal. Maria tried to feed herself on gossip, and innocently advanced that the sun was bright, that it was a beautiful day for a nice party among friends, that she was available for last-minute errands in case there was a need. Crystal sat at the table, feigning reading an article in the book she had opened, while she sipped her coffee.

———

Gerard sat in his car in front of the hospital, fuming. He was so angry he was clutching the wheel with a ferocity that was making his hands hurt. It was he who had been on Crystal's porch that morning. He had come to pay her a visit, as he had spent Thursday crafting plots to get back at her, to punish her for her stubbornness, for choosing to attend the New Spectrum anniversary party without him.

He had bought the airplane ticket for her to travel with him to Paris without consulting her, and had contacted a civil officer for an expedited marriage just to prove to her he was in charge, and planned on being the head of his family and the one ruling the show. He was in that state of mind when stepping out of his car, and had not seen the taxi that dropped off Arianne. He was annoyed when, spotting Maria on the sidewalk, she had told him Crystal already had a visitor. He had been about to leave when a crippling sense of insecurity made him stay, just in case the visitor had been a man. Just in case it had been Fritz.

Gerard climbed the steps to the porch with his temples drumming, his heart racing, his respiration panting. He trembled with rage and indignation. He was sweating in the cool morning. But it had been someone entirely different. Fritz's mother. Just thinking about that woman made him want to tear the wheel off the car and hurl it at something, or rather, someone. The audacity of that woman, to come to his fiancée's house and harass her in such a manner.

But that was just the beginning of what was really bothering Gerard. The whole time he had known Crystal, he had felt as though she had a secret, something she would not tell him. Now he knew what it was. Her history amazed him. She had been through so much. She had been betrayed by the family of a person she had loved. That fact hit Gerard like a stone, and that stone settled itself firmly in his stomach.

She had loved Fritz. Could she love anyone else the way she had loved him? Did she love him that way? Did he love her? No. The answer surprised Gerard. He admired Crystal; he thought the world of her. But love? The reason he had wanted her so badly, wanted her enough to marry her was because she would fit in perfectly with his life. Her brilliance would make him shine even brighter.

Gerard couldn't help but wonder if, had Arianne left things alone, Crystal would still be with him at that moment. She was with him because she had been exploited. A nasty taste came into his mouth. *Exploited.* That word reverberated in his mind. *Exploited.* He wanted to marry Crystal simply because it was a convenience. Wasn't that a form of exploitation? His thoughts drifted to the tickets to Paris in his pocket. He had gotten them without even consulting Crystal, assuming she would just go along with him. Wasn't that exploitation? Wasn't eavesdropping on her, his future wife, exploitation?

Now Gerard was seriously disturbed. The bad taste in his mouth got worse. He couldn't stand having something in common with that woman, Fritz's mother. At that moment a loud beeping noise burst from his pocket, catching him by surprise. He literally jumped out of his seat, bumping his head on the ceiling of the car. Rubbing his head, he reached into his pocket and drew out his beeper. It was blinking, which meant there was an emergency and he was needed right away.

Gerard rushed toward the entrance of the hospital, only to be cut off by a group of nurses pushing a wheeled stretcher holding a limp body, and speaking in hurried, agitated voices. From their voices and the general tumult around the body, Gerard determined that it was either a very important person, a grave case, or both. He watched, transfixed, as a man ran in after the wheeled stretcher, talking and waving his arms hysterically.

From the little Gerard could discern from what he was saying, he was the driver of the *tap-tap* that had collided with the patient's car. The nurses ignored the man and one of them pulled something out of the patient's breast pocket: his wallet. "Fritz Jean Lucas," she pronounced.

———

Arianne was lost. She had climbed into a taxi, and immediately a feeling of claustrophobia had overwhelmed her. She had gotten out near the hotel; feeling nauseated, she waved the taxi's driver away. She now wandered the streets of Port-au-Prince, in the hotel vicinity, deep in her own thoughts. Could Crystal be right? Could she really be that selfish a mother? Impossible! She had done it all for Fritz, for his own well-being.

But a tiny voice crept into her head and whispered, *Did you really?* She shook her head in confusion. If she hadn't done it for Fritz, who had she done it for? Her mind went back to Crystal's words. "Oh, no," she gasped. Maybe she *had* done it for herself. She thought of how fearful she was of the stinging words of others, how she feared her family would be ostracized from the Arab-Haitian society she loved so much.

It was then that she realized the difference between herself and Fritz. Fritz did not dictate his life according to what others believed; he did it according to his own beliefs and standards. She, on the other hand, was constantly comparing herself to others, making sure she never stepped too far out of line. Arianne came to an abrupt stop and looked up. She was standing in front of the Fabric Pro façade. She hadn't even realized that was where she was headed. She walked in and immediately noticed some of the leftovers of the previous day's blessing: paper plates, napkins, plastic forks and knives, and beer bottles scattered everywhere. It was a sure sign that she had not been there.

She felt hollow inside. If she had attended the party, the place would now be clean. She couldn't stand the sight of a mess, and had always been the one to clean up, right after a party, no matter how late it was. She looked around and noticed a door that was slightly ajar. It was *Fritz's office.* She knew what she had to do. She walked in and looked around her.

On the wall opposite the desk was a painting. She recognized it as the one Crystal had made for her son. A surrendering smile appeared on Arianne's lips. She shrugged her shoulders. That painting was the one he had carefully wrapped when leaving Cap-Haitian. It had adorned his Paris apartment, only to disappear in New York and resurface here, in his office.

She also noticed a beach bag that was obviously Crystal's. A deep feeling of sorrow washed over her. *Fritz really does love her,* she admitted one more time. She had to do something to make up for all she had already done, something that would begin to heal the wounds she had inflicted. She walked over to the desk, took out a pen and a piece of paper, and settled down to her new task.

Dear Fritz, there are so many things I want to tell you, but I shall start at the first. I want to apologize for missing the factory blessing ceremony. It was wrong of me not to attend. Normally I would try to justify my actions, but now I know that I was wrong, and all I ask for is your forgiveness. I realize now that you love Crystal, and I know that she is a worthy girl, sensible and lovely. I wish I had been here to see the two of you together. I sincerely hope that whatever I as a mother could not give you, she will be able to provide in abundance. I see now that Michael and your father were right all along. I missed the factory blessing, but I can assure you that I will not miss the opening party. Save a seat for Crystal next to me. I have a surprise for her, but I won't tell you what it is, or it will spoil the treat. I must go now. If you see your father before I do, tell him I went downtown to buy ingredients so I can fix as many Arab-Haitian dishes as possible for the gathering.

I love you more than you could ever know,
Arianne.

———

Gerard's blood ran cold, even as his heartbeat sped up. For a moment all he could see was black. Could it be? Could it really be Fritz? Crystal's Fritz? The connection between that man and his fiancée made Gerard's body spring into sudden action. He was no longer thinking with his mind, he just did what he knew must be done. "Only nurses in the room, please!" he ordered. His voice carried a tone of authority, and it was clear to everyone present that if they did not obey, there would be hell to pay.

Gerard tore off his jacket and rolled up his sleeves. "Draw the curtains," he barked. His blood was pounding in his head, and a slow panic was starting to rise in his throat, but he kept his cool. He looked down at Fritz, examining him. Fritz's chest was rising and falling with steady breathing, but Gerard knew he was in grave danger. His left arm was rotated outward, bent at a gruesome angle, and when Gerard called his name, he did not respond.

"Start the vital signs to be repeated every five minutes," Gerard commanded. "Place an IV site, start fluids at 50ml per minute, then get an x-ray of the thorax, abdomen, and left limb. Quickly, quickly!" Turning to Annette, the head nurse, he instructed, "Prepare the operating room."

Turning his attention back to the patient he thought, *He might be able to hear me.* "I am Dr. Armand," he said aloud, "I am the surgeon who is going to take care of you. I don't want you to worry, but I have a few questions to ask you." Gerard began busying himself with stabilizing the broken limb. Fritz made no sign of answering, but Gerard continued, "What is your name, sir? Do you remember your name? Can you tell me what it is?" Still no answer.

Gerard swore silently. He thanked God he was in a familiar environment, for even the nurses were familiar to him, and began examining Fritz more closely. In a strange place he would not have been able to control his reaction. But there, in that emergency room where he had reigned for almost eight years, he proceeded mechanically. He verified Fritz's pupils, noted that they were equal and reactive to light. He listened to his lungs, diminished but bilateral equal breath sounds, his heart was pounding fast but strong.

Gerard had always approved of his profession as being important and dotted with some degree of gravity. In the emergency room, having to take care of Fritz Jean Lucas, he added cynicism to the list, because even now protesting was not an option. He inhaled, silently cursing at the accident that placed him in such an awkward position. He looked at the white bare wall facing him, with blank, empty eyes; a slight tremor ran down his jaw muscles.

He suddenly turned his look inward as if responding to an interior voice that had just hollered his name. For a swift moment, he experienced the same feeling he had at the age of six when after a victorious ascent, he was perched on top of a tall coconut tree. He could not figure out how to climb back down, he was lost in the situation, but neither would he voice his fear, nor his insecurity.

He had then closed his eyes, tightened his grip around the trunk, and slid down. And now, as in the past, even though he felt betrayed by his success and power, he took the immutable resolve to confront the challenge. He distanced himself from the fact that the man lying in front of him could be a menace to his relationship with his fiancée and ruin his plan, and just considered him as a patient. Dr. Armand bent his torso slightly, pressed his hands against the stretcher's side rail, his fingers clenching the metal with great force. No one in the room had noticed the internal turmoil he had just conquered.

He resumed his task as a physician and began his physical examination of the patient.

When Gerard palpated Fritz's abdomen he noticed tenderness on the upper left quadrant, and he believed he heard a light groan. He thought the patient was regaining consciousness. Gerard checked the right lower limb and demanded, "Wiggle your toe." Fritz did. He asked him to do the same with his left toe. The patient did. Gerard now returned to the head of the bed to face his patient.

All that Gerard acknowledged was that in front of him was a young male in distress, his eyes closed, his face contorted with pain. The patient was taking shallow breaths and held his exhalation longer, too much longer. He was limiting his inhalation in an effort for his diaphragm not to push on his belly, which was hurting.

Gerard again questioned him, "What is your name?"

In a whisper Fritz answered, "Fritz Jean Lucas."

"Do you remember what happened?"

Fritz winced then feebly avowed, "I was hit by a car. I don't remember anything else."

Unconsciously, Gerard wanted to keep on asking him questions to prolong the agony of the man—the man on the stretcher that he sensed would cause him the biggest disruption of his life and with that, too, so much anguish. Gerard anticipated that it was his time, his turn to get some explanations from the intruder. He fixed Fritz with a cold, venomous glare.

Fritz opened his eyes and watched the doctor with a weak, trusting look that pierced Gerard's conscience like a burning sword. The effect on Gerard was enormous. For the first time he felt uneasy, and the immediate result was that he wished the man had died, in which case he would only have had to pronounce him dead. Crystal would be depressed for some time and he would use the grieving process as an opportunity to console her, to get close to his fiancée. Gerard became unsettled, frantic. He was seized by a sudden uncanny, devilish persuasion: to just let the man die, let the accident take him.

To justify the mad decision that crossed his mind, he had to blame Fritz, to accuse him of some wrongdoing, to condemn him. "Damn it, these bourgeois boys! This one was probably drag racing in the early hours believing that the road belonged to him. Poor bastard, he's going to pay for his error." It was justification enough for Gerard to go along with the devilish plan of causing Fritz's death.

In an icy, resolute tone Gerard ordered, "Wheel the patient to the x-ray room, I will be waiting in the operating block." He reasoned that with Fritz bleeding internally, the more time he bought, the graver the danger. All he needed to do was prolong the delay. It would be over soon. As Gerard was leisurely scrubbing, a nurse burst through the door with a wild, alarmed look on her face. "Doctor, there was a marked change in the patient's vital signs while he was in the x-ray room!" Gerard flinched involuntarily, a cold chill ran down his back and his heart began beating fast.

"What are they now?" he inquired calmly.

"HR+135, BP=90/60, and going down. He also looks diaphoretic, doctor."

Gerard began scrubbing vigorously, and ordered, "Quick, get him into the operating room! Is the anesthesiologist ready?"

"Yes," answered the nurse.

Gerard dashed into the room. Fritz was being transferred from the stretcher to the operating table, and the anesthesiologist was waiting at the head of the operating table, his machine bellow going up and down, pumping the hanging mask with blowing air. The patient was pale and limp. The anesthesiologist placed the mask on Fritz's face.

"Fluid wide open," Gerard said. "Did you get a cross and match?"

"Yes, doctor," replied the nurse, "as required by the protocol."

"Get some packed red cells ready in case we have to transfuse the patient." Gerard now had his head cap on and his mask was being tied by one of the nurses. He was donning his sterile gloves when his partner and an assistant walked into the room, the doctor fully dressed and looking like an astronaut.

Gerard gave him a brief report of the case. He mentioned that the patient was actively bleeding and that they would have to explore the abdomen first. Together they began the delicate surgery. Gerard was right. Fritz's spleen was ruptured, and he was bleeding profusely. Gerard and Dr. Colbert performed a splenectomy, then they stabilized the left arm fracture and placed the limb in an arm sling. After three hours, Fritz was ready to go to the recovery room where the nurses, under the supervision of the physician on call, would take care of him for a short period.

To the great surprise of his co-workers, Gerard announced, "You can leave. Thank you for your help. I will stay with the patient." When the crew reached the door Gerard reminded them, "Try to locate the patient's relatives. Send someone to the Arab store on LaLue; maybe the owners know how to reach his parents."

Gerard closed the door behind him and drew the curtains tight. In the small square of the recovery room there were only Fritz and himself. Poles with multiple bags on them swung slightly from side to side as they delivered various fluids and medicine into Fritz's body. It had been a difficult operation. Fritz had been bleeding, and to access the organ and the different blood vessels to be clamped had been hard work.

Gerard was relieved the surgery had gone so well. For some reason he could not explain, from the moment he had pierced Fritz's skin with the scalpel, his sentiment toward him had changed. Why? Was it because he had been actually operating on him, and he wanted to succeed in the operation, regardless of who he was operating on? It was one of the possibilities. But, now that the surgery was over he could not leave. Gerard wanted to be sure that Fritz was safe. Why? He could not answer that question either. Was his pride playing a trick on him?

While thinking and trying to enumerate the reasons to justify his attitude, the first ten minutes passed and the manual timer at Fritz's head reminded Gerard it was time to check the patient's vital signs. He checked Fritz's pulse, which was 95; he inflated the blood pressure cuff and listened for the beep. He exhaled, deeply relieved when he noticed the first beep at 115 and the last at 70. Gerard still looked at Fritz's body with concern, and addressed a silent prayer, "God, help Fritz to fight, give him force and endurance to surmount all the danger facing him."

Fritz was still zoned out. Gerard set up the timer for five minutes, and when it blared again, he repeated the same routine. That time the pulse was 115 and the blood pressure 108/65. Gerard shook his head in disbelief. *What was going on? Could a mistake have been made during the operation? Could it have been my mistake?*

He re-pumped the cuff pressure with anxiety. The needle on the quadrant escalated at 105, not 108. Gerard panicked. Trembling, he went to the IV poles and adjusted the different fluids and medicine being delivered to Fritz. Then he pulled the sheet off of him and examined the wound. It appeared to be normal, a little ooze, but no excessive bleeding. Gerard's head was now throbbing. He was sweating. "Is it internal bleeding again? Or something else?" he asked out loud.

He palpated Fritz's abdomen, relying on his experience. An expert surgeon's hand could discern when the patient was hemorrhaging. He repeated the gesture carefully, tenderly, pressing a little bit here and there. The result appeased his tense body. But suddenly, his worry increased. *This might be a pulmonary emboli. The fracture!* Gerard analyzed Fritz's nail beds. They were pink. *No,* he reassured himself, *What, then?*

He stared at Fritz from head to toe, covered him with the sheet, then went to his ear and whispered confidently, "Fritz, don't fail me. Fight, you have to live. Live so I can tell Crystal you are out of danger. Live so I can tell Crystal you made it and bring her to visit you. Remember that Crystal loves you. She is waiting for you. Wake up!"

Gerard set the timer for five minutes and sat by Fritz's side again. He held Fritz's hand and from time to time squeezed it. It was a gesture to pass to Fritz some of his vitality and to comfort the patient as much as himself. Gerard was possessed, he did not recognize himself. When the timer blared again he noticed the numbers had improved. Gerard took his seat again and for an hour he stayed at the bedside until the effect of the anesthesia wore off and Fritz was stable.

Fritz awoke disoriented. Gerard reassured him, informing him that he was just out of the operating room, that the procedures went well, and that the hospital had sent for his family. Gerard told Fritz he was leaving, that the day shift would take care of him. Fritz was in pain and voiced his discomfort. Gerard administered some analgesic intramuscularly because of the trial with Fritz's blood pressure earlier.

While injecting the medication Gerard scolded himself, *I was crazy to think I could have killed him. I would have never been able to live with the guilt.* When he was done, he pressed the bell for assistance. The nurse showed up. After writing orders for his patient, Gerard left the room.

Gerard was stopped in the hall by the Dijon twins. They were both restless, their faces displaying anxious, devastated looks. Gerard proudly edified them on the present situation after relating the specifics of the surgery performed. He entrusted Fritz's care to them and the head nurse. Gerard left the hospital with a brisk, light walk, and drove hastily to Crystal's house.

———

When the other members of the household awoke there was a sense of fretfulness in the air. Ifelie, Crystal's aunt, blamed the unsettling atmosphere on her brother. *Everyone is trying to please him,* she'd convinced herself. That conclusion explained to her why Crystal was first at the table, and Maria was officiating without the pleading.

She noticed that her niece's eyes were riveted on a spot in the garden, and that she was distracted. She admired her maid's zeal for an instant, thinking, *These maids, look at this one, she is acting concerned, just to buy my brother's appreciation and reap a hefty tip, but what can we do without their help?* She turned her attention back to Crystal, "God, I slept tight, so tight I did not hear you getting ready. How are you doing?

"I guess I am doing fine," Crystal mumbled.

Her attitude stimulated her aunt's interest, who recalled that it was the day of the factory inauguration. She moved closer to Crystal, curved one arm around her shoulder, and whispered, "You gave your all to that project. It's time to relax. Gerard should plan a vacation for the two of you."

Crystal remained silent. Her fiancé for the moment was the least of her concern. Her uncle and father arrived, waved to the women and continued their conversation, "The shoeshine man is out of control; he is a *tonton macoute* and comes early when he has to attend a parade, but today is no holiday. Why did he have to show up that early? Tell me, you don't have to deal with those nuisances in the countryside. Do you?" inquired her uncle.

Dr. Dijon did not have to condemn or defend the serving class. A commotion disrupted their exchange. Abandoning her niece's shoulder, Ifelie jumped into the conversation. "Where are you heading? You look so preppy, are you not done taking care of your business?"

Dr. Dijon raised his eyebrows at the sight of his daughter and the steaming cup. Worry tightened his gut, but he chose to give his sister's probing satisfaction. "After thirty years of wearing a tie on a daily basis, I feel naked when it doesn't complete my outfit." The tone of misery that accompanied his response excited the audience, and they laughed. The weariness evaporated.

The men filled their seats at the table, Dr. Dijon taking a seat next to his daughter. He eyed her. She looked tired, and even a little scared.

"Crystal?" he whispered. She looked up at her father. "Are you all right?"

Crystal smiled feebly, but she could not stop the tears that suddenly sprung to her eyes.

"What's wrong?" her dad asked. She took a deep breath. She could tell him, she reasoned. He would understand how she felt. He would reassure her, tell her not to worry. So in a low voice, making sure no one else could hear her, she began to tell him of all that had happened that morning: Arianne coming to see her, her notion that Gerard might have overheard it all, and how bad she felt for speaking so badly to Fritz's mother.

Dr. Dijon was about to answer all she had confided, but was caught off guard by Ifelie who, inspecting the living room because she had assumed some clients would pay her brother an unplanned visit, was angry to find it in disarray.

Her irate voice covered the morning sounds. "Maria, come here! What's wrong with you? Don't you know I forbid the living room chairs to be moved during the week, only on Saturday for the big cleaning."

Crystal was so surprised by her aunt's heated shout that she jumped. Her cup hit the saucer with a resounding *crack* and split down the middle, hot coffee spilling onto the table. Ifelie jumped back and raised her arms toward the ceiling, her eyes bewildered, and cried, "Division, separation!" She pointed a fearful finger toward the cup. It was cut in two.

Haitian superstition always stressed that whenever something broke into equal parts it was a precursor to a severance, or parting in someone's life. Everyone present was imbued of the knowledge; they were all afraid. The men chose to be brave and hide their concern. The women on the contrary manifested their worry with vivacity.

Maria quickly placed the basket of bread on the table and slipped outside to get the chocolate. She was pale, her hands were shaking. She feared her employer's predilection and prayed to St. Anthony to kill the bad angels.

Ifelie's comment hit Crystal like a bullet. Her heart fluttered, she swallowed painfully, playing with the broken cup to regain her composure. It was she who had caused the cup to break by putting it down so forcefully. It was also proclaimed that the person responsible for destruction of the piece would be the one to suffer the irreparable breakup. She had to contain her fear, and that of her family members, so she hastily proffered a reason to appease the disquieted witnesses, "There was probably a crack. I will buy a new one today."

They forgot about the displaced chairs, started breakfast with a timid appetite, the unmatched cup and saucer on the table reminding them of Ifelie's prevision.

The front gate creaked, followed by a firm stride and a fast knock on the front door. Their eyes were glued on Maria dashing out of the kitchen to attend to the visitor. In a flash she came back, and out of breath trumpeted, "Dr. Armand wants to see Ms. Crystal."

Dr. Dijon jumped up, his face distorted by anxiety. He advised his daughter, "Stay here, I'll speak to Gerard."

———

Dr. Dijon had sprung up, anxiety etched on every feature of his face. After what Crystal had just told him, he was sure it was Gerard who had been on the balcony that morning. And he was even more certain he had come to demand some kind of explanation. Deep inside, Dr. Dijon was grateful that Gerard had finally decided to come to see Crystal at her house and not in a public place, where a scene could be made. He was also glad he was there; he believed his presence could calm Gerard down a bit and keep him from doing anything rash. He could convince him of Crystal's interest in him, or at least deter the man's wild jealousy. When he entered the living room, he found Gerard standing with his back to him, facing the window. At the sound of Dr. Dijon's footsteps, Gerard turned around. A warm smile spread across his face when he saw the older doctor walk in. He was surprised as he extended his hand and asked, "How long have you been in the capital? Don't tell me that the public transportation made you miss the conference."

Dr. Dijon was taken aback by this display of friendliness. Maybe it hadn't been Gerard on the balcony after all? He gladly exchanged the handshake and offered Gerard a seat. "I have been sleeping in the capital's warmth for quite a few nights."

Gerard frowned and asked, "You were here on Wednesday and you didn't attend the conference? Tell me it's not true."

Anxious to bring his daughter's plea to light, Dr. Dijon responded, "I had other things on my mind. I came to visit Crystal."

Deliberately brushing that subject away, Gerard answered with some mystery, "Your vote for me would have meant a lot."

Dr. Dijon was now intrigued; he repeated, "Vote? What vote? Vote for what? Did you finally get the post as director of the hospital?"

Gerard did not answer, but simply fixed the older doctor with a victorious grin.

Dr. Dijon quickly evaluated the situation, and concluded that Gerard in a higher position would be more demanding. He played the social card. "Congratulations. The hospital really needs someone like you: motivated, smart, and reliable."

Gerard stood and began pacing the floor, talking all the while and exposing his new position with fame and glory. "I was the one chosen to participate in the training in Paris for laparoscopic surgery," he announced at last.

"Congratulations," Dr. Dijon wished him in an unconvincing tone. He scratched his head. "I guess it all came as a surprise. What are you going to do now, with your practice? When do you leave Haiti, and for how long?"

"I was planning on leaving next weekend after my marriage, for sure. But I have a patient at the hospital and I want to see him out of the woods, which will probably take another day. Where is Crystal?"

Dr. Dijon became apprehensive. He ignored what Gerard had said about the patient and said softly, "She's in her room, probably putting on the last touches before attending the Fabric Pro inauguration."

Dr. Armand exclaimed with conviction, "There won't be one!"

Dr. Dijon mistook what he said as meaning that he would not allow Crystal to go. "Gerard, for God's sake, be reasonable. Crystal worked so hard on this project. It was her first big one, and she did well. I will go with her, and if you want, you can come, too. But don't gratify yourself on exercising your fiancé's right to shun her from a place where she has invested so much."

Gerard squinted and fixed Dr. Dijon with a stare. "I have as much at stake as Crystal in this affair," he murmured.

Dr. Dijon was still not sure what Gerard was talking about. He warned him, "Gerard, Crystal is my only daughter. I won't let you harass her."

Gerard replied, "You really believe that I could harm her, don't you?" He continued looking at the other doctor for a moment and then said, "I came to pick her up."

Dr. Dijon replied vehemently, "Crystal is not going to her office today. She is going directly to Fabric Pro. Engineer Turnier is on his way to drive us."

Gerard touched Dr. Dijon's shoulder lightly, amicably, and for the first time addressed him with his first name. "Fernand, Fritz is in the recovery room being taken care of by the twins."

The shock of this news was so startling that Dr. Dijon was dumbfounded for a moment. "What do you mean, Fritz is at the hospital?!" he yelled. "What happened to him?!"

Crystal heard her father's scream and before Gerard could answer, she burst into the living room and demanded of Gerard in an anguished voice, "What happened to Fritz? Is he all right?"

Gerard moved close to her, hugged her, then kissed her on the cheek.

Crystal pushed him away and almost screamed, "Tell me what happened! Tell me that Fritz is okay!"

Gerard sat and pointed at a chair. Crystal ignored it and continued to stare from her father to Gerard.

Gerard took a deep breath and said, "Crystal, calm down. I came here with good news."

Crystal's aunt poked her head into the room, then her body followed. Slowly the room filled with people, all looking at Gerard expectantly. It was then that he realized the magnitude of what he was about to say. He couldn't help but wonder bitterly if they would care as much if it were he who was in the hospital, and not Fritz.

"Fritz is fine. He has a fracture and it hurts him a little, and we removed his spleen. But he is fine."

Everyone in the room let out a collective sigh. Crystal was still shaken.

"Thank you," she said quietly. "Father, can you take me to the hospital please?"

Gerard stood up quickly and said, "I can take you."

The reaction was immediate and forceful. Those simple words pronounced by Gerard caused a profound uneasiness among Crystal's family members and a state of shock in Crystal. The suspense grew to an unprecedented level.

Everyone in the room looked at Gerard with surprise and suspicion. He quickly explained himself, "I promised to... to...," he stammered, unable to bring himself to say Fritz's name, "to him that I would bring you over there."

Crystal was confused; she had always assumed her fiancé was proud, vindictive, but she could not retrace any of these traits from his present behavior. She forgave him for using so much emphasis while presenting the facts. What was important to her was that Fritz was taken care of, and that he was safe. She could not control herself anymore as she braced her courage to accompany the man in front of her to the bedside of her real love.

A slow panic gnawed at her insides, making her tremble, as she realized that danger awaited her. How would Fritz's family members interpret her presence so soon? Did they know the surgeon was her fiancé? His mother and her threat to trash Crystal's name, and after all, Fritz. Why was Gerard insisting on having her be so soon at his rival's side? Was it a way for him to take revenge?

She swallowed her pride and with searching eyes, her voice but a whisper, beseeched him, "Why? Why do you want to go with me that quickly to the hospital? Why the rush? Do you anticipate that he won't make it? That his life, Fritz's life, is on the brink of shattering?"

Gerard was startled by the suddenness of her request, the anguish of her probing. His body stiffened, his face darkened, he shrugged his shoulders, and did not answer. For a swift moment, he was haunted by the ghost, that devilish temptation to hasten the end of Fritz Jean Lucas. He pushed away with firm conviction that murdering impulse. In an uncontrollable shift, he had reversed his decision, adopted the resolution to save his rival's life with all his might, his passion, his will.

He was there again while his body decompressed, ready to explain to his fiancée his prognosis, sharing with her the joy that he as a skilled surgeon experienced with the successful outcome of a difficult case, even when the surgery was performed on the contender he despised.

After being on Crystal's porch that morning, he was imbued with a new problem, a new handicap—the fact that he was aware his fiancée shared true love with that young man. True love. It was not a money problem, nor a skin or race issue in his battle, just true love. The kind of love that was not in his arsenal.

He volunteered, shifting his gaze from Crystal to her father, to the audience, "He was lucky to be brought to the hospital right away. He reached it in time. His organs are not irreversibly damaged by the bleeding." He stopped sharply, as if to persuade himself that his patient would make it, that he was out of the woods, that he would survive. Then he added in a lower pitch, "He is young and strong, he will make it."

The crowd in the living room had noticed Dr. Armand's hesitation, but mostly they acknowledged how he had become somber at Crystal's inquiry. Crystal's family looked at each other with faces betraying their increasing doubt, while the option of foul play visited their minds. Crystal too had registered her fiancé's reaction, and became suspicious.

She abandoned her father's side, walked with determination and planted her nervous figure in front of Gerard. She fixed him intently with glacial eyes. Her stringent voice sliced the thick air, "Why did you operate on Fritz, Gerard? What kind of intervention did you do on him? How come you were at the hospital that early, anyway?"

Her body grew tense like a compressed spring before its sudden unleash. A new pressure filled the room. She kept her sight glued on Gerard while the other witnesses drew theirs on the floor, the window, the table, away from the towering dominating frame, afraid they were to discover a monster.

Gerard, sensing that he had sold himself, returned the ball to her camp; his question unsettled all of them. "Does it matter, Crystal?"

Her eyes widened, multiple interpretations of his question clogging her mind. *Does Gerard mean he had intended to kill Fritz? Or does he mean he had played his tune and Fritz's destiny was not in his hands anymore, that if his client died, it was not his fault.* She turned to her father to observe his reaction, to judge the effect of her fiancé's avowal on him. Dr. Dijon was impassive, a faint smile perched on his lips.

She directed her gaze back to the man who was playing tricks on her, making her worried to the point that her heart was beating at the tip of her mouth. She tilted her head, smiled. Gerard's hands spread in a gesture that a stranger would mistake as an intention to strangle her. But she recognized the posture he had adopted during his internship to intercept the babies abandoning their mother's womb, inhaling the fresh air with their first independent breath.

He uttered, "See my hands, these hands; they are here to protect, to save lives. How could I face you if I had killed him? How could I face myself after such degradation? No! No! I'm not a murderer, an assassin. I could never kill, not even Fritz."

No one moved; the dropped words hung in the space, hammered in the listeners' ears, impregnating their conscience. It was as if Gerard had just revealed a secret, liberated himself of a torment, confessed. A few minutes passed before the phase of astonishment dissolved. The different entities present examined him with a new kindness. They imagined the internal clash, and the misery he went through. They admitted that he had made a choice that would follow him for a lifetime.

The atmosphere bounced back to the everyday monotony, how the usual routine emerged with the stuttering of the morning: the cars humming down the road, the song of a bird, the water gushing free of a pipe, a street seller offering peanut and ripe banana to the neighborhood, the shuffling, quick exhalation escaping the chests that were inflated or tightened for too long.

Crystal's face transformed into an impenetrable mask, hiding the cascade of emotion swirling inside her. Dr. Dijon began pacing the room, his regard switched from the ceiling to the floor, his hands jammed in his pants pockets. He reached the door giving access to the hall, and stopped, hesitant.

He returned to the center of the living room, joined his daughter and her fiancé, and presented his concern about his colleague driving Crystal to the hospital. "Gerard, I don't share your enthusiasm about driving her to the hospital. Thanks for your help, and what you have done for us! I will go with my daughter." He grabbed her arm, tugging her slightly, inviting her to follow.

They were departing when Gerard raised his voice, exclaiming, "Wait a minute! Where are you going? Don't you get it? I promised, I promised to the man recovering that if he comes back, if he fights his way back, I will bring Crystal to him."

Dr. Dijon released his grip on Crystal. They were all lost, except her. She was flabbergasted, then puzzled. She looked at Gerard with incredulous eyes that progressively changed to stares of admiration. She had finally caught up with the explanation for her fiancé's action. She addressed her family members, "OH! Don't worry, I will be fine." Her input convinced them of his good intentions.

Her aunt proposed for the adults to pay the visit with her. They debated for a while the impact of the plan on the victim and his family members, and Dr. Dijon rejected his sister's proposition. He claimed that their presence in such force would intimidate the Arab-Haitians. "Remember the twins are already at the hospital."

That argument disarmed Ifelie, who divulged her next agenda to stay home and fix a beautiful fruit basket for Fritz, for by now she was fully aware of what had happened. She had seen Crystal with the Arab-Haitian owner of Fabric Pro at the New Spectrum party, and her quick mind had sewed the loose ends together.

Gerard grasped Crystal's hand and they exited the house under the wondering gaze of the audience.

Gerard let Crystal precede him, having retrieved her bag on her way out. She appeared solemn in her new role with her head straight, her movements sure. Her companion, before closing the door, waved to her relatives with a consoling glance. Close to the car, he opened the passenger side for his fiancée, watched as she climbed into the vehicle, and sat in no hurry. He sat in the driver's seat and started the engine after locking the doors.

The traffic that Friday morning was similar to what they had affronted on Monday: students packed the roads, happy on the last day of the state exams, impatient drivers jammed the streets manipulating their vehicles with address to gain speed and arrive safely at their destinations.

Crystal expected Gerard to be irritated by the congested routes. She reviewed the week's events to come up with a subject to distract him. She rejected the option to interrogate him about the conference because it would for sure remind him that each of them had chosen to attend a different celebration, that they did not act as a loving couple should have. She noticed that contrary to her assumption, he was relaxed, and was directing the car with more prudence than he had used in the past.

Fritz's accident brushed her mind, and she was once again tormented by the outcome, *Was he in such bad shape that Gerard was finally more cautious in his maneuvering of the car?* She was tantalized by the prospect of what awaited her at the hospital. *How was she going to react? Would she be able to control her feelings in front of Gerard? Was Fritz's mother there, in the room with her son? Would Gerard stay with them in that cubicle? Was Fritz awake? Did he know who the surgeon was? Was Fritz aware that he was at the mercy of his rival, that his life had been exposed in more than one way in one morning?*

Gerard's voice drew her from her tribulation. He asked, "How was the New Spectrum anniversary party?"

His question met with absolute silence. She was surprised by it, but resolved not to fall into the pit, not to satisfy his probing. Did he learn that Fritz had been one of the guests?

221

He pursued with the same amiable tone, "Your father probably went with you; this is why he abstained from honoring us at the conference! Poor guy, he is so devoted to his children's well-being!" Remorse smacked him, and he manifested his regret for his attitude. He avowed that he could have been with her, but preferred not to be, since three months before she obstinately claimed she would not bargain her participation at that feast for all the gold of the king of Spain.

He had needed to teach her a lesson, to subdue her, for her to appreciate the prestige that came with being in his company, a man of his tenure. He did not apologize; all he wanted was for her to talk, to confide her ordeal. After eavesdropping on her conversation with Arianne, his only desire was to receive from his fiancée's mouth the account of how she and Fritz had been separated. What were they subjected to? What had that awful dame done to them? He ventured, "What happened between you and Fritz?"

Crystal, taken aback, convinced herself that Gerard was aware of her recent escapade with Fritz. She considered that adventure her private life. She was angry, and through clenched teeth she protested against the invasion, "Please, Gerard, this is not the time for such a discussion. Don't push me into regretting having come with you."

Gerard understood her reaction. She had been through a lot: Arianne's visit, his own, the accident, the trip to the hospital, and he forgave her attitude, reasoning that she was at the edge of a cliff. He ignored her abrupt tone and insisted, "My dear, you must tell me; it's important, very important for me to find out."

She repeated slowly, to buy time, "Find out? Find out about what?" She debated in her mind the next course to adopt, *Was the car going too fast so she could not attempt a quick jump? Or could she wave to a passerby to solicit their help?* She played her last card, touching a sensitive chord, and pleading at the same time, "Don't let your jealousy prevail to spoil all your good deeds accomplished!"

Gerard shrugged his shoulders, remembered that he was skating on thin ice; since meeting his fiancée he had never approached the subject of her relationship with the Arab-Haitian man. It was a dead matter interred in an untouchable territory. But for his sake, he had to know. From what he suspected the answer would legitimize, absolve, his decision to withdraw his vows, give him an anchor to hook on, a balm to soothe his pride.

He couldn't help but be amused at how Crystal referred to saving someone's life, let alone her one true love's life, as a simple 'good deed'. It was then that he started to see the real difference between them, how Crystal really was much younger than him, and though she had been through a lot, still had much more to learn. He reassured her, plunging full speed ahead in the debate, "How could I be jealous? I had not even met you. It has only been two years."

Crystal's eyes were distant, her body shrunken like a deflated balloon, crushed by the recent events. Her mind was once more preoccupied with Fritz's ordeal. She could not concentrate and was not inclined to play any guessing game. She asked him bluntly, "What are you talking about?"

Gerard kept his eyes riveted on the road. He whispered, "Your relationship with Fritz Jean Lucas, how did it end up?"

Crystal sighed, lacing her arms in front of her like armor. A deep veil of sorrow spread across her face. She recalled Fritz's reaction when she told him she had waited three years for him, and he had shown devastation mixed with shock. The same feelings that had inhabited her for so long surged. She remained silent.

Gerard wanted her confirmation on the subject, so he risked, "What I heard from his mother, is it true? Is it true that she took your pictures with Alex and persuaded her son that you cheated on him?"

She acquiesced with a faint voice, "You said it."

The car was moving slowly, while she wished she could be at Fritz's side to measure the degree of damage. She suddenly came out of her stupor and blurted, "You were the shadow gesticulating on the porch this morning!" Baffled, she continued, "Why did you come so early, you knew I must have still been in bed?"

He reluctantly confessed his intention to harm her. He explained that he had figured out Fritz was back in Haiti and that she was the architect working on his project for so long. He wanted to hurt her badly for being stubborn and working against his will all those years. But after listening to Mrs. Lucas, he kept imagining what Crystal had gone through, to be set up and played with like a toy. "That woman is crazy. By the way, where did she get the nerve to come to your house after all her mischief?"

They arrived in the hospital's parking lot. He curbed the car and announced solemnly, "I have something for you." Fumbling through his pocket, he retrieved the airplane tickets, exposing them in front of her.

Crystal read their content and looked at him with bewildered eyes. She exploded, "You cornered me! How dare you buy me a ticket without my approval? Is this your vengeance? In a way, you are like Fritz's mother. Guess what? I won't travel."

He took back the tickets from her trembling hands, and retorted with consequence, "What an inconsiderate comparison. I have changed, Crystal." While talking, he tore her ticket into small pieces, then added, "You and Fritz have taught me a lot about perseverance and how to face adversity with hope, and forgiveness." He kissed her on the cheek and said, "I wish you luck, and all the joy this charming young man can give you."

Crystal could not believe her ears. Shifting in her seat, she cast an embarrassing glance at the scintillating diamond on her left finger. Gerard read her mind, and continued as if to himself, "It's yours, it will remind you that you are a fighter, and that I am your friend." She sat still for a moment, contemplating. Free, she was free. From what Gerard had just said, he was the one to break off their engagement. She closed her eyes to clear her mind. Gerard sensed a heavy weight lifting off his back, and he tapped her shoulder and reminded her that Fritz was waiting for her.

Crystal emerged from the car. Her head was throbbing. Fritz, his accident and surgery, came back to her mind with a force that pushed away everything unrelated to his health or safety. Dark thoughts clogged her mind, *What was he doing on the road at dawn?* The inauguration party was scheduled for 4 p.m. She recalled Arianne's morning visit and her proposition. Could it be that she angered her son with some silly proposition, and he was on his way to repair the damage he had anticipated?

How far did Arianne go? A new suspicion burgeoned as she remembered Fritz claiming they would leave the country if he met with strong opposition to their union. *What if he had upset his parents? What if he had been foolish enough to defy his mother and bring her to desperation? Or the contrary? What if his mother had brought him to desperation? Did Fritz try to kill himself to escape the Arab-Haitian tradition?*

Crystal refuted that possibility with all her might. *Fritz is a fighter, he would never resort to suicide as a solution.* She felt the sinking weight of the responsibilities befalling her. She faltered, shivered. She could not abandon Fritz, not after what he had done, not after his trip to Cap-Haitian to meet her father, to discover the truth, and to challenge his parents.

With her face withdrawn, her eyes sad, her shoulders slumped, she walked at Gerard's side. She grew scared. She slowed her pace involuntarily, so that she lagged behind him. He hurried with long strides to the hospital's employee entrance. He opened the door, and held it for her. After an instant of waiting, he realized she was not there.

He pivoted, and observed a devastated woman that he did not recognize. He flinched, thinking, *My God, why did I bring her? Is she going to collapse?* Regret assailed him; he swiftly considered whether his promise to bring Crystal to Fritz was an egoist, unsafe gesture, whether it was too late to back out. Rushing to Crystal's side, he took her hands, squatting to meet her gaze. Then he sprang up, pulled Crystal to him, hugged her, and murmured in her ear, "Be firm, Crystal, you have to, for yourself and for what lies ahead."

He rocked her like a father would to comfort his child. Her arms hung loosely, she reposed her head on his chest. Above them the sky bloomed like a huge azure parasol, silent birds flew the course of the yard to form an even row on the hospital roof, and the green bushes erected their leafy branches to salute the consoling effort of a friend.

Suddenly, the truth struck him. *I could never witness her suffering! I don't regret letting her go.*

He parted from her when she had regained some of her senses. She was affected the same, but her bearing exuded confidence; she was calm as she passed through the hospital door.

———

Arianne was satisfied with the note she had written to her son, which brought her some peace. Now she had to catch up with what she had missed: the factory blessing. She called the watchman, ordered him to get ready to go to the main, central market. She was bursting, pleased by the fact that she was going to surprise her family members with her planned intervention and at the same time buy her son's forgiveness and his former girlfriend's trust.

She wrote an extended list of ingredients she needed, as many Arab-Haitian recipes flew through her head. On second thought, she abandoned her initial plan. *Where am I going to prepare those meals? Kenscoff, at the Plantation, it's too far.* She reasoned, *I won't have time. Damn it! Why did I not think about that earlier?*

She tapped her fingers on Fritz's desk; her eyes were anxious, but slowly a confident smile spread across her lips, illuminating her face, chasing away the worries. She hailed the watchman back. The man advanced timidly, his face a mask of resignation, for he did not want to displease his boss's mother and jeopardize his position at the factory, now that he had met the owner and was sure he was lucky to have a young, conscientious man at the head of the enterprise. The first thing the owner had done was give the watchman a raise, a hefty one too. So he braced himself for whatever was to come, reminding himself that his boss would show up later. "Yes, Madam, at your service."

Arianne ignored the man's civility, there was no time to waste. "Get a *tap-tap*, you are going now to Petion-Ville.

Forget about the list I gave you, just ask the chauffeur to wait at Unique Pastry Shop, you know, the big store in the corner where all the public transportation turns to go to Delmas. I will meet you there."

Arianne was pleased with the solution she came up with—to buy all the prepared food at Unique Pastry Shop. She had decided to use the workers' tables at the factory to display her acquisitions. She hastily crossed the street to her hotel, solicited the right to utilize the phone, which was accorded to her with great cordiality by the secretary, and in the reception area under the inquisitive and amazed glances of customers and employees alike, she placed her order.

She emphasized that she was buying everything—cakes, sandwiches, pastries, etc—that had been fixed to be sold that day at the shop. She hung up the phone, leaving the hotel in a frenzy after thanking the clerk. Then she rented a taxi and rushed to her destination. She arrived at the shop in time to verify the packaging of the items she bought. She then busied herself acquiring all kinds of drinks: wine, cola, rum, and also ice. She hurried back to the factory.

The poor workers were worried for their boss; he had told them he would be there in the early morning and had solicited their help for the inauguration, but they had never met the woman who they all considered as strange. However, the watchman who was from Cap-Haitian and knew about his boss' mother's ways from the person who had recommended him for the job, had advised them to behave because they were going to have a day from hell. He knew about the woman's rigor and took pleasure in divulging that fact.

In that state of mind they witnessed Arianne as she came back, flushed with anticipation and excitement. She requested for the air conditioner to be turned on full blast, she felt hot; it would calm her and also preserve the food. She monopolized all the construction workers and employed them to arrange the tables and decorate the room. The owner of the pastry shop had come out to help her in her choices. How helpful that woman was, she would mention it to her friends after the feast. As the inauguration time advanced, she became irritated, more demanding; she wanted everything to be perfect. Relief announced itself in the form of a visitor of a most unexpected kind: an officer in a flaming red jeep.

Arianne had stepped into Fritz's office for a few minutes to stock up on extra beverages for late afternoon invites when one of the contractors informed her about the visitor. "Madame, there is an officer asking to see Mr. Lucas."

Arianne's face illuminated with interest and showed her pride for her son. She inquired with eagerness, "Did he give you his name?"

"No, but I told him you were here and he is waiting."

Arianne cast a sharp glance to inventory what had been accomplished. She launched more orders before exiting the office under the curious eyes of the workers. She mumbled to herself, "Fritz for sure is not playing; he already made important contacts with the military."

On her way to the factory she entered the small bathroom adjacent to the office. She dabbed her face with some Kleenex, checked her reflection in the mirror, noticing that her skin was shiny. She remembered Crystal's beach bag lying at her son's desk, and she went back to get it. She did not expect Crystal's powder to match her skin tone, but she

LASTING IMPRESSIONS

still searched it vigorously, trashing the paint bottles and brushes on the water tank of the w.c.

There was a small pressed powder of neutral shade; she grabbed it, dabbed her index finger in it, and rubbed the artificial dust on the wrist of the opposite arm. She smiled and wiped some powder with a Kleenex, smoothing it on her face. She appeared radiant. Armed with a charming smile, she ambled to the factory workers' shop. When she entered, the officer had his back turned to her, facing the street side of the courtyard, a long chain of smoke swirling above his cap.

Arianne lingered at the door, clearing her throat noisily. The officer extinguished his cigarette, pirouetted, recognized Arianne, took his cap off, and with a sure step, advanced toward her with his right arm extended. While the officer walked toward her, Arianne, after a swift assessment thought to herself, *What an impressive man; his profile is perfect, no bulging, a flat stomach, the golden tone of the Vs on his left shoulder reflected on his brown skin giving it some kind of glamour, his nose is thick but acceptable, his lips protrude but do not hang, which means charming.* The officer said, "Good morning, Mrs. Lucas, I did not expect to find you here today."

Arianne was shocked, she cleared her throat again just to buy some time and put the situation under her belt. In front of her stood Cap-Haitian's head of police. That presence gave a workout to her mind. How did the officer know about Fritz? Who told him about the factory? Was he invited to the party? She offered her hand, her inquisitive eyes searching him in an attempt to solve the mystery. She joined him and her air changed from surprise to great dignity. She adopted some distance and said, "Well, my son is having this party today, as you can see I'm helping him like all mothers would do."

The officer presented his excuses; he did not mean to interfere, just stopped by to announce his promotion to Fritz. He was now the assistant head of police in the capital. Arianne congratulated him for his promotion, reassuring him of their deep appreciation for his job in the countryside. Sensing that in the future they may need his expertise she decided to play the social card, "Cap-Haitian will miss you. It's a shame you cannot attend the party." He was on his way to Cap-Haitian to pass the command and his former house to his relief.

She moved aside with a great gesture of her hand and head and announced, "Let me fix a plate for you to take on your trip."

Arianne was in the process of doing so when Martine arrived with a deceitful stance in her look and way of acting. With much pretense and pride, Arianne informed the newcomer that her services were not solicited, that she could go back to her store. Martine feigned not to register her sister-in-law's rudeness. Her attitude irritated Arianne, who assumed Martine had come to help Fritz, and coarsely told her, "You can come back at 4 p.m., like the other guests."

Martine finally replied, "I came to get you, I have to talk to you."

Arianne, who had a grudge against her brother and his wife for assisting Fritz in the realization of his plan, took the advantage of what she assumed was her better position. She dismissed Martine with a look of contempt and continued to add pieces to the officer's plate, then casually invited her to reveal her confidence.

"Dear sister, this is Officer Josue Charles, he is a friend; whatever you have to tell me he must learn it down the road. Please speak!" Arianne knew perfectly well that what she had just stated was false. Arab-Haitians never discussed their private matters in front of strangers. It was her way of saying she had nothing of importance to say to her sister-in-law.

Martine reddened; she played with her hands, looked away, checked all the food on display, and swallowed with great difficulty, as her head was spinning. In her whole life, she had never heard of such a thing or experienced such an approach, having an Arab-Haitian family affair discussed in front of a stranger, and at worse, a member of the military. She darted a doubtful glance at Arianne. The officer too, was embarrassed; he began pacing the floor with his head down. When he was in front of Martine, he curtsied and said, "Nice to meet you."

Martine was a little relieved by the officer's attitude. She did not detect the blunt arrogance that they tagged the military with, but still she remained on her guard. She announced timidly to Arianne, "You have to come with me."

Arianne burst out laughing, shaking her hand to show her impatience and with finality told her, "No, my dear, you are joking, are you not? I have just enough time to get ready for the party."

Martine furtively scanned the food, the tables, the decorations. She sighed deeply and with an air of profound affectation she said, "Are you going to celebrate without Fritz or the other members of the family?"

Arianne stamped her right foot upon the ground, banged the table with the spoon she held in her hand, and screamed like a child who's preferred toy had been taken away, "Damn it, how dare they change the time or date without my approval!" She trembled with rage. Through clenched teeth she vociferated, "Fritz, it's all Fritz's design." She moved her head from side to side as if to shake a bad dream, and inquired, "By the way, where is he?"

Martine calculated her words, then in a mournful voice whispered, "Fritz had an operation, he is at the hospital, he is okay."

Arianne let go of the plate and spoon, and they crashed to the floor. She jumped in front of her sister-in-law, grabbed her shoulders and shook her frantically, all the while screaming, "Fritz is at the hospital! What happened? Tell me, tell me that my son is okay!"

Martine, after many unsuccessful attempts, managed to liberate herself from the claws that imprisoned her. They were both deeply colored, and Arianne was breathing fast. Martine rotated her shoulders to get rid of the pain. She announced, "Fritz had an accident this morning."

"MY GOD!" Arianne's voice was dying in her vocal cords. She brought one hand to her heart, the other to her forehead; her body became limp, rotated, collapsed. The officer hastily provided one strong arm for support while with the free one he grabbed a chair.

Her body slumped on the chair like a ripe fruit hitting the ground under fierce winds. Her eyes were withdrawn, her shoulders bent, she was shaking. Martine asked one of the workers to bring a glass of cold water. Small rivulets of sweat ran down Arianne's face as the shaking lessened. She was still flushed red like a hot iron. The officer improvised a fan made from cardboard, and handed it to Martine. She started to shake the air around Arianne, who was sipping the water, while babbling, "Poor son, poor son." Arianne seemed to recover part of her senses. She formulated the question her sister-in-law dreaded most, "Who is with him? Don't tell me he is by himself, my poor child."

Martine answered shyly, "Don't you worry, everyone is there, except you."

Arianne's pride took a blow. "Except you" resonated in her ears. It was as if she was living in a bad dream, she was sweating and she could not fight the reproach or the accusation hidden in those two words, "Except you." She insisted, "How is he doing? Is he okay?" Martine explained that when she left the hospital, Fritz was in the recovery room sleeping like a baby.

Arianne did not reply. She absorbed all the information provided, and readied herself to visit her son. She appeared drained, but her spirit awoke, and she proposed, "Hospital food is cold and not tasty, and we can expect a lot of visitors. Let's bring some of the food, the workers can share the rest, if there is still some left over, give it to the homeless in front of the churches." She addressed the officer, "Now, you can't leave, you must see Fritz and wish him a speedy recovery."

Arianne's body ached and her head throbbed. How could she miss something like that? Usually what she called her sixth sense warned her of any impending bad event. Her encounter with Crystal came to her mind.

In the car with Martine, she experienced profound regret; she blamed herself for what she called her blindness and felt guilty. *I must change!* she persuaded herself. She recalled her companion mentioning that everyone was at the hospital with Fritz. She kept rewinding that sentence in her mind but she did not have the guts to inquire whether Crystal was one of the people mentioned. Instead, she noticed how little progress their vehicle had made.

Crystal entered the building trailing at Gerard's footsteps. The vibrant life simmering inside the enclosed partitions caught her by surprise: the odor of cooked food lingering in the air, the flow of passing figures, mostly nurses, acknowledging Gerard with a smile and an interesting gaze, the housekeeper pushing a cart knocked on a door as if she was testing delicate china, the pharmacist with a tray of medicine advanced as if he was carrying eggs, a group of grandparents standing in front of a glass window talked animatedly to a newborn lying in a crib, offering them total indifference with his eyelids shut, his whole body tightly wrapped in the blue blanket.

That sight awakened Gerard's interest, and he approached the jubilant pack, congratulating each one of the performers for their achievement. He continued his tour, a nascent smirk brightening his face, and he addressed Crystal, "I feel sorry for the father, the way that woman was screaming earlier is enough to discourage him from exploring further intercourse." The allusion sent a chill through Crystal, but she chose to remain quiet. It was not a good time to present the differences in concepts between men and women on childbearing and childbirth.

Gerard entered a corridor and progressively the atmosphere changed. It was a naked space filled with still air pierced by vivid rays of sun that splashed on the wall in gigantic reverberations. A strange fear gripped Crystal. What lay at the end of the hall? Was it the recovery room's back door, giving access to new life and hope, or was it the morgue signaling the end, the disintegration of all designs? One must think about that option when immersed in such a deafening silence! Her insides grew taut, but she persevered on her march, deciding to withstand the cruelty of her destiny.

They arrived in front of a polished wood door carved with domestic scenes of the countryside. It sat in the sterile wall like a challenge inviting any visitor to peer inside so it could unveil a treasure. Gerard threw a complicit glance at his companion. Her heart drummed loud beats against her chest as the man at her side reached in his pants pocket for a set of keys. He grasped the long one with a head like a crown and dipped it in the lock hole, gave a simple turn to the right followed by a brisk push. The door glided open, and he advanced with one arm extended while the other disengaged the key. He said with a voice full of emotion, "Welcome to my niche."

Crystal stood at the door, her eyes perusing the crowded office. She was lost, and demanded, "Where is Fritz?"

He offered her the only seat, an antique high bamboo chair towering behind his desk. He informed her, "I am going to see what happened during my absence. You relax, everything is fine. I will come back to get you in a little while."

He moved close to the door and asked, "Do you want the light on, or would you like something to drink?" He pointed to a small refrigerator nestled in the corner behind his desk. He cracked a joke, "I don't think it is a sin if you drink from my cup." They both smiled at the remembrance, and his deliberate sense of humor. Without transition, he became serious, reaching for the phone sleeping on his desk and dialing.

A soft voice at the end of the receiver announced, "Good morning, recovery room, how may I help you?"

"Good morning, this is Dr. Armand. Has the patient Fritz Jean Lucas been transferred or is he still in your department?"

"No, doctor, he is in Room 26. Dr. Dijon made the arrangements for him."

"Thanks for the information." He hung up. *Room 26*, he thought. *Damn, Fritz is lucky; it's the coziest room in this place, if there is such a qualification in a hospital.*

Gerard's attitude and the woman's answer on the phone instilled some peace in Crystal. She eased herself into his chair while he waved to her before closing the door. After a few minutes in his office, she admitted how foreign her ex-fiancé was to her. His office was a stark contrast to hers—no radio, no flowers, no paintings. Only plain sketches of the human anatomy exposed in all positions adorned the walls. However, on his desk paraded a frame displaying a photo of his mother and father.

She slid the diamond ring from her finger and placed it at the bottom of the frame, then wrote a consolatory note to justify her decision: *Give it to your mom; she always wanted one like this.* She felt relieved with her finger undressed, as if she had gotten rid of a heavy weight.

She spotted a romance novel buried under the pile of medical journals, and retrieved it to fill the waiting time. She was engrossed in the chapter that she admired the most, the scene where the protagonist had found the source and was presenting to his girlfriend the importance of his catch, when after a shy knock on the door it unfolded to give way to two radiant men: Gerard and her brother Gregory.

Her eyes wandered from one to the other. They had donned their snowy lab coats, the white contrasting with their complexions, giving them an added sense of accessibility. Gregory was in a joyful mood; he kissed his sister, scanned the room, touched the almanac, the anatomy cut, then teased Gerard, "It was time for the world to visit your pit. Interesting, you keep all these materials in the shadows, away from your beloved students and colleagues."

Dr. Armand accepted the disguised reproach with dignity; no one had ever seen his office before, except for the old man responsible for cleaning it. He was his friend per se, sharing the intimacy of his retreat, complimenting Gerard for his success, blaming his failure on bad luck and envy from the competitors. Now Gerard admitted his domain had lost its reclusive reputation. He protested in the most unexpected terms, "Thanks to the patient sleeping up there, we are all victims of intrusion, our lives are upside down. From now on this office will welcome the public." He pronounced the last stretch in a whisper.

Crystal stood, and as she exited the room with Gregory, she understood Gerard was not accompanying them. He stayed at the entrance with an air of mystery on his face. She turned and asked him, "Are you not coming?"

"No," answered Gerard with determination, "my place is here. If you need me, you know where I am." He waved goodbye to her, and restrained himself in time not to kiss her.

Gregory tucked his arm around her, Crystal pivoted after waving to Gerard. Side by side with her brother, she began the ascension to assume the responsibilities befallen her. She felt secure, her brother teaming with her as he had since she was a young girl, always protecting her.

They shared a special kind of understanding, and that morning she needed him, needed his support, needed his strength. He pulled her out of her thoughts by commenting, "Fritz was lucky, he not only made it on time to the hospital, but benefited from Gerard's scrupulous care. His father and uncle are in the cafeteria. Do you want to meet them before going to his room?"

She caught his arm, looked at him with clear eyes, and manifested one more time her concern, "Not really, but tell me, Greg, how is he doing? Are there any big surprises in store for me? Why all the mystery?"

They were now at the bottom of a flight of stairs, and he grabbed her hand, interlacing his fingers with hers. Walking on, he reassured her, "No, Cryst, he is okay." And that was it. They climbed the steps, their plea sealed by their knotted fingers. They arrived on the first floor where a cacophony of noise assaulted them. Gregory let go of their link, liberating her. Her hand fell to her side. They advanced toward Fritz's room like two soldiers fighting the same war on different planes.

Fritz's room was just a few steps from the stairs. Greg signaled his sister to wait on a small balustrade perched on the stairs they just climbed. He disappeared to emerge a few minutes later talking to a nurse, and he invited his sister to come. She left the spot, her eyes transfixed on the two medical employees, and advanced mechanically.

Crystal heard her brother's voice from another world introducing the young woman to her. She just shook her head, and together they entered the room. It was an anteroom, a sort of sitting area, empty at that time, with a coffee table with cups, and a coffee pot. Crystal ignored the empty sofa, directed her eyes on the half-open door giving way to another room where Fritz was reposing. She crossed the unwelcome space that deferred her visit with renewed vigor. Gregory almost had to run to keep up with her.

He pushed the door to a ninety-degree angle, and then she stood, her eyes pinned on the form in the bed, absorbing Fritz sleeping peacefully under crisp, white sheets, his left arm in a sling, grotesque with a large bulging bandage, a beige strap protruding from the corset snaking around his shoulder to stabilize his fractured limb. Her chest decompressed slowly, she molded her lips in a pout of approbation that translated the relief she had just experienced.

Gregory motioned her to the chair he had placed on the opposite side of the bed for her. She walked with great caution, as if afraid of breaking a delicate object in her path. When she was close to the bed she repeated the same gesture Gerard had a few hours earlier: she lifted the sheet to observe the patient's body. She watched his chest rising and falling in voluptuous waves under the gown, she perceived the pads on his abdomen, his lower limbs appeared intact, but his face was drained. She covered him.

She moved the chair closer to the bed, sat, closed her eyes. Greg had left. She was the only one in the room with Fritz. She could not think, and as in every moment of despair or great joy, she addressed a prayer to her God. She thanked him for saving Fritz's life. She did not have a lot of knowledge in the medical field to ascertain the risks Fritz was exposed to, but from the experts' attitudes she assumed they were great, that the odds had reacted in their favor, that one more time what they termed "chance" had prevailed.

She reached for Fritz's arm so she could keep his hand in hers. She poised her head on the bed and just kept watching him, trying to record every single signal from his body. She sensed his eyelids flutter, and her heart jumped; she thought she had hurt him. She released his hand, and patiently, her body still while her heart derailed, she watched him, ready to activate help at the first panicky sign. She held her breath.

Yes, this time, she was sure; Fritz slit his eyelids open a little longer than the first time, as if adjusting to the daylight. She advanced to the tip of the chair, expectant, her eyes strained on his face. Slowly, he opened his eyes, then shut them quickly. He tried to move his body, growled, breathed in then out, reopened his eyes slowly. He scanned the room, frowned when he saw the IV pole with the hanging bag of medicine. When his sight met Crystal, he smiled and murmured, "What are you doing here, love?"

She returned the smile, touched his hand lightly, and warned him, "Don't move, you winced when you attempted to earlier."

Fritz was in a fog; he asked her what had happened.

Crystal became as restless as before and full of worries. She was puzzled and mired in the fact that maybe he was suffering from a bout of amnesia. She forced him to think, just to ensure her peace, challenged him, "Don't you remember what happened? Try to, at least you recognize me; that I'm sure."

A moment of silence followed that seemed like an eternity to Crystal. Her head was heavy as she looked at him, and the question hammered in her ears, "What happened?"

He had shut his eyelids again, shut in his world, a world apart from hers where he was fighting to regain possession of his past, and direct his future. She wished she had been with him; at least she could have given him some clues to help him remember.

As a tree growing from a rotten seed, he opened his mouth and confided to her in one spurt with his eyes still closed. His words resounded in the room, "I was on my way to the factory. At the corner of Laboule 12, I saw a boy of about 10-years old walking on the sidewalk, his books in one hand, a stick in the other to command the band of goats that preceded him. A baby goat abandoned the group, and ran in front of my car. There was the boy on my path, right at the wheels. I swerved the car and collided with a *tap-tap* turning the curb. The odious bang of the crash is the last fact I recall."

She was appeased by the report. It was a long one for someone who just had an operation, then she remembered that as a swimmer of his caliber, he had practiced how to hold his breath for a long run. She felt relieved. She sat mesmerized by the account he had just given. The scene when she fell on the boulevard runway flocked to her mind: Fritz, rushing to lend her a hand and help her stand. The memories swarmed in a rising tide in a raucous sea where the waves collided, crashed, pushed each other, entwined, kissed, engaged, ran away to collapse at her feet in a soft murmur.

Her eyes welled; she folded her fingers and bent her shoulders like a flower smacked by a hurricane. Fritz opened his eyes, caught a glimpse of her and for an instant regretted having told her, regretted having pained her with his rambling. Scrutinizing her figure his sight fell on her finger, her left ring finger was denuded, stripped, untied. No, he was not wrong, the diamond was missing. It was not there. He chuckled, moved slightly, and cringed with pain. Crystal leapt to her feet, and exclaimed, "Are you okay, Fritz?"

Fritz swallowed the surprise, voicing only his physical concern, "Damn, my stomach hurts like hell!"

Crystal abandoned his side, reached for the door to summon assistance. He called her back, his voice a tender whisper, "Crys," which crawled inside her, made her stop sharp. She turned her head and looked at him in wonder. Their gazes locked, and between them passed myriads of connections, myriads of exchanges, silent promises, and eternal vows. She closed the door tightly and came back to her previous spot at Fritz's side. She knew it was where she belonged and where she was to spend the rest of her life.

The silence in the room grew thin. Crystal sat, fixing Fritz with eyes that betrayed her emotion. She was pale, if there was such a thing for a black complexion, and she was trembling. She did not move, she was like a ripe fruit suspended, pampered by a shy breeze from the branch before falling to the ground.

She remained still, trying to catch every moment of it, to retain every second of the transformation, to enjoy every phase of the metamorphosis. Because just like when a baby cries for the first time and his lungs pop open, something happened between Fritz and her. Just like that they were close again, enmeshed in the same skin with no difference, as if it had not existed before, just like all that mattered now was them, succeeding.

Fritz's face brightened with his charming smile, where one guessed jealously that he was repressing a voluptuous thought, which made you envy him, curse him, and want to die to explore his secret. Crystal returned the smile she could not hold anymore. She planted a kiss on Fritz's lips to catch some of his contentment.

Fritz's voice filled the room, a melodious song that bounced on the walls to reverberate in her ears, impregnate her body; he confided to her that he was aware of who had operated on him, from the time in the emergency room when Gerard presented himself as Dr. Armand, the name kept resounding in his soul, and when he was in the recovery room he had heard Gerard's promise to bring her to visit him. He had thought he was hallucinating and had rejected the implication; he did not want to hope and observe his expectations crushed one more time. He had concentrated on the physical pain, inhibiting the prospect to nourish such ambition. But now he darted a long, meaningful glance at her finger. They both remained silent, the quietness a seal of their attachment.

An uproar distilled the serenity, bringing them back to reality. An anxious voice hammering questions, a timid tone offering elusive answers, heels tapping the floor in a hurry, flat shoes slapping on the ground with precipitation, a probing silence, a hesitating knock on the partition, a forceful response from Fritz's throat.

The door gaped open, in the breach a flurry of red faces sprouted with a dark one perched at the tail of the troupe like a guard. Curtis advanced, his face turning white with anticipation and anxiety. He pointed a steady finger to the bed where Fritz was lying motionless. He presented Fritz with a hint of sarcasm, "There is Fritz, still in bed for once. I'm sure his arm will hurt him if he even winks."

Turning the finger in Crystal's direction he continued his entertaining tirade with, "There is Ms. Crystal Dijon, the firm's architect and our physician's sister."

Arianne slapped Curtis's finger down, and eyed him from head to toe with both envy and disdain. Swallowing her pride, she approached her son's bed, and with care and great affection traced Fritz's facial features with her hand, then bent, rested her head on his, remaining in that posture for a while with her eyes closed, both mother and son swimming in a world of their own. Then she kissed him again and again.

The newcomers aligned against the wall, waiting. Fritz, who reopened his eyes, was also waiting. Crystal, who had folded her arms across her chest and crossed her legs, was also waiting. Arianne stood up, and all eyes were fixed on her as she rounded the bed, extended her arm to shake hands with Crystal, then kissed her on her forehead, and finally talked to her for the first time. "Thank you for coming, Crystal. Thank you for being here for my son."

Crystal swallowed with difficulty. Her throat was tightening; she was either going to explode or pass out. She searched her brother's gaze for support, but he was looking at Fritz. She turned her head to see why Gregory was watching him, the fear of Fritz sliding down the scale gripping her again. No, Fritz had that smile on his face. She drank it in and melted.

Three men and two women in the cubicle were lost. Curtis, Michael, Martine, Gregory and Crystal exchanged a flare of curiosity and astonishment—was it love, affection, interest, respect, fear, surprise, civility...to explain Arianne's attitude. She was the only one that could provide all the facets of the dilemma, for Crystal would never betray her by telling anyone, even Fritz, about her visit that morning.

Turning to Gregory, Arianne asked, "Doctor, is it all right with you if I stay for a while?"

The request took Greg by surprise. His timidity reappeared, he shrugged his shoulders. Arianne had regained her composure, and made all of them laugh when she continued, "Imagine, Doc, that I remember when you, as a young boy, were running, always running in short pants with those mosquito legs of yours."

Fritz warned his mother, "You better watch your words, now he can order those injections that you detest. I'm tired, come back later." The patient had made known his will. They all left.

———

The blazing sun baked the city, its implacable rays licking the stretched garments exposed on tidy ropes by laborious washers, roasting the tin roofs protecting packed houses that creaked as if ready to explode. The heat monopolized

245

the engaged activities, setting the rhythm for a languor that established a warranted laziness. The clanging dishes disturbed the stillness, the intrusion lingered in the air, carried by a soft breeze which had awakened and lavished the metropolitan area with its absolution. Gone were the nurses, the pharmacist, the housekeeper. The hospital exhaled intonations of veiled conversations escaping from shadowy cubicles with their doors ajar.

Greg took the lead, with his sister parading at his side. Fritz's parents joined them. They ambled like a marching band toward the waiting room, with the music and conductor missing. Crystal's mind was preoccupied with her father's comment before she had left the house. Dr. Dijon had argued that her family would outnumber the true relatives if they chose to impose their presence all at once.

For the first time in her life, she became aware of the obvious fact: even if the Dijons were counted by the thousands and the Lucas-Kahlils were just a sprinkle of ten, the small group would not be eclipsed. They would stand out, succeeding or failing depending on whether they were accepted by the larger community, and if they were rejected, how strong their desire to fight.

She admitted that Fritz had dealt with duality his entire existence. Next, Gerard's remark popped up in her thoughts, "Thanks to the patient sleeping up there, we are all victims of intrusion, our lives are upside down." Gerard was right; Arianne's attitude in her son's room, her presence with the Arab-Haitian community, was a stamp of the new order. A sudden, precipitated stride superposed their muffled steps, and a gentle form crossed the blended bunch. It was Fritz's nurse.

She was a young woman in her twenties. She held her head high, her bearing exuded confidence, the ways of someone used to being in charge. Her face displayed a severity that betrayed the weight of her profession on her. She addressed the small crowd with a detachment that proved she was unaware of the profound impact contained in the message she was to deliver. In a neutral voice she presented her patient's request: "Mr. Lucas wants to speak to Ms. Dijon."

That was it. It was like she had just announced a condemning sentence. A lethal silence plagued the atmosphere.

Crystal waved dismissively, signaling her departure.

They all stood together silently. It came as a surprise to them and they let the significance of the last blow impregnate them. Fritz had not asked to see his father, or mother, or aunt, or uncle; he had requested Crystal.

The sentence fell and the crowd was paralyzed for an instant. Arianne was crimson, regurgitating what she had already recognized: that Crystal was to mingle in their business with the consequence being the fading of her own influence. Martine inspected her shoes, checked everyone's attitude, and inwardly congratulated herself for being an expert diplomat. She had tied her tongue, not offering any earlier suggestions that she could recommend a rich Arab-Haitian partner for her nephew.

Now, to ensure a friend on the plantation because she predicted the architect would be her selected neighbor, she employed her craft as a mediator. She glanced furtively at the three men. Their stance exuded great embarrassment. Gregory, the only black man there, could not come up with any subject to distract the disgruntled bunch. Michael and Curtis delighted in each other's desperation. Martine broke the stillness with a declaration that startled them. "Who knows how long he will keep her in there. Let's go to the waiting room."

The casual way with which she presented the unappealing truth cheered up the assembly and buffered the deteriorating effect of the displacement. Resigned, they accepted with some reserve not the invasion, but their constrained position.

They proceeded to the waiting room, void of visitors at that time, since everyone was with their beloved connection in their hospital rooms. Reaching for the second shelf of a decaying console, Gregory fetched a plastered memo proudly brandishing the note: "Room not available." It was the space favored by the medical staff to inform family members about the decline in recuperation of their loved one, and it was shied by the general public.

One more time Greg admired the Arab-Haitians for their adaptability; they were all comfortably seated and planned to fortify their roots in such difficult passage. Curtis took refuge in the darkest corner and manifested his usual penchant: he offered to help. Michael rebuffed his brother-in-law's advance with the pretext that the capital's warmth would shock the countryside man. By then they were all laughing. They tasted the delivered food and declared that it was delicious.

Except Arianne, who noticed that the bread was too crusty, that the salad looked fresh but exhaled a strong odor of lemon. She concluded that the salad would be unpalatable with an acrid taste when she added some vinaigrette. Measuring her gestures to mask her disdain, she steered away from the sandwiches and salad, considered trying the drinks. She was thirsty anyway. She checked the pitcher and repressed on time a smirk of repulsion. A large barge of ice swarmed on top of the pitcher, which meant the warm soda lingered at the bottom. She compared the mixture to a purgative. She hated the sight of ice floating in her glasses. At home she made sure her drinks were kept in the refrigerator until they were ice cold.

She could not show her displeasure. Everyone else was enjoying the delivered food. She flashed a synthetic smile as she recalled her own harvest, the fine goodies from Unique Pastry Shop she had stuffed in the car before coming to the hospital. She repressed the urge to propose her items, the ones she had purchased for the party; she was not fit to provide a satisfying answer to any probing by her family members. She was not ready to avow that she was on a shopping spree while her son's life was in danger. It was too early to expose her defeat to the whole family.

She realized then that she must learn to be less competitive, not try to always be the one, the first one. She silently thanked God for saving her son's life, then she prayed in her heart for herself and her family members. She looked at each one of them and admitted how simple they were, her people. She would not let them down; she grabbed the pitcher and poured soda into her cup. The liquid was warm, but she emptied her cup with no remark or disdainful gesture.

Feigning that she needed some fresh air, she asked Gregory to please show her a peaceful area where she could regain her senses. As soon as they were outside, she presented her real motive: she must hurry to find a safe preserve for the food in the car or else it must be sent to one of the churches' soup kitchens. They settled for the last solution after Gregory convinced her it was tactless to impose such a burden on the hospital's personnel.

In the parking lot they met with Lieutenant Josue Charles. After Arianne presented him to Dr. Gregory Dijon, Lieutenant Charles inquired about Fritz's health.

Dr. Gregory Dijon reassured him the patient was sleeping, and should be fine in a couple of weeks. The lieutenant declined Arianne's invitation to visit Fritz. Instead he handed her a farewell card for the patient. He reminded Arianne of his trip to Cap-Haitian in case she wished to send news of Fritz's accident to relatives in the countryside. Arianne thanked the officer and said she was sure her husband or brother already had. Lieutenant Charles exchanged a handshake with each of them, bowed, and returned to his jeep, which he had parked close to the hospital's entrance.

Gregory signaled to the orderly waiting on the hospital's steps to advance. He charged the orderly with the task of disposing of the food, summoning him to act fast before the soup kitchens closed.

As Gregory toured the hospital premises with Arianne, she thanked him for his help.

After dropping Arianne in the reception room, where everyone was guessing why Gregory did not come back sooner, he left, not answering their questions. His pretext was that he had to solve their problem of communicating with the outside world, since there was no telephone at their disposal; only a select few businesses benefited from that technology, so he was to delegate a *garcon* to inform the more distant relatives.

A sudden panic surged in Crystal as she walked toward Room 26. The limbo of her situation hit her. She compared herself to a shipwreck coming to shore with no anchor. Down in the basement was Gerard who had withdrawn his commitment; she could not blame him, it was long overdue. Closer to her was the man she had told two nights before not to nourish any hope because she was not going to default on her engagement. For one thing now, she advocated that Fritz was in a better position than she was. He had disappeared, but he had never said no.

How can one interpret silence? Anyway, it was a better weapon to manipulate than the harshness of her definite negative response. And now she was tortured, tortured by the fact that maybe Fritz could question her reliability; she had created a breach in his trust for her. She was miserable, not because she was with no fiancé or boyfriend, but because she wanted to gain Fritz's complete trust as she was sure now that Gerard trusted her, did not see in their separation an act of treason, but the logical ending of a thwarted case. She persuaded herself that she should abide, back off. Let him present his argument, but that option did not carry any peace either.

Her head slightly bent, her eyes on the floor, she walked at the nurse's side. Her temples were beating hard, her mind was clouded. She kept repeating silently the question: "Why did Fritz call me back?" She was upset, unsettled. She searched for a justification for her condition, reasoning that Fritz soliciting her presence would not create that deep perturbation in her. It had to be something else that triggered the uneasiness.

She replayed the last minutes elapsed in her mind, concluding that the attitude of the Arab-Haitian group upon learning of Fritz's request, to see her alone, was what had tipped the balance, made her unsure of herself. She had never expected the unconditional cooperation of Fritz's family members, of the Arab-Haitians. Still she was vexed and distressed by the unrestrained manifestation of their surprise mixed with resentment.

She had masked the immediate effect on her with her dismissive wave, but she was tormented by their attitude. She had to find a way to shield herself against their blunt arrogance, she persuaded herself. She raised her head. Contrary to the tidy, crowded, single-family houses, conveying a sense of limitation she just turned her back on, at her feet lay a luxuriant carpet of tropical plants. She admired the new panorama of tall, leafy trees sliding in palisades to end in the capital's bay.

It was a powerful image evoking infinity. It expressed, when coupled with the blue sky and the bright sun, deep love. It reminded her of Fritz. She looked closer, at the shrubbery parading in the hospital's courtyard. She discovered two pigeons cooing intimately in the early afternoon, making love. She looked past them at the sea and remembered her outing with Fritz at the Birds of Paradise Garden.

She smiled at the recollection of Fritz presenting his plea like a trained lawyer, for her now a gesture, a proof of his love. It came to her that she would be fine with Fritz, safe. He would protect her against any destructive behavior. Her heart swelled with her love for Fritz. And suddenly, she was aroused by a new feeling. She did not want to lose Fritz after all they had gone through, all she had gone through. She wanted to be at his side, to one more time make sure he was doing okay. She quickened her pace, almost running, opened the door, stormed into the anteroom, and flew to Fritz's bedside.

He was lying in the bed the way she had left him, immobile like a granite statue, untouched by the swift torment that racked her soul. His face, a plateau of serenity, disarmed her insecurity. Out of breath mostly because of her excitement more than the exertion, she fixed him with eyes that betrayed the turmoil she had just experienced. She caught his hand and in an almost supplicating tone avowed, "I'm under a lot of pressure. Please don't condemn anyone for my state of mind." Silence. She inhaled deeply, exhaled in one scoop, and blurted, "I need some time, I need some time to think, to recoup." He let go of her hand and whispered, "I don't want you to worry so much. Everything will be fine."

She grabbed the chair, pulled it to the place it had occupied before, and sat, preparing herself to discover what he had to tell her.

Fritz blushed as his eyes met hers, the blushing that had produced the same result even after years apart, and her insides grew taut. He tilted his head to the side, opposing her as if to gather momentum. She was suspended, expectant on the edge of her chair. With a voice full of tenderness and concern he reminded her, "I left your beach bag in my office."

The directness of his observation and the implication attached to the material proof of their escapade swirled her back to their encapsulated realm. "Oh, Fritz," she exclaimed, "how can you think about that bag lying there?" As if for her that renegade was not important, in fact it was the only piece of evidence that had to be destroyed, that must be eliminated to save the appearance, and conserve the reputation of faithfulness imposed by their society. To save the three of them: Fritz, Gerard, herself. But what mattered most was Fritz's health, so she reproached him, "Who cares about the gossip, you should be worried about your health, concentrate on healing."

With his usual wisdom he wrapped the effects that the deteriorating speculation could cause on their environment saying, "It's our responsibility not to encourage rumors." With an air of malice he added, "Don't contemplate resigning from your post at the firm. I have some new orders for you, young woman!"

She adopted an affected air that confirmed to him she was aware he was up to something. Not giving her time to protest, he laid out his plan; it was simple. "The one-bed-room apartment designated as my office must be finished before my discharge from the hospital. The most important deed is that I can keep away from my family so they can digest the new turn of events while I recuperate. Is life not wonderful?"

"What? What do you want me to do?" exclaimed Crystal.

"Do you recall the discussion I had with you about the apartment in the factory? I need the arrangements to be made quickly. Will you please make sure I have a sleeping area behind my office? I intend to stay in the city," he answered casually. "We have enough time to draw the canvas." In a more serious tone he stated, "I'm pooped, I need some rest, see you tomorrow."

He closed his eyes. Crystal did not move; startled, she absorbed the meaning of Fritz's demand on her career. In fact, it was the second time that she, as the architect, was discussing her work directly with a client without the firm's directive. She was always treated as a subordinate and had to receive from the engineers the information she needed for her assignment.

She was trusted, encouraged, admired by the engineers as long as she remained on the back burner. It should have been the contrary. As the architect, her job was to prepare the plan for the house, and she must know about her client's taste. But Haiti was not ready for that stage. If she was to obtain directly the information from the clients, the male engineers would have felt displaced, diminished, threatened. This explained why she had only met Michael Kahlil twice in a two-year span and why she was never acquainted with the intricacies related to the ownership of Fabric Pro.

With Fritz's attitude, she was in charge. Michael and the firm would learn from her about Fritz's decision. She observed him, mesmerized by his determination. Sleep had submerged him. She prayed involuntarily for their sake. She left the room as she had entered it, in a hurry, and announced to the nurse who was waiting in the anteroom that she was leaving. She selected the back stairs that she had climbed with Greg earlier, glanced at Gerard's office, its door tightly shut.

She turned to the path opposite the one she had walked with her ex, landing in a garden blinded with wild roses. She adopted the single alley crossing the lot, which ended at a rustic wooden door that was unlocked. She opened it, finding herself on the street at the extreme back of the hospital, the corner facing the convent school back yard. She decided to reach the main road, not Canape-Vert, the one passing in front of the hospital, but Bourdon, the one that was near the firm.

She melted in with the pack of students clanging in the alleys, and felt revived. She hailed a taxi, opting to go back to her house. In the taxi she repeated with conviction Fritz's comment that life is wonderful. She was free.

———

The capital's main streets buzzed with the effervescence of joyous students. They felt relieved, the state exams were over. Crystal identified the provincial ones with their timid air agglomerated in a corner to discuss their answers to the last test. She recognized the local ones from the capital with their characteristic indifference, planning to expedite the weekend in fashion by going to the movies or the discos. She remembered her time at the boarding school, and how

Fridays were the hardest because she was confined within the sisters' house. But now she was free. The meaning of the word struck her again as she hailed a cab, gave her address to the taxi driver, and entered the back seat.

To someone who has never experienced constraint, freedom is a natural state devoid of any thrilling effect. That was not the case for Crystal. The new feeling brought her great happiness. She was also conscious of the responsibilities that came with it. She acknowledged that, for her, being free meant first being accepted by her community as an adult capable of reasoning and making choices.

She admitted she was lucky because her father did not oblige her to enroll into the medical field he had advised her to pursue. She had entered the architectural field despite all the warnings received. She had paid a hefty price for her stubbornness; she was never included in any big decision-making at New Spectrum, since her uncle had not wanted to ruffle the engineers' pride. The result was that she met Mr. Kahlil a few times when her co-workers could not relay the specifics of the information their client had requested.

The offer Fritz had just made to her reversed her role. She was now in direct contact with the owner and would inform New Spectrum about Fritz's decisions for his office's alterations. And suddenly she realized it was the same for Fritz. He had not called on his uncle or his parents to first expose his intentions, as was the custom of Arab-Haitians, did not solicit the advice of others; he was firm, confident, and ready to go ahead with his choices. His attitude sealed his independence. Crystal smiled at the feigned, casual way he had endorsed his responsibilities. She realized it must have been hard for him and his family members to accept the change.

Gerard and his impositions and rhetoric about women and work and their place in society crossed her mind. Crystal shrugged her shoulders and her face darkened as she admitted to herself that if she had married Gerard in a rush, it would have been a big mistake. They had never been a true couple. There had been no intimacy in their relationship. She concluded that she would have destroyed herself, her personality, her dreams.

She was lost in these thoughts and did not identify her neighborhood. The prudent voice of the taxi driver stated her address and pulled her out of her analysis.

Startled, she mumbled an apologetic, "Thank you," tumbled out onto the sidewalk and paid her fare, signaling to the cab driver to keep the change. She entered the house by the side gate, which was wide open. Maria had been stationed in that post since Crystal left with Gerard that morning. The maid had presumed the day was to be full of surprises and was watching the street in quest of strangeness. Crystal passed her, murmuring a distant, flat "Thanks" that discouraged Maria's curiosity. Crystal completely disarmed the maid's eagerness by not inquiring why the household was empty at that time, contrary to the usual.

She emerged later from her bedroom, refreshed, wearing a floral dress with her hair subdued in a ponytail. Fritz's comment at the beach about its texture brought a smile to her lips. And soon they parted to spill the high notes of *Ave Maria*. She was happy.

She stepped outside into her garden, a small lot in the back of her aunt's house, nothing to compare with the luxurious hills of the plantation. However, she had cherished that plot since joining her aunt's household. Except for the past week; since her brother's visit to announce Fritz's return, she had not set foot in her garden.

That day, she was there to assess the results of her abandonment. The blooming petals of the roses smiled to welcome her. Their lavish fragrance confided to her that they had awaited her return. She neared a branch and mechanically sorted out the yellowish leaves. The victims were accepted with warmth by the compost pile. A light veil of flies escaped the decaying mound, swirling in a merry-go-round dance. Crystal admired their performance and remembered it was June, that the mango's harvest was near at hand and that the unbearable summer heat would soon reach the city. That unforgiving heat she would have to fight to preserve her vegetable garden.

The new concern made her turn her attention to the corner where tomatoes, peas, and pickles grew. Contrary to the flowers, the edible plants brandished their amputated legs with revenge. During the whole week they had endured a constant assault, a perpetual attack that had deprived them of their most beautiful crop. Alarmed, Crystal tucked in her dress and squatted to nurse the injured.

She entangled the denuded branches with budding stems and fresh bunches of foliage to mask the wounds. She gauged the effect and was pleased. She was thinking about who to blame for the damage. Maria or her aunt, but instead decided to teach them how to harvest the crop without any harm. She did not see her father standing on the back porch.

Dr. Dijon, his hands resting on the rail, admired his daughter. He interpreted her communion with nature as a healing process, and an opening to new avenues. He could see the metamorphosis accomplished by Fritz's return and the time he assumed the couple spent together. Crystal's bearing exuded a new assurance; there was some kind of satisfaction emanating from her.

On the other hand, he was visited by a profound sadness. Crystal, his closest child, was gone. He chased his grief away with the consolation that a scandal had been averted. And from Crystal's attitude he guessed that the Gerard saga had a decent end. He contemplated the arrival of his grandchildren as a fair compensation for his loss.

He neared his daughter and interrupted her thoughts. "How is Fritz doing?" he asked simply.

"Papa!" Crystal exclaimed, her eyes gleaming with wonder like when she had been a little girl running to land in his arms. In a whisper she confided, "He is doing fine." She tried to find the right words to express her feelings. She joined him, walking now at his side. She touched his shoulder, looked him straight in the eyes, and voiced her apprehension, "You know Fritz, Dad, you were his soccer coach during his years in high school."

Her father, surprised by her enthusiastic outburst said, "Time flies. Can you imagine Fritz being an entrepreneur, changing the course of his people's business in this country, not exploiting the population, but creating jobs?!"

"Dad!" she murmured, "you should have come to the hospital."

He did not have the time to answer. With no preamble, a tapping noise advanced rapidly from the tin roof toward them. Fat, copious droplets pounded the earth with delight. Father and daughter ran inside the house, just in time to avoid getting drenched by the unexpected rain.

She teased her father, citing the countryside anecdote, *"Diable ap battre madam li pou la soupe sale!"* [The devil is beating his wife because she served him salted soup.] Crystal added, "Why do they always blame women in this country for all mistakes, even in this case where nature is in fact providing us with some relief?"

Dr. Dijon retreated, "Anyway, we were taught not to follow the devil's example so we know it is forbidden to raise our hands to our wives. It is siesta time, 2 p.m."

They were now in the living room and without thinking reached for the seats Arianne and Crystal had occupied earlier that morning. Dr. Dijon sneezed, took his handkerchief, swept his face as if he were tired. Crystal's comment bothered him. He opined, "It is very unfortunate that the general population is biased against women."

Crystal remained silent. It was a painful subject for both of them. Dr. Dijon was hesitant when he proposed, "Are you coming home with me? A few days of rest will help you catch up, regain some energy after all this turmoil. There is no comparable sight to help someone relax than the Cap-Haitian Boulevard at sunset, or better, the beach at Cormier or Rival."

Crystal's face brightened with gratitude. She thanked her father for his consideration, but declined the invitation. She explained the duty that awaited her.

"I have to finish Fritz's office. He would like a one-bedroom apartment. He plans on staying in the city during his convalescence so he can manage the factory."

"Fritz is mature and more cautious than one would assume. It is good judgment for him to supervise the functioning of his factory from the beginning. I hope his mother won't interfere."

"She was at the hospital and surprised everyone when she thanked me for being there for Fritz."

Dr. Dijon exclaimed, "I don't get it. Do you mean she had the nerve to say those words in front of her son, her husband, and her brother? This is too much for me. This woman is really unpredictable."

"You have found a nice way to describe her attitude. Anyway, her arrogance paid off. She provided Gerard, while he was spying on the porch, all the useful information that persuaded him to withdraw his proposal. Her zeal to free her son served the purpose of easing the difficult task of clearing my path. Can you imagine how shocked I was when Fritz showed me the pictures of myself with Uncle Alex? Today her accusation appeared ridiculous to me: Uncle Alex engaged to me! But I must tell you that I was at first very angered when Fritz avowed to me the cause of his silence."

Dr. Dijon placed a soothing hand on Crystal's shoulder. He mumbled, "There we go again. This is Haiti where a young woman seen in the company of a young man is always stimulation for gossip." He stopped sharp, then in a lower voice added, "It was a mistake, Crystal, the mistake of an overzealous, conservative mother."

Crystal looked at her father with a smirk on her face. She was not surprised by his reason. She braced herself to accept the pending advice.

Her father continued, "You must forgive her. She has been punished enough for her imprudence. I dropped Fritz at his house Tuesday afternoon. He was furious after he found out that Turnier was your uncle. I would not want to be in Arianne's place. It must have been embarrassing for her to admit she was wrong and to apologize."

Crystal's laugh filled the room. She retorted, "It's probably why she was here this morning with the stupid proposition of me being a 'mistress' for her son."

Her father cut her off. "Arianne is not a regular Arab-Haitian wife. Her husband spoiled her, and let her go with a lot, meaning unopposed familial decisions. They both paid a hefty price. They almost lost their son. Fritz was ready to leave the country. His mother's last attempt translated her despair. It shows us she admitted Fritz was serious about you."

"I imagine that learning about Fritz's accident a few hours later unsettled her world for good. She was the last one to be at the hospital. How come?"

Dr. Dijon answered, "It does not matter anymore. Now you are the link, the person to bring peace to both parties—mother and son. I count on you." The pouring rain stopped as it had started—with no warning. The aroma of fresh mud blended with swollen grass. The house was cool, the sky limpid, the plants refreshed.

———

Toward the end of their conversation Crystal noticed that her father was somber. She attributed his pain to their pending separation. But she could also detect that he was preoccupied, that his mind was dwelling on something important. So, when he abruptly ended their meeting with the excuse that he would come back with the twins for supper, she accepted the proposition without a remark.

Dr. Dijon retreated from his sister's house, hailed a cab, and requested to be dropped in the university area. He was willing to wander in that vicinity until he could locate Gerard's clinic. His task was easier than anticipated. Most of the parking lots were empty on Friday afternoons. As the cab glided between rows of stern buildings that lined the streets, Gerard's solitary car sprung out in the little private entrance at the side of his clinic, contrasting with the vacant front parking lot.

Dr. Dijon sighed, halted the cab driver to a stop. He paid for his ride, but hesitated on his way to the entrance. He reckoned he would find Gerard in his clinic, but was it fair for him to intrude in the man's private life? He was sure that was what he was about to do in a certain way. However, he could not abandon the course. He had to reach the finish line. He knocked gently on the wooden surface of the entrance. The door gaped open almost immediately, as if someone were expecting a visitor.

Gerard stood in the doorway with his arms wide apart, a bright smile warming his face. They hugged. When they parted, he offered Dr. Dijon a seat in his private office. They sat like the patients in quest of treatment and healing, talking at first about the clinic.

Dr. Dijon asked, "Do you have someone to take over your duty on such short notice?"

Gerard admitted he had always predicted something like obtaining a grant could happen. "It was one of my goals, and the reason why I collaborated so closely with my partner, Dr. Potelli, for my patients not to feel at a loss during my absence."

They then broached the subject of the bustling life of Paris. Dr. Dijon warned him of the traps his new position held. "The city of lights is very interesting at night." He restrained from adding that a fresh bachelor with a broken heart would find solace in the liberties of the modern world. They did not mention Crystal, or Fritz, or the morning's incidents. Instead, they browsed on the miniskirt and the current fashion trends.

Dr. Dijon reminded him, "Will you please send me any medical material you find interesting?"

"It would be my pleasure," murmured Gerard. There was nothing left for them to discuss. As Dr. Dijon readied himself to wish Gerard good luck and leave, the coarse crushing of tires sliding in the parking lot startled them. Surprise and anxiety spread across their features. Hurried steps hammered the ground followed by a nervous pounding on the door. Fritz's family members and Gregory filled the entrance. Their arrival increased the two doctors' sense of awkwardness. Gerard and Dr. Dijon appeared confused.

Gregory eased himself to let Arianne pass. As always, she preceded her family members in the file. She bowed graciously in front of Gerard. As soon as they were all seated she presented the subject of their visit.

"Doctor, we are not here to discuss money with you. What you did is priceless. We are here to thank you for your generosity and good heart."

Gerard, who was toying with his belt, trying to decide how to start a conversation, was relieved by Arianne's overture. He mumbled a shy, "Thanks. I just did my job." He was touched by the woman's spontaneity and the sincerity that emanated from her being.

Arianne's family members looked at her with astonishment. Curtis disrupted the delicate silence that invaded the room after his wife's intervention. "Doctor, we learned that you are the recipient of the grant from the French government. Don't look stricken! You know news travels fast in Haiti; it was the talk of the hospital today. Please feel free to contact my two younger brothers who reside in Paris. They will be glad to honor any request from you." Handing the doctor the piece of paper where he had scribbled their addresses and phone numbers, he added, "I will call them tonight." He shook hands with Gerard, "Thank you again for your help."

He then addressed the elder Dr. Dijon, "When are you going back to Cap-Haitian?"

Dr. Dijon answered in an evasive manner he assumed would not hurt anyone present. "I must be there for my patients by Monday." He got to his feet and voiced his desire to finish his errands in the capital. It was as if he had signaled to the bunch the completion of their mission. They all stood and presented individually their farewell to Gerard. Arianne for once was the last one to depart after she shared a long, meaningful hug with her son's surgeon.

The short distance from the clinic to their cars served the purpose of formulating the design for new plans. Michael, who had remained silent inside, bounced back to life. He proposed, "Since you two must be in Cap-Haitian Monday morning, why don't you travel together?" Michael was pointing at Dr. Dijon and Curtis while talking, and Arianne showered her brother with eyes that beamed with gratitude. She confirmed her desire to stay in the capital. She cuddled with her husband and said, "Curtis, darling, you know I must be here with our son. I will stay at the plantation."

Dr. Dijon nodded his head in approval of all that was said. His face sported a dreamy air as he boarded his son's car and the Lucas-Kahlils theirs. He was thinking about the future trips Curtis and he would be making, and maybe Arianne, if she did not elect residence on one of the lots on the plantation.

Gerard pulled the curtains closed. He had to finish the review of his private patients' charts, then travel to his parents' house in the countryside of Leogane. He had to be the first one to bring them the news of his success.

———

The third week of June swirled, for some, over the island of Haiti with the blatant sameness that period offered every year. It was the end of the school year with the preparation for final exams and summer vacation looming ahead. The events of the week touched the Dijon and Lucas families like a storm: it blustered, created turmoil, and exited, leaving behind its indelible stamps. From the simmering havoc exhaled the possibilities of clearing the path, reorganizing, securing the foundation for reconciliation.

Crystal spent the weekend hibernating in her bedroom. Her family members understood her reaction. They excused and accepted her deliberate absence from their gathering. She employed the time to adjust to her new situation and to draw the design for Fritz's one-bedroom apartment at Fabric Pro. She only received Gregory, who came to give her news of Fritz's progress. He was healing fast.

On Monday, Crystal landed at Fabric Pro for the remodeling of Fritz's office. She was bemused by three discoveries. The first one was her beach bag that lay on the w.c. and revealed the blunt invasion. Crystal then appreciated Fritz's concern with a new light. The beach bag was the concrete proof of their escapade. Arianne could use it as a derogatory tool if she still fancied pursuing her initial endeavor. But Crystal had read her letter to her son; it had been left open on his desk. Crystal had placed a box with her name that the foreman had handed to her upon her arrival at the factory next to the letter. She noticed that the date was Friday.

Crystal gave instructions to the foreman about the modifications to be made to the actual office design. She left the factory for her office at New Spectrum carrying the box that Arianne had confided to the foreman for her. She believed the familiarity of her office would shield her from any impending doom. Her father's soothing advice did not quell her apprehension. Fritz's still blooming bouquet welcomed her, partially quieting her anxiety. She finally presumed her alliance with Fritz would annihilate any form of obstacle from Arianne, or whoever chose to oppose them.

With that new disposition she liberated the card attached to the box. Its content was the following:

> *Dear Crystal,*
> *These are our family pictures that Fritz had kept during his sojourn in the United States. Will you be so kind as to display them on his office's walls? I'm sure he will appreciate their exposure when he learns you are the one who arranged them.*
>
> *Thanks for your help, Arianne*

With moist eyes, Crystal reached for the framed pictures that had been caged for four-and-a-half years, the same stretch of time she had not been in touch with Fritz. She admired them. She recognized some of them as the ones he had shown her the first day when they were on the porch at his house. His mother's wedding, his baby pictures, his grandfather in front of their house, Fritz straining with a fish almost his own height. Crystal guessed he must have been about four-years-old in that picture.

And at the bottom was a crumpled sheet. Crystal hesitated. Should she read it? She surmised that it was a letter. She unfolded a delicate paper, and her name popped out in the middle of the first line. The handwriting was that of Fritz. The page was stained; the ink blotched like someone's tears had fallen on the print creating the smear. Someone who had been crying profusely at the time of pause during a painful task. Crystal read the content at once.

> *Dear Crystal,*
> *I just spoke to you. I imagine you standing in that sordid box at the telegraph with a quizzical glance on your face. Your voice distorted by statics had reached and touched*

me the same. I could still recognize Crystal, the one who loves me. That voice disarmed my resolve to present to you the accusation that my mother implies with the pictures she carries. Talking to you, I realize that I could not expose you to the town's gossip, could not endure having your name trashed. Our relationship had been the buzz of the town for a long time, so let them guess. For now, I cannot do anything to fight those pictures, your pictures with that handsome lieutenant. Except that I hate him with fervor.

However, if you have decided that he deserves your love, if he were to be that lucky, I will respect your choice, even when it condemns me to eternal chagrin. But if my mother in one way or another had caused you to abandon me so soon, three or four months after I traveled away, by convincing you and your family members that I will only marry an Arab-Haitian woman to comply with my race's tradition, be certain that I will come back and defy her. I can see her and the pictures she spread out on my coffee table. Damn, I'm angry at her! Why did she have to expose them there? I'm going to New York, to live with my cousins. It was my family's decision, the safe way to separate me from you by assuring the presence of my relatives to distract me. I'm so afraid and lonely. Those damn pictures..........

Crystal's trembling hands transmitted her emotion to the letter she had never received. The letter that was never mailed. The letter that was interred with the framed photographs in that box. Their discovery eliminated all of Crystal's second-guessing about Fritz's intentions.

The letter was not signed, it did not contain a farewell; it was not even finished. It was as if it embodied a pending issue, an unresolved mystery waiting to be elucidated. Crystal's tears were now falling on the already overworked parchment, imprinting it with her dedication, engraving it with her devotion as Fritz had years earlier. But hers was different, a mixture of relief and reassurance that eliminated the last trim of doubt that could ever arise in her subconscious about Fritz's intentions. It was also the firm witness to what her father had predicted for her to be a link to ensure peaceful exchanges in the family. She carefully folded the letter, weighing whether she should bury it again in that box and let Fritz find it and know she was aware of its existence, or let Arianne discover that piece if she had not done so yet.

She sat, mesmerized by the implication—that they would have to go over that painful episode again. No! She did not want that. She did not want Fritz or his mother to be exposed to any more hurtful subjects. Right there she decided she would never reveal to Fritz her argument with his mother that Friday morning, or her visit.

She would instead highlight her efforts to please him by fixing a party for him, unaware that he was at the hospital. That was how she would begin her mission as the link. She took the letter, the beach bag, and the box to her house.

Crystal focused on remodeling Fritz's office into the one-bedroom apartment he had requested. The change was easy because at the time she had designed it she had anticipated a space to nestle a secretarial office in front of his in the future. Now she crowded Fritz's furniture in that area. A partition was raised in the back. The half bathroom was transformed into a full one.

———

Fritz spent his birthday, June 24, in the hospital. She wrote him a card for the occasion where she renewed her

269

love for him and wished him a speedy recovery. She assigned its delivery to her brother, Gregory, who every day had visited to inform her about Fritz's progress.

Fritz was released from the hospital on July 2, 1965, fifteen days after his admission. He felt like he was a reborn man dotted with a new sense of wisdom, thanks to the experience of entrusting his body to Dr. Armand. Having his rival save his life imbued him with that conviction. He happily boarded his family's car for the factory. He was curious to discover the metamorphosis improvised by Crystal.

During the course of his stay at the hospital, he did not question any of his family members about how they were making out with Crystal. As soon as he set foot in his office, he knew. He glanced at the walls and admired the photographs artfully displayed. He knew Crystal was the one who did it, and ascertained that between the two most cherished women in his life reigned peace. He knew his mother had played her tune and Crystal, with her democratic stance, had reasoned and forgiven his mother.

In fact, in Paris, Arianne had witnessed as Fritz, enraged by the condemning pictures, wrote a letter. She had seen him crush the message in that letter under his angry fingers, dump it in the box, and smack with fury the family photos on top of his desperate plea, then seal all of them with a resolute determination. He was sure she had brought the box to Crystal. Had she opened it before? It did not matter. Was she aware of the letter's contents? That did not matter either.

He interpreted her gesture as an act of contrition. His mother had accepted her faults, and was begging for forgiveness. Fritz concluded that for a proud woman like Arianne to expose her family's secret and her condemnation was an act of great expurgation, a gesture of restitution, a cry for redemption and a token for reconciliation.

Fritz in one swift moment acknowledged the significa-tion, the symbolization of the sacrifice. Like Crystal had done before, he elected not to turn the ashes, not to inves-tigate the evidence and provoke an uproar. It was time for unity and the true realization of his dream. Like the budding stems that emerged from the smoldering pile of a forest's fire, he pronounced his first thanks to them, these people who were his family, with Crystal fully included as part of their circle.

He exchanged a complicit smile with his mother after they both purposely eyed the photographs on the walls. Everything was set up for his comfort. Arianne and Crystal had never met during the time of the renovation, but each one of them discreetly placed their stone, added their mark to raise the castle that would host Fritz's well-being. He was pleased by their orchestrated effort and the palpable result.

Arianne left with her brother and sister-in-law to share the rest of the afternoon with them. She had been living at the plantation since Fritz's accident. Curtis, who came back for his son's discharge from the hospital, had offered to sojourn with his son in the factory during his stay in the capital. A twin bed was added to that effect in Fritz's bed-room. Fritz did not mind. His father had been strong lately. He needed some encouragement and the manifestation of understanding for openly opposing his wife.

Curtis surprised Fritz before supper while he was feed-ing him the latest gossip about Cap-Haitian's events. He said, "It's four o'clock. I think I can brave the traffic now. I will drive you to Crystal's."

The neighborhood would grow accustomed to the love-birds' presence each afternoon on the porch. Fritz proposed six months later. Their engagement was celebrated at Crystal's aunt's house. Arianne refrained from suggesting her Arab dishes for the occasion. Ifelie deliberately lavished the table with Haitian recipes that the bunch honored to her satisfaction. Maria's admiration for the couple doubled her energy to show off her talent. She fought with Vonise, who had been there as a member of Fritz's family. Maria claimed it was her territory and that Vonise was a guest. Crystal settled the feud by reminding Maria of her reverse position for the marriage in six months.

Crystal and Fritz were married at the Cathedral of Cap-Haitian. The same people who used to comment, "It will never do, they will not make it, it has never been done before," crowded the park across from Dr. Dijon's house to witness when Crystal would be leaving with her father. Their fresh opinion for the occasion was "They were deeply in love; we knew it was going to happen, what a lovely couple they make."

As soon as the bride left her house, the populace hurriedly crossed the park to get the better spot on the other side facing the church. Holding their breath, they recorded Dr. Dijon passing his daughter's hand to Fritz. It was a time when emotion cruised the arena to liberate the chests filled with love, the eyes moistened with joy, and the enthusiastic legs to carry the execution of the ballade. The family members and guests gathered in the church's middle aisles, the curious occupying the empty benches on the side.

The ceremony reached its climax when Father Ignacio asked the formal question, "Fritz Jean Lucas, do you accept to take as your spouse, Crystal Dijon? Do you promise to take good care of her in health, disease, richness or poverty?"

Fritz's voice filled the expecting silence with a thunderous, "Yes I do!" His moist eyes were fixed on Crystal as she answered a strong, "Yes I do" in return to the same question.

They exchanged rings and the priest announced, "I now pronounce you husband and wife." A collective exhalation swept the church to blend with the music that spilled over the snuffling noise that sprinkled the cathedral. Many guests were dabbing their eyes.

The flood of guests enlivened Dr. Dijon's house. Mr. and Mrs. Fritz Jean Lucas officiated the first span of the party. They greeted their guests and thanked them for their consideration. After they fulfilled the social requirements they left.

Fritz and Crystal spent their honeymoon at Rival, the beach just a few minutes from Fritz's house. Crystal had chosen the small cottage passed down to her husband by his grandfather. Fritz had made all the arrangements for the place to be fixed. When they entered the facility, soft music was playing. Fritz swept Crystal off the floor and held her in a tight embrace. He covered her with kisses and murmured, "I love you, Crystal, I love you, I love you."

When he set her back on her feet, she whispered, recovering her breath, "I love you, too, Fritz."

The honeymoon lasted the weekend. They relished their privacy and stayed mostly indoors during their honeymoon. During one of their few promenades on the beach Fritz asked Crystal, "Now tell me, did you hate me twice as much as before, when Gregory informed you I was the one who owned Fabric Pro?"

She turned, laced her arms around her husband, closed her eyes, and inquired, "Now tell me what you thought when

Uncle Alex opened my office door and our music stirred in the background?"

She offered her lips, Fritz bent and kissed her. It was a fulfilling answer for both.

———